Nothing to Lose

Books by Consuelo Baehr

Report from the Heart
Best Friends
Nothing to Lose

NOTHING TO LOSE

Consuelo Baehr

G. P. Putnam's Sons
New York

For Andrew, Nicholas and the amazing Amanda

Second Impression

Copyright © 1982 by Consuelo Baehr
All rights reserved. This book, or parts thereof,
may not be reproduced in any form without permission.
Published simultaneously in Canada by
General Publishing Co. Limited, Toronto.

Library of Congress Cataloging in Publication Data

Baehr, Consuelo Saah.
 Nothing to lose.

 I. Title.
PS3552.A326N6 1982   813'.54   82-7519
ISBN 0-399-12749-6   AACR2

PRINTED IN THE UNITED STATES OF AMERICA

1

IT WAS EARLY MARCH in New York. One of those days when the sun shines stubbornly through sprinkling rain. A sign, her mother had told her, that the devil was beating his wife.

April Taylor sat with two other applicants—a gray-haired woman, a thin young man—in the waiting room. The fluorescent lights, a generous wattage considering the miserly furnishings, did nothing for them. They looked picked over.

The logo on the door, chubby magenta letters all in lower case, was gay but the rest of the space was dingy in the same forlorn way small town bus depots are dingy. The furniture was bunched up in the center of the room in hygienically neutral space. "Our 30th year of finding great jobs for great New Yorkers," said a poster. They had been too busy to dust.

April shifted restlessly in her seat, a friendly school-type chair with an extended arm for filling out the form which she had long since completed. The gray-haired woman cleared her throat repeatedly. April began to count the number of times she did so. After the twentieth time, she steeled herself for something weird. Would she beg for help the way some people now did on the street? *Please*, you've got to help me!

April fixed her gaze on a far wall on which was posted a message that might have been written expressly for her: "You just might blush . . . because our professional employment counselors aren't content with reeling off your previous employers. They talk about all the intangibles that make you you."

She expelled a pent-up sigh and tugged her skirt over her knees. Within a few minutes a thin woman with a stiff blond pageboy fished out her nameplate from a metal desk and waved her over to take a chair.

The nameplate said Sondra Greene. She was wearing a hot pink sleeveless top, a brave choice for such an iffy day. The same pink graced her lips, her nails and the dizzying chevron pattern on her discarded jacket. "These samples aren't worth much." She had been flipping disinterestedly through April's slim portfolio, which she now pushed halfway off the desk. April jumped to retrieve it.

"What about the car ad? That's a big account."

"Doesn't amount to beans by itself." She seemed to begrudge her an explanation. Time was money. "You have one car ad. The rest are newspaper ads for . . . ugh . . . paper plates . . . shoes . . . Barney's Boystown. There's no TV. One campaign. Nothing national. And . . . everything's at least two years old." She chewed on her number two pencil, satisfying every notion of what a tough job broker should be. "I have nothing for you."

"Nothing?" April's mouth hung open. The upper part of her body felt congested. "I've got to work." Her voice sounded overly loud and theatrical. "I'm good at copy . . . please, look again."

Sondra gave her an exasperated stare. She needed work and Sondra was an employment counselor. What could be less exasperating?

"You want the truth?"

The truth? How had they arrived there so quickly? "Yes."

"You don't look the part."

"I don't understand."

"You don't look the part for the kind of job you want."

She proposed this as such unassailable logic that April couldn't defend herself. "What do my looks have to do with it?"

"Plenty. They want lookers." To her credit, she didn't look embarrassed or sheepish, which would have made it tragic. She yawned and studied her nails.

"They?" April waited but no answer was forthcoming. "They who?"

"The big agencies want good-looking girls." She folded her arms neatly, pushing freckled breasts to their full allure. It was cold in the office and her arms were so thin. April wanted to urge her to put on her jacket. "I'm not trying to put you down or anything . . . but . . . uh . . . most of the copy chiefs are men and if they have a choice they're going to choose the most promising girl."

"Promising for what?"

"To look at. To flirt with. How do I know for what?" Her patience was gone. "Every office is a stage," she said daintily, as if this was going to be her last word on the subject, "with many, many dramas being played out. I don't want to get a reputation for sending them . . ." *If she had said dogs* . . . "Look," her voice softened, "take off forty, fifty pounds, get yourself some clothes that show off your tits and come back to see me."

April had always suspected that the people she most disapproved of in life would, by some devilish trick, be the ones who held the key to her heart's desire. At that moment, she suspected Sondra Greene held the key to her heart's desire and would liberate her if she could detain her long enough.

Surely, she would rally to April's support if she knew about Harald. *Ms. Greene . . . Sondra . . . I'm not what you think. I've been married to a man who outwits thousands with his stock market know-how with the full consent of the U.S. Government. We lived in a limestone building on Park Avenue. It had thick mullions and delicate muntins—built for beauty, not for profit. He made me wear a silk wrapper at breakfast. It had a scalloped edge and sometimes—you know how unreliable silk can be—my breast would fall out, which is what he hoped.*

Then, as if it hadn't been a full year since Harald had left her, the pain and desperation came over her so acutely that Sondra's disdain was ludicrous by comparison. She could see clearly now how to get what she wanted.

"Isn't there an agency run by one old man who needs an all-around girl? I'll do mail order. I'll answer the phone and send out bills." Her eyes filled with tears. She had left her apartment that morning determined to find herself a place to go each day. Suppose she sat there all day crying? They'd find her something soon enough. Who could move her? "It doesn't have to be terrific. Please, look again." As bad as it sounded the speech didn't leave Sondra unmoved. She rifled through a metal box quickly as if looking for a preordained spot and extracted a soiled white card.

Had she been tricked? April wanted to grab the card and devour the information. "Well," sighed Sondra as if they had been negotiating for days, "this might work. It's in Newark. They're looking for someone to commute in reverse." She gave April another appraising look that made her feel untrustworthy. Then she dialed. "Mrs. Briggs, please," she said into the phone, "advertising . . . Hi, Top of the Line here. Have you filled the copywriter's job? . . . Good. I have someone. Very good experience. Hard and soft goods. Wouldn't ordinarily consider a department store but she's been out of the country for a couple of years and is getting her bearings. She's not crazy about the salary . . . considering the commute and . . . everything. Any chance of upping it a little? . . . uh huh . . . uh huh . . . that's a little better. I'll see when she has an opening to come out." She put her hand over the mouthpiece. "Can you go there first thing in the morning?" Her voice lost all sweetness.

"Yes."

"It turns out," she returned to the phone, "she's had a cancellation. She'll be there at 10:30 tomorrow. Fine. Bye now. Well," she said, writing busily on a piece of paper, "you've got an interview. Don't blow it."

"Where is it?"

"Newark. A department store chain. Six stores."

"I thought Newark was all burned out . . . the riots . . ."

"It is. Don't walk from the station. Take a cab."

"What's the job?"

"You'll be writing advertising copy for soft goods."

"What are soft goods?"

"Things that are soft." She didn't look up. April pictured clouds and cotton candy, satin pillows, pussy willows. How did you sell pussy willows?

"What's the name of the place?"

"Burdie's."

"Birdies? As in tweet tweet?"

"No. With a 'u.' As in burlesque." It didn't seem to April that she was smart enough to be ironic, but there you were. Sondra swung her legs out to end the interview and April noticed through her sandals a corn pad on her smallest toe. Worrisome corns before thirty do not point to a carefree childhood. Her heart began to melt for Sondra Greene. They had known each other barely half an hour and she had already negotiated a small raise for April out of simple human caring.

"Are you going to wear that rag?" Sondra now took in

April's fragile cotton overblouse and nondescript pants. She had spent the better part of the night fanning them dry in front of a tiny oven. She had pressed them carefully at seven that morning. It was the only outfit she had left that fit her.

"No, of course not. Why would I wear this?"

"Good." She eyed April suspiciously. "I don't have another thing to send you on, so don't screw up. Remember, this is a fashion situation."

April didn't have to remember. Among other things, she was blessed with total recall. If you named a year, she could tell you everything. How she came to be so heavy. And jobless. And at the mercy of this person called Sondra and another called Harald, both needlessly awkward names.

2

APRIL FULLY INTENDED TO keep her appointment at Burdie's following her interview with Sondra Greene. She listened carefully to Channel 7's "Accu-Weather Report." The weathergirl winked at the anchorman and warned that a wedge of cold Canadian air would push the existing warm, moist air, creating thunderstorms and high winds most of the following day.

She laid out her wardrobe—a Ship 'n Shore blouse whose color had once been labeled madeira pink and a shapeless A-line jumper of gauzelike material that was faintly stylish for the first hour of wearing, after which the seams shifted, making it hang unevenly. Panicked by the unfamiliar roundness of her face, she began to snip at her hair. Suppose it rained and she arrived at Burdie's with soggy hair and a certain to be soggy outfit? At least in its new length, her hair would curl, giving her the look of a woman who had many years of creative work still ahead of her.

She shaved her legs and under her arms. She emptied her handbag, beating out a year's accumulation of cookie crumbs, peanut bits, bobbie pins. She put egg white on

her face and let it dry to tighten her pores. While she
waited, she massaged Nivea into her knees and elbows.
She would give herself every chance.

In the morning, contrary to the Accu-Weather, everything was sunny and calm. She climbed on the scale as
she did every morning and when it showed 185, the figure so alarmed her she returned dazed to the edge of the
bed.

She hadn't eaten her usual quota the preceding day,
partly due to the time spent at the employment agency.
She had even walked around the city, casually window
shopping, and had purchased thirty-five dollars' worth of
better underwear at Bloomingdale's, having read in a recent issue of *Ms.* that " . . . you don't have to weigh 100
pounds to wear pretty underwear and vibrant lipstick."

How could she have gained two pounds on one of her
most active days? Was her body now a sly enemy, maliciously retaining water and slowing her metabolism to a
crawl? Already her heart felt squeezed and the beat
irregular.

Too unnerved to leave the apartment, much less find
her way to Newark, she waited for Sondra's call, invent-
ing things for her to say: "You fat slob, why didn't you
go? I'll kill you!" Sondra's fury was rising out of the subway gratings. Maybe Sondra was right. She certainly had
every chance to bone up on human nature. Everyone assumed that the overweight had lost control of more than
their weight. Perhaps it was true. Perhaps there had been
no possibility that she would keep the appointment.

"April Marie," she went to the mirror and spoke softly
to her image, "do you want to sit and rot here in this
somber apartment where the only place the sun hits is the
refrigerator?" Her eyes looked back narrower behind her
puffy, polished cheeks. She now had slitty eyes. Toward
the end, that's what Harald had hated most. "You look,"

he had hissed at her across the bed one morning, "as if your IQ dropped ten points during the night."

Somehow the day passed.

By the following morning, the two pounds had disappeared as mysteriously as they had come and she left for her appointment only twenty-four hours late. She was sure to be met with aggrieved, angry faces. She saw doors closing one after another. No, thank you. Still, she had to go. She needed someplace to go every day. To hook up again with life. As Sondra had said, there wasn't another thing to send her to.

The main selling floor of Burdie's was wide and spread out with a maze of aisles created by huge glass counters trimmed with polished wood. It looked like an ocean liner and she wouldn't have been surprised to see Bette Davis at a railing looking meaningfully into the black depths of the sea.

Sleeveless blouses dangled over counters. THE SHELLS OF SPRING, said a sign. The advertising department was on the seventh floor, a warren of grimy cubbies behind major appliances. A matronly woman was making cocktail knishes in a food processor for a sizable audience. The smell of onions was in the air.

She passed a display of a holiday dinner complete with Easter ham, succotash, deep-dish apple pie and a family of four, depicting the virtues of freezer-to-table ware. It seemed so handy and cheerful, she made a note to purchase some with her first paycheck.

Missy Briggs, her contact, was on the telephone when she was ushered to her door. She looked young enough to be a child.

She had known one other Missy in her life, a girl renowned for mischief. There were stories that Missy had set fire to a cat or hacked up a rabbit, but April never believed them. Missy was a name alien to evil. They could have been saying Missy pressed her satin ribbons or Missy combed her pony. She mentally airmailed this hopeful message to the Missy in front of her who had completed her call and was looking at April with pale, inquiring eyes.

"I'm April Taylor. There was a mix-up. I was supposed to be here yesterday."

"I don't know what the mix-up could have been. I was told you'd be here at 10:30."

"I'm here now," she said too brightly. "Is it convenient?" She edged into the office hiding behind her giant portfolio, which she unzipped and placed before Missy. After a wary pause, she began to turn the pages.

When she came to the final ad, Missy sat back and studied the resumé. Occasionally, she glanced from it to April. It reminded her of a segment on "60 Minutes" in which a private eye told Mike Wallace how they could reconstruct anyone's life from checkbook stubs. They knew where you shopped, where you went on vacation. If you had your own home, your own car, your own teeth. She began to fidget with her fingernails, trying to wedge one between the layers of another."

"I don't understand," Missy had put everything back into the binder and zipped it neatly. "Ms. Greene said you had soft goods experience. Why do they always send the wrong people?" She looked ready to cry.

"Oh, I do. I do." April felt sorry for Missy, who was rejecting her for something real—her lack of experience—and not for her weight. "Why don't you give me a test? Let me write an ad for something you need right now."

Missy rolled this over in her mind and, seeing it made sense, nodded toward a corner of her desk. "All right. Write me an ad for that ghillie."

April looked in vain for something that looked like a

ghillie. Was it a fish? There was no fish on the desk. "A ghillie?"

"This shoe is called a ghillie. It laces up the front and has a closed toe . . . and this blouse," she gestured to a softly bowed white blouse that hung on a peg. "Write me an ad for the shoes and the blouse."

She directed April to a small booth, one of about twenty that flanked a long, narrow aisle. There was a Royal manual on a gray metal desk. "There should be paper in that drawer," she said and left.

April looked around the partition, which was half wood and half a rippled plastic. There were two full-page news-paper ads taped to the walls. One was for a lawn mower: *The workhorse you can guide with your pinkie! Adjusts to seven cutting heights.* The other was for bathroom shelving: *Hold everything! Behind the bathroom door.*

She stared dully at the wide-planked dusty floor, feel-ing displaced. There was a perpetual buzz in the air like the noise they played to comfort assembly-line workers. She assumed each cubicle held a person like herself, their mind abuzz over some piece of merchandise.

She stared at the blouse. In the overall scheme of things, you could live out your life happily without a blouse, especially a blouse you had to tuck in. She had tucked nothing in for years. Three weeks before her mar-riage to Harald, unable to eat or drink, manic with her strange new body, she had worn a sweater tucked into her jeans for seven days.

During that week, she thought of little else but the sweater blousing delicately over her waistband, her stom-ach flat. The contours of her back, brave and optimistic, were finally visible. At the end of that week, she fell into a stunned, dreamless sleep for most of two days.

April took the shoe Missy had given her into her hand. It was the type of shoe worn by people who had lost interest in sex. It was square-heeled, perforated in front and tied sensibly up the instep. In desperation, she wrote: *CLUNK! CLUNK! CLUNK! For those secure enough to go in comfort.*

She tiptoed to Missy's empty office and placed her headline on the desk. Minutes later, Missy waved her in. "Why would you want to point out the deficiency?" she asked, as if April's intentions were malevolent.

"It's reverse chic, ha ha. Whoever buys them *wants* to look clunky. They're saying, 'I'm wearing these *on purpose.*'" She hated her high-pitched, nervous voice. She hated what she had written.

"I don't think so," said Missy.

"What would you say?" April asked numbly.

Missy didn't hesitate. "The shoe you need. The shoe you'll wear most. The shoe that's you . . . in your own words, of course."

"Of course." She returned to her cubby and within five minutes typed: *If this shoe fits, wear it! Wear it walking, shopping, around the house.*

Missy smiled approval and April felt giddy with relief. There was a formula to the ads. She could learn to do them in her sleep. It was a piece of cake to do the blouse ad: *The blouse you've always wanted. Clingy, supple—so fickle, it goes with everything.*

Wear it mucking, trucking.

"What do you expect to get out of this job?" Missy asked soberly when April was seated primly across the desk.

A place to go. "Try my hand at something challenging and worthwhile," she answered.

"We do our best for Burdie's and take it seriously," she warned.

"Absolutely." It would have been more courageous to say nothing, the appropriate response to a thinly veiled accusation. But she was too overcome with gratitude.

She stopped in the ladies' room, peed, and then sat there exhausted by the interview. With great effort, she roused herself, washed her sweaty hands and waited for a blast of hot air to dry them. Her eyes burned and she felt stiff and tired, as if she'd been driving on a hot, dusty road for a long time. She left the store and began the walk to the train station.

The streets looked war-torn. There were grave miscalculations everywhere, too many stores out of business. Yet several corners sported crisp white signs: *We're Putting the New in Newark.* It seemed too optimistic. She sighed, bought two slices of pizza from an unhealthy looking woman in a luncheonette and ate them walking along the street. Still, she was starved when she boarded the train. It was a train that had come from farther south and was littered with food wrappers and soda cans. In front of her was a poster: *Four days, three nights in Grand Bahama complete—even a welcome rum swizzle—could cost as little as $199. Call American or your travel agent.* She had four days and three nights before she began work at Burdie's and a little sun would do her good.

On the way home, she stopped at a deli and bought a bag of Fritos and a quarter pound each of turkey breast, salami, and Swiss cheese. She added a box of croutons and a jar of Marie's Bleu Cheese Dressing. She would make a big chef's salad when she got home. The thought of the salad made her feel cheerful and calm, but when she got home the head of lettuce was frozen and the leaves stiff and translucent. She had told the super that the refrigerator froze lettuce on one. "Well, that's as low as you can set it," he replied. He looked as if he didn't believe she ate lettuce.

She opened all the cold-cut wrappers and began to roll the individual slices and put them in her mouth. Then she put the turkey breast and salami between two slices of Swiss cheese and ate it like a sandwich. In between bites, she popped a few croutons into her mouth. The croutons were fantastic, cheesy and crisp, a little oily, with a hint of oregano. She made herself a plate of the croutons and the cold cuts and ate sitting on her sofabed and staring at the opposite wall. The room was totally quiet. She felt safe and contented with her plate of food and tremendously relieved, as if she had climbed a cliff—the escarpments on the edge of the Sahara. How treacherous the business world could be. And how brave she had been to try. It could have all gone the other way and she could be sitting here no better off than before.

She made a resolve to rid herself of at least part of the weight as soon as she settled into some sort of routine. It would be pointless to start now when there would be all that stress ahead of her. Better to wait. She finished the box of croutons and the cold cuts and opened the bag of Fritos, which had a different taste from the croutons but were just as crispy and just as good.

When she finished eating she called American Airlines and told the clerk who answered that she wanted the four-day, three-night package to Grand Bahama beginning the next day and was told to pick up her ticket at the airline office in midtown. She had never done anything so spontaneous in her life but it seemed the perfect thing to do.

She arrived at Kennedy Airport two hours early, which turned out to be the only way to get a seat. The flight was hopelessly overbooked. After checking in she went to stand by the window to watch the planes taking off. She turned away and saw coming into the lounge a man whose looks and demeanor completely absorbed her. He had the kind of magic, carefree stride they catch for cigarette ads to take your mind off the seriousness of cancer. His hair and heavy tweed jacket trailed a few millimeters behind him, as if it were windy, which it wasn't. There was a woman with him wearing a sweater that fell below her calves and a gypsy-style scarf on her head, the kind that made real gypsies look alien but made her look powerful.

The man stood in line, glancing reassuringly at the woman from time to time. When his turn came, there seemed to be some problem. He argued earnestly for a few minutes, then went to stand next to the woman. He rubbed the back of his neck as if deciding what to do. He cupped the woman's chin in his hand and said, "Don't worry." Or at least that's what it looked like he said. It could have been, I'm sorry, or You're pretty.

He looked around the lounge slowly as if trying to find someone he knew and then, inexplicably, he began to stare at April. There was no mistake, he was really looking at her. She regretted not wearing her raincoat, which had needed cleaning but was more appropriate than the green melton tent that made her look large and matronly—the meat loaf queen in a bake-off. Her new sunglasses, which only turned dark in sunshine, gave her some protection to stare back at him without looking stupid.

He was coming toward her. Yes, it was her he wanted. She pushed back her shoulders and waited. His eyes were outstandingly blue, inconsistent with the rest of his coloring. "Are you interested in selling your seat?" Momentarily, she thought he meant something lewd and didn't answer. "They're overbooked," he said, "and my friend needs a seat."

"Who's your friend?" He needed something only she could give him. Who would have thought.

"She's over there." He pointed to the blond on the other side of the lounge.

"I can't sell my seat," she said conversationally, as if

she'd known him a long time. "I really need this vacation."

"Of course you do, but there are other flights and I would give you a bonus."

"What kind of a bonus?"

"Money."

"Oh . . ." she said thoughtfully, as if it were an unexpected answer, "money." What had she thought the bonus would be? A kiss? A hug? A night on the town? "What good would money do? I need the sun as quickly as possible. I'm starting a new job. This may be the last time off I'll have for a while, so I can't take any chances." He was becoming edgy. He had further canvassing to do but she wasn't ready to have him leave her. "I took this trip on the spur of the moment, I'm not ordinarily a spontaneous person. People should do things once in a while that are against their nature, don't you think?"

He was writing on a piece of paper. "If you change your mind, page me," he said. "I'd be willing to go as high as two hundred."

"What makes you think I'd change my mind?" She crumpled the paper and put it in the ash receptacle to show him what she thought of his idea.

"Nothing," he said apologetically. "Nothing would make me think that. You're a woman with a will of iron." Then he smiled and walked away.

My god, he must have been crazy about the woman to spend all that money, practically the cost of the whole vacation. When everyone else was walking out to board the flight, she retrieved the paper with his name and smoothed it out. Luis O'Neill. She folded it carefully and put it in her wallet.

Throughout the flight, which both he and his girlfriend finally boarded, she stared at his neck and profile. He read *U.S. News & World Report* cover to cover, then dipped into his chocolate brown duffel for the *Wall*

Street Journal—a serious businessman. They drank two bloody marys.

"I'm glad you made it," she offered when they disembarked and she was close to him.

"Thanks." He smiled again. He was so attractive it made her shy. "Have a good vacation."

The sweetness and sincerity of his response was so unexpected it made her think of him as someone to love. She felt foolish, but there it was, a surge of feeling, an incorporation of him into her heart and mind.

She looked for him each of the four days. It was an island, how far could he go? She bought an orange and white batik beach wrap—an oblong cloth that tied over the breasts and fell to the ankles. You could be out of it in three seconds. At least two of those nights, she imagined that she would be out of it in three seconds for Luis O'Neill.

It was wonderful to have someone to love again even in such a circumscribed way. She had been so sure it wouldn't happen to her again.

3

BURDIE'S AT 8:45 IN the morning. The lights blinked on dramatically, highlighting leather gloves, personalized stationery, business machines, closet accessories, an executive jogger. If he closed his eyes, Luis O'Neill saw it all moving out in the full, happy arms of the women of Newark. The worst thing was to see the same things there, unsold, day after day.

He himself bought very little at the store despite the generous discount accorded senior personnel. His suits were custom-made with Burdie's labels sewn in should anyone look. His bachelor apartment on New York's East Side had no need of furniture, Burdie's or anyone else's. They called it the New Minimalism—carpeted platforms with four loose pillows. It had looked good on the plan but, in practice, he mostly used the sleeping platform with its flexible reading lamp and extraordinary view of the river.

He was no newcomer to river views. As a child in the projects, he had had a good view of the wrong river. His mother was from Puerto Rico. She liked to freeze grapes and suck on them while watching television. She es-

pecially liked two shows: "Mi Vida," a Spanish soap op-
era, and "English for Aliens" with Conchita Riva. Your
wallet . . . *su cartera.* Your wallet . . . *su cartera. ¡Mucho
cuidado con su cartera en la calle!* Watch your wallet in the
street. *Hay* muggers. *¿Sabe que es esto* muggers? Bonk *en la
cabeza.* In the head. Bonk. Bonk. Bonk.

"*Ay, que loca,*" said his grandmother, who also lived with
them. "Crazy woman."

His mother said jes for yes, dun for don't, jew for you
and chips for ships. "Dun expek much," she had warned
him repeatedly. Despite her pessimism, his life had taken
some extraordinary turns.

When Luis was in his junior year at Princeton, a repre-
sentative from the First Commercial Trust Company took
him to lunch at the Alchemist and Barrister, the most ele-
gant eatery around the campus.

"Let's be honest with each other," said the representa-
tive, Mr. Saladino. "My company is very interested in hiring young men like yourself for our trust division. I like
what I see. You know how to listen and . . . I would guess
you're smart as hell." When Luis failed to comment, he
continued: "Being smart as hell is important, but"—it was
a big "but" punctuated by a large swallow of his drink—
"not as important as you might think. Looks, for instance—*very* important. A certain look. Voice. Tone of
voice. *Very* important. Your voice has no discernible re-
gional accent. It's strong—a pleasant voice."

"As long as we're being honest," said Luis, "why should
I go with you?"

"Aha. Why, indeed?" He threw his hands into the air as if
to show Luis there was nothing hidden there. "No reason.
We're solid, a growing company, but so are others. We pro-
mote from within and have high starting salaries—like others. Sooo . . ."—a big "so" during which he pushed himself

away from the table—". . . we have to make it attractive. What would make it attractive for you? You tell me."

Luis realized if he asked for too much he would be thought to have poor judgment, and if he asked for too little he would be thought to be a small thinker. "The work's the main thing," he said. "If the work's not challenging, all the perks in the world won't make it right."

"Well answered," said Mr. Saladino, raising an eyebrow in admiration. "However, we like to ease our young men into city living by helping them out. How can you struggle to live and also do your best work? We're prepared to pay half the rent on an apartment up to two hundred and fifty a month and, initially, since the wardrobe is work-related, we will open a charge for you at Paul Stuart with a thousand-dollar credit."

"It's a generous offer," said Luis. "I'll certainly keep it in mind."

He had not expected to take the job. He didn't particularly like Mr. Saladino or the ten other reps who offered similar positions during the next few months. There was a basic insincerity that disturbed him. As if conducting business was rooted in pretense. They wanted him as a prototype. He saw himself as an original. They wanted him to walk primly. He was ready for dynamic leaps. His roommate, Fred Burdette, repeatedly offered the entire Burdie's chain of department stores, which his father controlled, as a job source, but Luis wanted to test his own muscle and drive.

He accepted the job with First Commercial Trust and arrived for work on July 5th, one month after his last day of school. During the first week, they sent him home with a history of the company and its divisions as well as a mimeographed sheet of suggested dos and don'ts:

Only dark blue or gray suits, please. And let's see some cuff below the jacket sleeve. Dark shoes that tie are in. Boots, high or low, are out. Three bootblacks make the rounds each day, no cost to you. Hairstyles with a definite part inspire confidence. Cologne or jewelry—other than a simple watch or class ring—are distracting to others. A slim wallet—without picture bulge—is desirable. No slang expressions. Hello is preferable to hi. Good-bye is preferable to bye. Introduce yourself as Mister (your last name) and address customers as Mr., Mrs., or Miss, never Ms. During a business lunch, consider eating fish, omelettes or veal, and drinking wine. Red meat and hard liquor are associated with excesses people don't want in their bankers. Hamburger is what children eat. Enough said.

Initially, he was assigned to solicit customers with large checking account balances and try to sell them on transferring their investment portfolios to the bank's trust division. There was a protocol to the calls and Luis, along with four other young men, practiced the dialogue. They were to begin each call by asking How are you today?—a greeting Luis considered backslapping and dumb.

He made ten calls his first day and discovered that people with healthy bank balances seldom answered their own phone or were available to come to the phone. He left messages with his name and by afternoon the return calls began to dribble in.

"This O'Neill?" asked a man's voice.

"Yes. What can I do for you?"

"What can you do for me? I don't know. *You* called me. This is John McNally." The man sounded annoyed. More than annoyed.

"Oh, yes. Well, Mr. McNally, how are you today?"

"How am I today? I'll tell you how I am. How would you like this phone up your ass? I don't talk to people who ask me how I am today. What, are you selling something? You want to sell me something and have the nerve to leave a message for *me* to call *you*?" He became angrier as he spoke.

"Yes, sir."

"I wouldn't have even returned the call but my wife's lawyer is O'Neill. Must be the name. He's an asshole, too."

"Yes, sir."

"Why do you keep saying, 'Yes, sir'?"

"Because I think you're absolutely right. I shouldn't have asked how you were."

"What are you, a wise guy? Who do you work for? I'm checking you out. What's your company?"

"No company. I . . . work for myself."

"I'm having this call traced."

Luis hung up.

He didn't say How are you today to anyone again. Three more calls were returned but no one really wanted to move their investment portfolio to the bank's trust department and no one wanted to have lunch and find out more about it.

Within three months of joining First Commercial Trust, Luis knew the banking business was not for him. It was needlessly secretive. All information was treated on what they called a 'need-to-know' basis, making employees feel untrustworthy. Progress and rewards were impossible to gauge since no one knew the objectives. During the time he worked there, he never met the chief operating officer or made a close friend.

He was mystified as to how the banking business maintained its aura of sophistication and financial muscle. Banks were the softest touches around. There was a childish optimism over the borrower's success quotient. Inflation had left most lending institutions holding long-term loans at ridiculously low interest rates. Periodically, cash bonuses were offered to mortgage holders if they would pay up, but few were dumb enough to accept. Extravagant sums were loaned to countries which had no compunction about defecting on both interest and princi-

pal. What was the bank going to do? Go to some remote
part of the world and overthrow the government? Non-
federal debt had gone from four hundred billion in 1955
to eighteen hundred billion in 1973. Where was all this
money going to come from?

By the time he was twenty-three years old, he decided
he had given First Commercial Trust enough of his time
and went to a management placement firm to help him
work out his future. He didn't even know if he was
management but when the interviewer, Henry Patten,
saw Princeton and First Commercial Trust and his
starting salary of $25,000, he said it would be no
problem.

He called Luis two days later. "There's an extremely
desirable situation available and your name came to
mind. In your favor, you're an unknown quantity in the
field. A fresh face."

"Is that a nice way of saying I have no experience?"

"On the contrary. It's an advantage not having been
around. They want somebody new and young and
classy—all of which you fit nicely."

"What's the deal?"

"The situation is this: an organization that buys oil
from two major oil-producing countries, Kuwait and
Venezuela. You would be the liaison until you learned
the ropes and possibly eased into heading the department. A lot of traveling, a lot of entertaining, ninety
percent PR, until you eased into the actual buying, in
which case it would accelerate into deal-making at a very
high level. Nerves of steel, a quiet manner . . . grace
under pressure." There was a long pause. "Are you
interested? The major honcho interviews for this and he
does it over lunch." There was a second long silence.
"You want to get back to me? Think it over?"

"No. I've thought it over. I'll go."

"Good." Henry Patten made the arrangements and

called him within the hour. "It's set. The Four Seasons. That's Thursday, June two at 12:45. Wear a dark suit, no sports jacket. Good luck."

He arrived early and rose when his host, Hunter Garrison, walked toward him. He was at least six feet four but would have been intimidating at four feet eight. His face was like a missile, pink and beefy, ending in a perfectly bald, round head. His neck draped a half inch over his immaculate, high collar.

He ordered Tanqueray on the rocks with three olives.

"Would you like a side dish of olives, sir?" asked the waiter with a straight face.

"No," said Mr. Garrison. "I'll eat too many. Just the three."

Luis, although he would have preferred not to drink, asked for "the same, without the olives."

"Normally," said Hunter Garrison, rubbing his hands together, "I would consider team sports an essential for the man I need, but with your background, it's not important. I'm sure you had plenty of competition growing up in a ghetto." He lowered his eyelids and looked off to the side. "You had to compete to survive. There must have been plenty of clawing and gouging at Stuyvesant High as well." He took a sip of his drink and looked at Luis over the rim of his glass.

Luis had never tried to hide his background. Why then did he feel so guilty? He was being goaded for a purpose. Well, since no question had been put to him, he would remain silent . . . and listen. He, too, would take a sip of his drink and look at Hunter Garrison over the rim of *his* glass. "When I was at Brown," continued Mr. Garrison, "we called you guys the hot pavement sportsmen."

"Well, Mr. Garrison," Luis felt more relaxed knowing what was going on, "I never even played hot pavement sports. I was what you might call a sissy. Not a homosexual, but somewhat afraid of the streets. The boys in the neighborhood liked to beat me up." He said it calmly and without emotion. "And I didn't like getting beat up. So I stayed in."

Hunter Garrison relaxed in his chair, as if he had found out what he wanted to know. "I don't blame you," he said, and motioned to the waiter that they were ready to order. Luis chose turbot, but in his anxiety he misread it for tournedos and asked for it rare.

"Are you certain, sir?" the captain asked.

"Yes, rare," Luis said forcefully. The chairman's eyes went to half mast and he was oddly silent for the rest of the meal. He skipped dessert and barely shook Luis's hand before signing the check and leaving.

When he dialed Henry Patten's number, he was told by the secretary to hold on. It was a while before Patten got on the line. "It's not good," he said.

"Why not? One lunch and he's sure?"

"Didn't you sense something? Tell me what happened."

"He tried to put me off guard, then I said something he liked, he relaxed, we ordered lunch but then he went suddenly ice-cold."

"What did you order?"

"Fish."

"Okay, nothing there."

"I didn't know it was fish. I thought it was those little medallions of meat and ordered it rare."

"Uh oh. That must have been it."

"What's wrong with liking your fish rare? The Japanese eat it raw."

"Yes. But not Americans eating at the Four Seasons with Hunter Garrison. He's a stickler for finesse at the table because most of his business is done over meals. He knew you had made a mistake."

"Well, what do we do now?"

"We look for another situation," said Henry. "I'll get back to you."

Was it only his imagination that Henry's voice was less enthusiastic? He felt uncomfortable. What had happened was trifling and, in any case, couldn't be undone. Still, he felt he had let himself down. Turbot. Tournedos. Turbine. Turhan Bey. Damn.

During the next three weeks, Henry Patten sent him on six interviews. Two he refused because the immediate superiors were not men he respected. Four refused him. "I want to know why," he said to Henry. .

The personal idiosyncrasies of executives were legion. Curly hair made them suspicious. Under six feet made them edgy. Nongolfers weren't well-rounded. Certain religions were liabilities. Of course, no one said this out loud, but it was so. What it boiled down to was that by some uncanny turn of fate, no one that he wanted wanted him. We need someone with more experience, they said, and then hired a kid just out of college. He felt his confidence erode.

"These are the paragons who are running American business?" he asked Henry Patten with disgust.

"You know what you do when you meet a four hundred pound gorilla," Henry answered philosophically, "you do whatever he wants."

Luis had been transformed by Princeton. He had grown sure and patient. He had acquired that unblinking gaze that's often thought judgmental. He never spoke out of nervousness or to fill lulls in conversations. He was kind to women but not patronizing. He had never mooned over a woman or become lovesick. He was very handsome and when he entered a room, he heightened the reality of everyone present. His features had lost the roundness of adolescence. His nose had thinned out, his jaw was more defined and his eyes looked both intelligent and serene. His mouth occasionally tilted ruefully to one side, which added a vulnerability that heightened his appeal. Yet, with all of that, he couldn't find a proper job.

Six months passed. He stopped getting phone calls from Henry and went to another firm but they wanted to know what he had been doing for six months and they weren't as excited over his prospects as Henry had been.

One night on television, there was an ad for Oriental rugs that could be purchased at Burdie's New York store. "Burdie's gives you more of whatever you're looking for," said the announcer. Luis became very excited and put in a call to Fred Burdette in California where the family lived. "Mr. Fred's in Europe," said a nasal English voice. "Celebrating the birth of a son." Luis was somewhat hurt that "Mr. Fred" hadn't let him know he was about to be a father. Maybe the California air made you forgetful. He went to Burdie's anyway, the next morning, to the headquarters building on the Avenue of the Americas behind the sign for San Salvador and Costa Rica. He filled out an application and told them he would like to join their executive training program. It felt good to visit a personnel department and ask for a job. No lunches. No playing games. Two days later, they told him they'd be happy to have him on board. His first stop? Burdie's Georgia—in the flagship store in Atlanta. Position? Assistant buyer for linens and domestics. Salary? $16,000 per annum. Could he leave for Atlanta a week from Monday? He could.

He would not have predicted that going to Atlanta would make him feel so hopeful. It was an exotic place for a boy from the projects.

4

As a child, Luis was the only one in the family who spoke without an accent. His father, Robert O'Neill, seldom in residence, spoke with a Brooklyn accent but Luis spoke like Beaver in "Leave It to Beaver," whom he sometimes pretended to be. At every opportunity, he said Gee whiz, Awh, Mom, Cut it out, and Oh boy, exasperating the women. From their apartment on the eleventh floor, they could see bits of the Hudson River and the *France* and the *United States* when in port. "See the chips?" said his mother. It was such a clear advantage to be able to gaze on those splendid, hopeful liners, he took it as a sign that he was different and singled out for luck.

Luis's eyes were blue. When he played hard, two red moons appeared on his cheeks and made him look feverish. His looks didn't help him much inside or out of the West Side projects unimaginatively designated on maps of Manhattan as Penn. Sta. Housing South.

When he was seven, he begged his mother to make or purchase a Batman costume for Halloween. "I want to dress up," he said.

"What jew want to be?"

"Batman."

"I dun know nathing about Batmans."

"I'll show you," he said eagerly. "There's a little black bat on his chest with yellow around it, a long cape, a black tight hat."

"*¿Que es esto* Bhat?" His grandmother opened one eye.

"*Murciélago,*" said his mother. "*El quiere ser un hombre murciélago.*"

"For what?" his grandmother squinted as if looking for evidence to convict him.

"To go in the street," said his mother.

"Trick or treat," he interjected.

"*¿Como?*"

"*Engaño o convite,*" said his mother.

"*Ay, que loco.* Crazy. *Completamente* crazy *y tambien no me puede llamar abuelita.*"

He was an American and wanted to do what Americans did. Mrs. Anderson on "Father Knows Best" was well groomed and energetic while his mother spent her days going to clinics for vague illnesses. Even "The Courtship of Eddie's Father," an offbeat one-parent situation loosely similar to his own, was a rebuke. Did Eddie, for instance, have a huge white FUCK painted on the walk to his front door?

The dissimilarities between himself and the rest of America weren't all harmless. On a sunny spring day when he was looking out his window, straining to see the smokestacks of the *United States,* he saw a ball of colored clothing falling past him from above. When he went downstairs, he heard a woman say a baby had fallen out of 14F. He saw the mother howling. She took off all of her clothes and the police had to take her inside.

For weeks, a big splotchy reddish stain remained on the walk. Fredo Montenegro who was nine and still embarrassingly unable to read told him that was where the Orlando kid's guts and brains had spilled out and where Luis's, too, would spill if he didn't watch out. He knew that Fredo's ambitious plans for his brains had to do with the fact that he read very well.

When he was eight a man came from a government agency and told Luis's mother she must enroll him in Project Discovery, a pilot school for disadvantaged children who were thought to be gifted, instead of at P.S. 11

"The school . . . ees no good?" his mother asked incredulously.

"Project Discovery is better," said the man.

He didn't want to be discovered, but his mother put him in the program anyway. The first week, she took him every day, but the second week, she made him walk the ten blocks by himself.

Project Discovery was hardly what the man from the agency had promised. Some children still soiled their pants. Others hummed continuously, stopping only to throw paint or food. Classes were constantly disrupted by a stream of visitors, for the school was a pet of the media. Rich, well-dressed women came to help the children read.

Mrs. Anita Schwartz, who came to help Luis read, told him that because he was poor and foreign, the world was eager to cheat him. "When a neighborhood is poor and the mother can't speak English, the shopkeepers do bad things," she said. "They sell dishonest hamburger meat with too much fat . . . perhaps not from cows at all. They charge more for vegetables. Tell your mother to be careful." She handed him a booklet to take home: The Thief in Your Food Basket.

Another time, she told him it would be difficult for him all his life. "You see, Luis," she explained as if waking him from some foolish daydream, "you're not the typical American. You're worse off than the Jew, who can at least laugh at himself. You're neither here nor there.

You're the bottom layer." He considered Mrs. Schwartz crazy, but liked her nevertheless.

The following year, the school had a scandal it didn't survive. The free lunch program was found to be nutritionally unsound. "Protein is a phantom guest at the Project Discovery lunch table," was the quote of the day in the *New York Times*.

Luis returned to P.S. 11 and Mrs. Schwartz returned with him. He was her special project and she came regularly to his apartment. His mother was tolerant but impassive. "Jew wana cupa coffee?" she would ask.

One day, his mother surprised him by saying to Mrs. Schwartz: "I always tought that America was really heaven country. Everybody drives car. If I come to America, I can drive. I can watch TV. I tought I was really heading to heaven."

It was a shock to Luis to realize that his mother was someone who had once had hopes and dreams similar to his own and that she had been disappointed. Yet she didn't seem unhappy.

In the fifth grade, part of Luis's social studies class was devoted to a short history of Puerto Rico. As the teacher described the country in the 1930s and 1940s, she painted a picture of indescribable poverty. Shoes were rarely worn and the ground was infested with sewage and parasites. Grinding poverty, she had called it. He pictured his mother as a small girl being ground down, twisted this way and that. On the other hand, there was a love of dancing and singing, an idea that appalled him. Too often, he'd seen his mother shuffling around the linoleum, dancing. He wanted her to be serious and ambitious. At least ambitious for him.

When the semester was ending, the class wrote a composition on what it meant to be a Puerto Rican in New York and Luis was asked to read his to the class. "In

Puerto Rico," he began, "it was important for men to be macho, but here macho doesn't go. You need brains. You need to use your head, not your strength. You need to know how to operate a machine. In Puerto Rico, people like to sing and dance but here in America, singing and dancing aren't important. Making money is important. In Puerto Rico, there are all shades of skin. Some are a little tan, some dark and some very white. Nobody cares. In New York, we don't know where we stand. If New York is a three-layer cake, man, we are the bottom layer."

After school, Fredo Montenegro took him behind the school and smashed his thumb with a rock. "Let's not hear anymore about the bottom layer," he said and walked away. Still, Luis didn't feel sorry for himself. He felt sorry for Fredo whose life would probably include tattoos, life behind a counter in a luncheonette where they sold dishonest hamburgers, no satisfactory girlfriend.

One day, Mrs. Schwartz, well versed on the bad luck that befell the poor, brought him a small, blue, soft-covered book. "According to the 1950 census," she read, "unskilled Puerto Ricans showed three great categories of occupation—porters, kitchen workers and elevator operators." She left him with a brochure from an organization called Aspira. "A helping hand can turn the tide," was the message. He felt as much Irish as Puerto Rican but he knew he needed help.

Aspira did turn the tide for Luis. He was granted admission to the academically superior Stuyvesant High School. "This is just the beginning," prophesied the director of admissions with more accuracy than he knew. "With any luck, you'll receive scholarship money to a fine university."

The road to Princeton, the fine university that finally granted Luis a full academic scholarship, was not all smooth. That first semester at Stuyvesant High, it seemed to Luis that the film of his life had been speeded up. The students appeared to be middle-aged, bug-eyed with alertness, pale and unpleasant. The competition bordered on mania.

Luis became ill. First with bad colds and finally with pneumonia. When the pneumonia cleared up, he complained of pains in his knees and his mother began taking him to the clinics, but they couldn't find the cause of his pains.

One day, as they were coming home, a young woman, Carla, who lived on their floor, spoke to his mother. "Hey, Marie, how ya doing?"

His mother shrugged. "Okay."

"You heard I got a job? I'm doing keypunch at Klein's." Luis's mother said nothing. She didn't think much of Carla, who insisted on anglicizing everyone's name as if she had a bigger share in America than anyone else. "They sent me to school. IBM keypunch school." Carla shrugged impishly as if she'd put one over on her employer. "You know IBM?"

"I know IBM," said Luis's mother in a more neutral voice. The elevator stopped at several floors.

"Why don't you come and do keypunch, too?" said Carla.

"I dun know nathing about keypunch," answered his mother, but Luis could see her expression had changed.

"They'll send you to school. Come on, don't be foolish. You know numbers. Numbers are numbers in Spanish or English. Don't be foolish: $2.75 an hour. It's better than hanging around this shithole all day."

In the morning, his mother was up early, ate breakfast and set her hair in small rollers. "I hab the appointment," she said when she emerged looking remarkably businesslike.

At noon, she returned, a secret smile on her face. "I'm going to do the keypunch," she announced decisively, as if she expected an argument. Then, turning to Luis, she added firmly, "Jew go back to the school, okay?"

"Maybe," he said grudgingly.

"No maybe," she answered. "Jew go back tomorrow."

5

When April Taylor was two days old, her mother had a shot of Deladumone to dry up her breast milk and put a bottle of Enfamil into her baby daughter's mouth. Right away April took long, choking gulps, snuffling and swallowing. From the beginning, she loved her bottle.

By eight months, she was a chubby, adorable baby who said Hi to anything that moved and also Da Da. She could drag herself around on all fours and sit doubled over. She ate jarred beans and carrots, jarred beef and chicken and jarred peach cobbler, a name meant to stimulate mothers into believing their babies were having a glamorous dessert. She tripled her birth weight, astounding the pediatrician.

"God bless her," said the neighbors and pinched her thighs. Except Mrs. Beck. "All that fat's not doing her any good," she would say, hoisting her own frail Sylvie comfortably on her hip.

Bernice was neither proud nor sorrowful. She was two weeks short of her nineteenth birthday when April was born, an indolent young woman with beautiful breasts and a flat behind. It was sex, not motherhood, that had enticed her into marriage. She couldn't think of many things to do with a baby except feed it. She seldom spoke to April because she couldn't talk back. Talking aloud in the empty house made her feel irresponsible.

In 1963, when April was in the fourth grade, the children were studying words that ended in 'nce' and their teacher, Mrs. DeMont, asked them to use those words in simple sentences. April wrote: I can make my pony prance. I have a chance of winning the race. I can bounce a ball. I can dance very well.

"Very optimistic," wrote Mrs. DeMont in red and put a sticker of a smiling kitten on her paper. After class, April asked Mrs. DeMont what optimistic meant.

"It's when someone has a happy view of life even though the facts point to something quite different."

"You mean they point to *unhappy?*"

"Yes, my dear," Mrs. DeMont pursed her lips as if she had more information but didn't care to share it. "Have a talk with Mother."

The suggestion made her chilly. April knew Bernice had nothing to tell her. Sylvie had those kinds of talks with her mother every day, *every hour:* Did anything happen in school today? Were you called on? Did you answer? Was it right? Was the teacher pleased? Did she tell you how nice you looked? Mrs. Beck had an insatiable desire to know what kind of a little girl she had. Her parents never thought that way. They were unaware that things could go wrong with little girls. She was vaguely aware that something had gone wrong with her already.

Her parents were so crazy about each other, she was always the third party. Once she saw her father approach her mother with a garden hose in his hands. "Stick 'em up," he said and shot her with water in both breasts. Then they both went into the house. April shut off the water and waited on the porch.

There was never legal neglect. She was clean, fed, inoc-
ulated. Every other spring, Bernice bought her an Easter
coat and hat and Easter underwear.

Until the fourth grade, April had no idea that her
weight would have consequences. That just blocks away,
on Charlecote Ridge, there were mothers who would
have cried and lost sleep to see their daughters start out
with all that against them. Bernice didn't cry. On 170th
Street, fat wasn't good or bad. It wasn't anything. No one
was shaping their children's future when they were nine
years old. They were thinking about cleaning the leaves
out of their gutters and rewebbing their lawn chairs.

Every day, Bernice packed the same lunch: a bologna
and cheese sandwich with mayonnaise and lettuce on
white Bond bread, a small bag of potato chips and a
Hostess cupcake or Devil Dog. Sylvie had egg or tuna
salad on whole wheat bread, an apple or an orange. Sara
Davis brought a thermal mug of soup, cheese with
crackers and grapes or a banana.

"If I ate potato chips," Sylvie said, "my mother would
smell them on my breath. They could send her to find
lost children by smelling their lunch bags."

Once April had visited Sara's house after school and
was taken into the garage, where Sara opened the lid of a
freezer that would have made her father whistle. There
were rows of steaks neatly labeled: porterhouse, shell, sir-
loin. Next to that were stacked boxes of Birdseye vegetables, Celebrity crabmeat, Louis Sherry ice cream in three
flavors. Sara found a box of Fudgsicles and offered one
to April. They went outside and sat on a small wrought
iron bench in the middle of the lawn. There was a bird-
bath nearby with a carved fish spouting water. Sara wasn't
eating her pop and it began to drip on her hand. "I've
got to get rid of this," she said and walked to a coiled
garden hose and ran the water over the pop until it
melted.

April was shocked, as if someone had slapped her face. She had never in her life not finished a dessert. What's more, she would have gladly eaten Sara's pop and was about to tell her so before she melted it into a puddle of brownish water.

Bernice had a simple cooking style that was similar to every blue collar mother in Queens. She made meat loaf once a week. She browned her onions, put them in a large bowl, added ground chuck and pork, two eggs, a cup of bread crumbs and half a cup of ketchup. She blended it all with quick strokes, first taking off her wedding band, then shaped the mixture into a loaf which she wrapped in bacon. The side dishes included mashed potatoes made with margarine and evaporated milk, plus canned corn and lima beans. She bought Gravy Master and every night made gravy which was poured generously over whatever meat they ate. She always put out a dish of olives and celery sticks.

She was proud of her cole slaw—the only salad she ever served. It was made with an irresistible dressing of mayonnaise, evaporated milk, crushed pineapple and sugar. For dessert, she often made Jell-O with whipped topping or Royal chocolate pudding. Heart's Delight peaches—which they preferred to Del Monte—was their favorite fruit. For Sunday breakfast and lunch, Bernice would pick up a coffee cake or salt sticks from Smilen Brothers, a small specialty market close to home. Smilen Brothers were more expensive than King Kullen and when she served these treats she would say, "These are from the gyp."

It was cooking that was hot, tasty, filled you up and needed little chewing. Bernice and her father were proud and satisfied to live this way. They considered themselves a thousand times better than the Italians down the street

who had soup on Mondays—to clean out their systems—
and spaghetti on Wednesdays and all kinds of tomato
sauce and grated cheese. Her father had never eaten a
Chinese or an Italian dinner or even pizza. "I wouldn't
have it in my stomach," he said, as if he were talking
about Red China being in the U.N.

In eighth grade, April took the state aptitude tests and
was scheduled for a conference. She picked all the pills
off her white Orlon turtleneck and wore pantyhose instead of socks. The night before, she used Geminesse
peel-off clay masque although there was nothing wrong
with her complexion. Someone was going to help her
plan her future.

"Do you have any idea of how you did?" Mrs. Cal-
derone, the counselor, asked in a teasing way. April
shrugged. "Look here, verbal reasoning, 95," thump went
her hand, "numerical ability, 91," thump, "abstract reasoning, 97, language, 93, spelling, 92," thump, thump,
thump. "You can compete at the very best institutions
and have a fine academic career—a *future*."

That night after dinner, she approached her father
and told him she wanted to talk to him about her future.
Harlan laughed, genuinely amused by her seriousness.
"Your future," he said, wiping his eyes, "is what comes
along when you're eighteen and have to find a job."

When April was eighteen and had finished high school,
however, she didn't look for a job. She was five feet five
and weighed 180 pounds. She was certain she could control her future by simply losing weight. The ideal man
would love her. Important work would be hers. But she
couldn't quite galvanize her will.

Mrs. Beck was billing Sylvie as pre-law. Sylvie had a job

at the New School in Greenwich Village for the summer. She was going to take courses to apply for credit at Brooklyn College where she would use her Regents scholarship. "You could do the same," she told April. In August, Sylvie urged her to be her replacement at the New School when she started at Brooklyn the following month. She brought home an application and made April call Jamaica High and have her records transferred. She was entitled to two free courses. That was a start. She could come in a couple of days before Sylvie left and learn the switchboard, which would be one of her duties. Having had a taste of Manhattan, Sylvie was impatient with anyone who *chose* to remain in Queens. She had a boyfriend who came to pick her up in a red Ford convertible. He was in advertising, an account executive with an agency that had Rice-A-Roni and Bond Clothes among its clients.

Harlan warned April about the fairies and the creeps that hung around downtown New York. "At least we know she won't be raped," said Mrs. Beck.

"So I guess I'll go," said April.

"It's done," said Mrs. Beck.

"You'll see," said Sylvie. "It'll change your life."

6

IF HARLAN HAD STOOD outside the lobby of the New School on any evening, he would have declared it a Communist outpost. It had an adventuresome leftist air about it. Yet you had only to study the catalogue to see that many of the courses were how-to's for getting ahead in the capitalist system or for repairing a damaged spirit jaded by the good life.

When she walked the streets of the Village, April felt daring and sophisticated. There was something about that liberal wind sweeping across the sidewalks that made her feel intellectually superior to almost anyone alive.

No one at the New School cared about her weight, her experience or the fact that she wore the same outfit three days of the week and another outfit for two. She was one more ship passing through in a world of transients. They showed her what was necessary and went about their own pursuits with the distracted, saintly air of serious scholars who also had to earn a living.

Between her lunch hour walks and the unavailability of Bernice's handy, carbohydrate-loaded snacks, she lost ten pounds and was so exhilarated she made a conscious effort to lose ten more. She could now fit into a size 16, which allowed her more fashion possibilities. She went to Bloomingdale's and picked out two bias-cut skirts, two turtleneck sweaters, brown leather boots and a tan raincoat. By the time her classes began for the spring semester, she was someone with a recognizable waist and vastly upgraded dreams. And what she dreamed about was love.

In 1972 there was no air of goodness about celibacy. Everybody was hugging and kissing. On the street. In the movies. In books. Everyone but her. Worse, she was pure, not through self-restraint, but lack of opportunity. It was the worst thing you could know about yourself. In this state of continuous arousal and recrimination, she saw the man of her dreams around every corner and, one day, he materialized.

The first time she saw Harald Tierney was at 6:30 on a sweet January evening. It had been a bizarrely hot day, a record-breaker. She was waiting in the corridor of the school near the public telephones. He was searching for something in his pockets. He touched his breast, his hips, his sides. He was standing in half-light wearing a charcoal gray suit with a soft blue shirt. He saw her and smiled, not in an intimate way but as if he smiled at the world in general. He turned and a recessed light lit the back of his neck. The expression on his face, the texture of his skin, the bold cut of his jaw, the play of the innocent blue of his shirt against the pale, damp flush of his face were tremendously appealing to her.

He found what he was searching for, waved it to her as if in explanation and disappeared inside a booth. She edged closer and watched. He smiled as he spoke into the telephone and hung up reluctantly. When he rose to leave, she almost followed him.

By midterm, April had dropped her initial courses and chosen instead Writing Advertising Copy and a seminar entitled Change Your Emotions and Win in the Market. The stock market course was overenrolled, and at the first meeting they had to move to a larger room. The audience was affluent. The women wore dresses instead of jeans and the men wore dark suits and watches without numbers.

When the instructor walked in she was surprised and excited. It was the man she had seen in the hall. "Ladies and gentlemen," he said to them in a slightly mocking voice, "would you believe me if I told you that it is not only simple but almost inevitable to amass healthy sums from the buying and selling of common stock and the only thing keeping you from doing so are your emotions?" He took a deep breath and the class took this pause to put down their papers and books and give him their full attention. "It's not the big boys," he continued, "or the institutions, not the wheeler-dealers or back room deals, or insiders, or European cartels that are keeping riches from you. It is the pervasive inability of humans to sell a stock that's rising and buy one that has plummeted."

His audience settled back in a collective trance. He spoke with a quiet sincerity and each person thought only he had caught it. He appeared agile without looking athletic and had that straight Episcopalian hair that ended in a neat spill over a broad forehead. He looked to be about thirty.

"Now," he folded his arms in a loose embrace, "tell me what you hope to gain here. Did you take the course for a specific purpose or were you beguiled by the catchy title?"

He went around the room asking each of them to reveal their investment objectives. The answers were sincere but unintelligible to April, who couldn't keep her eyes off of Harald Tierney.

"I want to create capital," said a fortyish woman with a raccoon coat draped around her shoulders.

They all knew exactly what they wanted. To create capital. To conserve capital. Some wanted to trade. Some wanted to live off their dividends. Some wanted to speculate. Harald Tierney nodded agreeably at each answer.

"And you?" He reached April and she wasn't prepared.

"I was beguiled by the catchy title." She was the first to say this and everyone laughed. She didn't laugh. She was constricted by her own sudden interest in him, a quiet riot in her temples.

"It sounds catchy but it isn't," he said. "It's absolutely true. Are you in the market at the moment?"

In the market for what? "No."

"Do you have some capital?"

"You mean money?"

Again everyone laughed. "Yes," he, too, smiled. "Money."

"Yes."

"Would it be too personal to tell us how much? I'm asking for a reason. Perhaps we can make some money with your money."

"It's seven hundred dollars." It was all the money she had ever saved. She thought of where she kept her money, in her underwear drawer. Would they ask that, too?

Everyone looked at their hands and she knew they considered it a silly figure. Harald Tierney's expression didn't change. "It can be respectably increased when our class ends. If you won't mind, we can make an example of your investment."

Mind? Her eyes were locked on his face, dazed with his unexpected attentions. "No. I don't mind."

He smiled and his dark eyes sent out beams of light. "You will be our model portfolio. Your seven hundred dollars."

She hadn't intended to do any such thing with her money. She needed it to pay for her clothes, her food, in case she developed a toothache and college tuition if that ever materialized. "Fine," she said.

He outlined a practical procedure for them all. He would recommend half a dozen stocks, under twenty dollars. They would buy any combination they chose, the investment not to exceed one thousand dollars. They would lock in predetermined buy and sell prices on the day they entered the order. This would eliminate second thoughts, the jitters and other human foibles. The orders would be revised only if lack of price movement made it impossible to complete the transaction. Buying and selling would go off automatically when their price came over the ticker.

"We could do it without money, but it wouldn't mean as much," he said. "Your tuition will cover commissions. Your profits will be free and clear."

"So will our losses," said a man in the back and everybody laughed.

"Now, now," said Harald Tierney. He smoothed his hair back off his brow, the only time that evening he showed self-awareness. He wrote out April's specific recommendations on a piece of paper, folded it, and handed it to her: American Fan and RCD Corporation were written in a backward, slanted penmanship. She stared at it for the remainder of the period.

After class, a woman picked him up at the outer door where he stood and waited. He seemed totally delighted—which, according to his investment philosophy, meant it was the ideal time to dump the woman. Ha ha. Very funny. At least he had her money. He was going to stimulate her seven hundred dollars into growth, which, now that she thought of it, seemed a very intimate act for someone she'd just met.

Having nothing much else to do on her time off, April devoted herself to studying the business pages and find-

ing out what there was to know about the buying and
selling of common stock. She noted quickly that the reasons the columnists gave for falling or rising prices had
little to do with facts or prudent decisions. Stocks went up
or down because people were either exhilarated or frightened by the daily news. But nothing had a long-range
effect. Whatever volatility took place after a big news
event usually calmed down.

To her surprise, the financial news was written in extravagant, emotional language. It was a tumultuous time
in the market. President Nixon had devalued the dollar,
sending currency markets "skittering in confusion." An
initially "exultant market" became a "nervous market,"
and finally a "bewildered market skidding by 16.85
points." The price of gold "skyrocketed to 72.30." The
London bullion market had orders flowing in from all
directions, creating "chaos on the floor." Bond prices rose
and soybean futures hit historic highs. The American
tourist, vexed by the currency plight, said, "I'm going
home. I can't buy any presents or souvenirs."

Before she put in her orders for the two stocks Harald
had recommended for her, she checked on the trading
range for the past month in back issues of the *Times*.
American Fan had a pattern of going up a fraction—an
eighth or a quarter—until it hit a new high, then crept
back down the same way. Each upturn, however, continued half a point beyond the previous high and each
downturn stopped within half a point of the recent low.
Deducing that the current price of 8 would drop to 7
within a week, she put in a buy order at that price and a
sell order for 10⅞ which she calculated to be the new
high. She did the same with RCD Corporation, buying it
at 9½ and selling at 12.

She wanted to stun Harald Tierney with her new

knowledge. "Why did the market go up after the devaluation?" she asked. "It 'rose exultantly' according to the *Times*."

He smiled. "The market hates indecision of any kind. When the announcement comes, good or bad, it reacts out of relief. As you noticed, it quickly went down again."

"Yes," she said weakly. She noticed a small scar over his right eye. He was half sitting against his desk with his legs crossed in front of him. She felt nervous and disoriented.

She lived only to return to the class twice each week. The rest of the time was spent in mental and physical preparation. She massaged her body, steamed her face and slathered on skin preparations. She experimented with her hair, parting it in the middle and letting it flow around her. She bought rouge that looked dark brown in its case but turned russet on her cheeks. It took her an hour to prepare herself for his class, but he continued to give out his lecture in an impersonal way. People detained him after class and she felt an instant, leaden jealousy toward anyone who held his attention.

She knew the market was down. The news was both joyful and troubled. Consumers had boycotted meat, but there was another lunar landing. The Dow Jones average was the lowest it had been in years. Maybe he was losing money. Maybe he had taken their money and used it for his own purposes and lost it, too. She didn't care about the money. She hoped he *would* lose it and feel apologetic. She only wanted some sign from him, a nod or a particular word. When she left the classroom her mouth tasted dry and bitter from excess emotion. Her makeup, the lipstick and the eyeshadow felt heavy on her face.

One weekend, she looked up his name in the Manhattan telephone directory and saw that he lived on East 91st Street. She walked by his building twice, certain he would spot her and call the police.

With a success that surprised everyone, including Harald, April's initial transactions in the market netted her two hundred and sixty-four dollars. She wanted to put all the money plus profits into one stock but he advised her to split it up again. "It's less risky. A successful investor is always aiming to minimize his risk." He said this with a smile, as if there were several levels of meaning. Was he flirting with her?

It turned out to be good advice because the stock she had wanted went down, hitting her stop loss price three days after she purchased it. The other stock, however, gained a respectable two points for an additional one hundred dollars. She now had one thousand and four dollars, which she put into American Fan for the second time—the stock had again reached its low cycle. She bought one hundred and thirty shares and put in her sell order for 11¼, which it reached a month later for a whopping profit of four hundred eighty-seven dollars. She had more than doubled her money.

Harald referred to her as the whiz of Wall Street and only half jokingly invited her to be their guest lecturer. "Miss Taylor has again cut a giddy path through Wall Street," he announced to the class. "She's raking it in."

Sometimes she felt he was making fun of her. As if she had declared her love and he had handed it back. No, thanks.

The summer loomed ahead lonely and awful. He asked them to close their accounts or have them transferred to their own brokers. It was neither profitable nor convenient for his firm to handle twenty-three tiny accounts. Even though they knew it was coming, they all felt abandoned.

"I don't have another broker," said April after class. "Who'll take care of my money?"

"You will. You've been doing a better job than any broker could do for you."

"But it's knowing you that gave me the confidence."

"I could recommend a broker . . ." He was putting all his papers into a soft-sided briefcase. Why would he want to give her away to someone else? He wanted to be rid of her.

"I don't want another one. I want you."

He smiled. "Being a broker is not my main business. Besides, you don't need me. Whatever system you're using, you'll do just fine."

"Please let me stay with you. Please." She knew that was too many pleases but she couldn't let him walk out of her life without a struggle.

"All right," he said finally. "But I'll be in and out all summer."

When she called his number in June, an assistant answered and offered to take her order. Mr. Tierney was away. *Where? In Europe? On the Riviera?* He had some nerve leaving her and her money. She didn't make any more transactions for the rest of the summer, letting her money ride where it stood. She longed to see him again and decided that longing was important. Longing was almost as good as having the thing itself.

That summer, tropical storm Agnes struck Pennsylvania, devastating a wide area. Sylvie, triumphant from her year at Brooklyn College, was going to Europe, Mrs. Beck's grand gift to her honor roll girl. Sylvie had changed. Her face was totally new. A face that had always seemed gaunt and too long was now interesting, a landscape with peaks and valleys. She wore jeans *with* heels *and* white lisle socks and a man-tailored jacket. Only a candidate for Creedmoor State would have dressed like that in high school. Now it was a dazzling combination, promising adventuresome sex with a stern business mind.

Sylvie no longer spoke in slang, either. Turd and fart, her two favorite nouns, and turdy and farty, her two favorite adjectives, were no longer in her vocabulary. April was at a loss with this new Sylvie. She was afraid of boring her.

Two events in early July helped take her mind off Sylvie and Harald Tierney. She was offered a sublet two blocks from the New School by one of the psychology staff who was going upstate to study autistic children. It was an oppressively somber two rooms over a dry cleaning store. There was a pink bedroom, a living room and a closet of a kitchen with a greasy rotisserie instead of an oven. The price was right: $200 a month.

Every other night she ate a rotisseried chicken with potato salad from a deli down the street. When she looked out of her two front windows after dinner, she saw an Italian restaurant, a Kwik Kopy photocopy place, a plant store and a place where you could get help with your tax forms and buy insurance.

There were twin beds in the bedroom and two windows which opened to a view of rooftops and fire escapes. She locked the windows, pulled down the shades but still slept in the living room, where the windows could be reached only by birds.

The second important change in her life was initiated by Martin Bell, partner in the advertising firm of Bell and Adonesio, who was continuing to teach his class in writing advertising copy through the summer. April had enrolled again.

Martin Bell was a short, dapper man with clear gray eyes and a full, jowly face. "You know," he told them in the beginning, "the words people say in television commercials and the words accompanying the pictures in magazine and newspaper ads are all carefully written, sometimes mulled over for weeks. I'm telling you this because there's a misconception among the general public that these words just . . . appear . . . form themselves out of the ether. 'You mean somebody *writes* those things?' is a question I'm repeatedly asked at parties. Yes. Somebody writes those words and gets paid handsomely to do so." Martin Bell rocked expertly on the balls of his feet and buttoned and then unbuttoned his blazer. "I'm going to teach you how to write those words, too. I'll teach you to sell goods."

By Easter he had had many of them writing credible, selling copy: *We don't just take the money and run.* (For a small insurance company stressing personal service.) *Hey, shirt. I hear you're permanently pressed. Wanna prove it?* (For a sexy shirt.) *Plain Jane, the funny-looking dolly you love to love.* (For a sensibly homely doll.)

April liked Marty Bell and he liked her. He said her copy was conversational (good), not preachy and static (bad). Toward the middle of the summer session, he asked her to do catalogue copy for a small mail order book his firm put out. There was little creativity involved other than to squeeze merchandise description into the tiny space provided. "It will teach you economy of language," he said wryly.

There were thirty listings to a page, selling everything from old-fashioned muslin sheets to toilet paper printed with the Best of the Times Crossword Puzzles. She became a genius at abbreviating:

Children's all-cotton undershirts. Yr. choice messg. I'm a good/bad, boy/girl. I'm an angel/stinker. Red on wht. Szs. 3–6x, 2/$8.

Toward the end of the summer, in addition to the hy

pothetical ads which they all did, April contributed an acceptable headline for one of the agency's real clients, a sports car manufacturer who was having shipping problems for a car that was much in demand. *The prettiest thing that ever kept a man waiting.* Her headline was considered better than anything the agency could come up with and Marty Bell promised her fifty dollars if she could add some snappy body copy to go under the picture.

By Labor Day, she could see how seriously her life had changed. She had her own apartment, she worked as a freelance copywriter and, as an employee of the New School, she was entitled to get an education at a very reasonable price.

Sometimes she went out for an evening walk through the Village. A breeze circulated up her summer skirt, through her legs and thighs. She'd walk down to Washington Square Park, pretending that Harald was beside her. She looked at everything through his eyes.

When she looked out of her window and saw the couples entering the restaurant across the street, she could plainly see herself entering with Harald. He would have his hand on her shoulder as they waited to be seated. He would look into her eyes. As she sat eating her rotisseried chicken and her potato salad, she imagined that he could see her. She put down her fork between bites and chewed softly, hardly moving her lips, and it took her about fifteen minutes to swallow a spoonful of potato salad. She lost another seven pounds. When Harald came back in the fall, she would be ready for him.

7

THE SUMMER BEFORE HE left for Prince-
ton, Luis got a job with Lande Brothers Construction on
Third Avenue near Fifty-first Street. Mr. Lande was a
man he had met through Mrs. Schwartz. "Come see me
about a summer job," he had told Luis and, true to his
word, had been available and accommodating.

"I haven't had any experience," said Luis when they
met.

"Experience doesn't mean a goddam thing," replied
Mr. Lande. He waited for a startled response. "It all depends on what's up here," he pointed to his right temple,
"and what's in here," he tapped his chest. "You'll do fine.
Better than fine."

They placed him with the sales subsidiary, Aubernon
and Cagney, responsible for setting up sales offices and
model exhibits, hiring photographers and approving ads
for the real estate sections. Two or three times, Luis went
to the model homes located in the suburbs of New York
and New Jersey. The families that came to inspect the
homes seemed cheerful but overburdened with young,
fidgety children who begged to be held. Luis didn't want

any children. He wanted to be free to take full advantage of whatever life held in store.

It was right after he had decided that he wanted no encumbrances that he walked into Jim Aubernon's office and found a girl there spreading photographs out on the desk. She was blond, athletic looking, with chunky hips. Blond fuzz covered her tanned arms up to her shoulders, which were bare, and around her ears and lower jaw. She was wearing a tank top, a soft bra that showed her nipples, peach colored cotton slacks and sandals. Her hair looked bushy, as if she had stayed out in the sun too long and it needed conditioning.

There was something sure and businesslike about her, in contrast to her looks and way of dressing. While they both waited for Jim Aubernon to get off the phone, she stared at Luis as if daring him to look at her. She didn't care if he liked to be stared at or not. Then she smiled. He looked determinedly out the window and didn't return her smile. Then he thought it over and changed his mind but she wasn't smiling anymore. He tried to catch her eye but Mr. Aubernon was off the phone and she was hoisting a black portfolio onto his desk.

Luis left reluctantly and asked the secretary who she was.

"Her name's Barbara Traynor. She's a photographer's rep. She tries to get work for the guys in her stable by going around showing their photographs."

"The guys in her stable?"

"It's just an expression, don't get offended."

He wasn't offended. In fact, the expression made him feel kind of sexy. Thinking about Barbara Traynor with her bushy hair and her chunky bottom and her nipples pushing through her tank top made him feel like being one of the guys in her stable. He hung around the office hoping to catch her eye before she left.

The next time she came he was in Jim Aubernon's office but this time, since no one asked him to leave, he stayed to watch her make her spiel. She turned the sample photographs slowly, doing a first-rate selling job as she went.

Mr. Aubernon said, "This is great stuff, Barb. We'll let you know by four tomorrow."

"Good enough," she said with just the right indifference and again zipped up both portfolios, looked at her oversized watch and left the office. Luis followed her out. "Uh . . . hey . . . wait . . ." He caught up with her at the bank of elevators. "Uh, you go out or something?"

"Yeah," she turned around and peered at him. They were the same height. "I go out . . . I don't know about the . . . 'or something.'" She tried to imitate his husky voice and he laughed.

"Want to go out tonight?"

She looked at her watch again. "I have two more appointments and then I need forty minutes to scrub the soot off. How about 7:30? 23 West 83rd Street . . . push the bell marked TRAYNOR." The elevator came and before he could answer, it closed on her satisfied smile.

He thought about her thighs all afternoon. He knew they would be thicker than they should be, but it didn't matter. These small imperfections made her accessible to him.

Her building was an extra wide brownstone with two small stone lions flanking the door, which was a cheerful red. He began to have doubts over their short acquaintance. He couldn't remember what she really looked like. Maybe she was more unattractive that he had originally estimated? Chronically undatable. Well, he was already there. He rang the bell and after a long wait—had he misunderstood?—she buzzed him in. He looked at his watch and realized that he was fifteen minutes early.

She answered the door in a loosely belted wraparound robe. They stood there staring at each other. She looked clean and rosy from the shower, no makeup. He sighed with relief. He could see quite a bit at the parting of the robe and most compelling was the fact that he could see a tan *and untan* portion of her breast. For some reason, being witness to that line of demarcation, normally beyond public view, greatly excited him. He could not have been more aroused had she met him totally naked. He must have looked embarrassed because she gave him a suspicious look. "Something wrong?"

"I'll just wait while you finish dressing."

"But something's wrong. I can see it in your face. What is it?"

"No, it's nothing."

"Yes, it is."

"I can see part of your breasts." His eyes returned to the parting of her robe.

"Oh, god," she rolled her eyes upward and pulled the belt tighter around her. "You think I'm coming on to you? Is that what you're saying?"

"Oh, no." He hadn't thought that but now that she said it, it became a distinct possibility. "I think it's perfectly accidental. I'm a little early and you're in your robe. But . . . it . . . bothered me."

"Bothered you?" Maybe she was coming on to him. Maybe he was supposed to do something. Should he kiss her? "You don't like it?" she asked sarcastically.

"No. It's fine. I like it. I just thought I should tell you." He backed away in confusion. He had yet to say one sentence he was proud of. "If I didn't tell you, you wouldn't know."

"Jesus," she said. "How weird can you get? You come here knowing me for a total of twenty minutes and the first thing you say to me is that you can see my breast."

"I'm sorry," he said. "Don't be mad."

"How do you expect me to feel?"

"I don't know." There it was again. The tan/untan

breast peeking out. Beckoning. She saw him looking and she looked at it, too. Then she looked at his eyes and at his agitated hands crossing and uncrossing in front of him. His ears began to buzz. He looked for a place to sit down.

"How can you get so excited over half a breast?" She challenged him but he could tell by the new softness in her voice that she was pleased. Maybe she was more than pleased. It gave him the courage he needed.

"I've been thinking about you all day."

"You're crazy. You're really crazy. How can you talk like that to someone you hardly know?" After she said this she did a very surprising thing. She took off her robe and sat on his lap and put her arms around his neck and kissed him on the lips. He kissed her back, letting his hands roam all over her body, still warm and damp from the shower. She smelled lemony and sweet. As his eagerness grew so did hers.

"You should take off those lovely clothes," she said. When his scholarship to Princeton came through, Mrs. Schwartz had given him a navy wool blazer and a silk tie—repeating horses' heads on a field of red—both of which he now removed. He left his trousers on, feeling suddenly shy and she led him to a sleeping alcove.

When she became really excited she called him lover, which pleased him. "Oh, lover," she said, "that feels so good. It's as good as it gets." This encouraging talk plus her agitated movements spurred him on. Every part of her was oversized, even her teeth which he could feel and see. She guided him expertly, parting herself to accommodate him, raising her hips to fit him better, looking him straight in the face and then losing control. He had read that women couldn't get clitoral contact during intercourse and he put his thumbs there to please her. "Oh, that's wonderful. You're great. Don't stop. I'm almost there . . . almost. . . ."

Through the commanding thunder of his own excitement, he considered her monologue extraordinary. Except for his very first woman, who had been primly efficient, he had never experienced or heard of anyone conducting intercourse in anything but complete silence and complete darkness. To be suddenly atop this tan, fleecy, appreciative, love-abandoned woman was eye-opening and invested him with a new and thrilling power.

They made love again before going out to dinner. "This is the first time I paid for my dinner before I ate it," she said with mock sarcasm.

"I've got thirty-two dollars," he said. "Let's go out and blow it."

"Okay." She went to the bathroom but came back before entering and sat on the bed. "I don't even know your name. You've just screwed me twice and I don't even know your name."

They ate dinner in a small Italian restaurant on Columbus Avenue. She ordered for both of them and then apologized. "Sorry. I have to be pushy all day and it's hard to turn it off."

He asked a lot of questions about her work and was surprised to learn the men she worked for were all older, some old enough to be her father. "It doesn't matter how old they are," she said. "If they had to sell their own work and someone told them it wasn't exactly what they needed, they'd probably kill themselves. They take rejection personally."

"So you take it for them?"

"With me, it's a job." She attacked her salad and began eating it quickly and he knew she didn't want to talk about her work anymore. He didn't want to talk about anything either, certainly not himself. She had pulled her

hair back and tied it with a scarf, which wasn't as becoming as when it was loose around her face, but her lack of
beauty made him feel protective. He wondered if she
would let him in when he took her home. He needn't
have worried. As they lingered at the window of a small
boutique, she squeezed his hand and said, "Let's go
home. I feel like screwing."

He wondered if he would ever get used to her offhand-
edness. It was still a jolt.

Later, in bed, she asked him to stay the night. That was
the last thing he'd thought of. "Sure," he finally answered. "I'll just make one phone call."

The following day, Barbara Traynor called him at the
office and invited him to dinner. "Come by around eight.
I'll cook you a nice dinner."

"Fine."

"I've been thinking about it all day," she said seductively. He had no trouble identifying what "it" was. "You,
too?"

"Of course." He looked around the office.

"Tell me one thing you've thought."

"Well . . . ah . . . all of it." He was conscious of at least
two secretaries possibly listening to him and watching his
face.

"Come on, come on," she insisted, "one thing."

"The conversation . . . during," he said as soberly as
possible.

"Ah . . . you like that, huh? Well, it would be nice to
hear a little of that from you. It works both ways, you
know."

He saw her that night and the next. They parted for
the weekend because she had a business appointment in
Boston. Finally they settled into a pattern of spending at
least three nights a week together in her apartment. His

mother was calm about his comings and goings and asked no questions.

As for Barbara, she didn't tell him she was thirty, which he guessed her to be. And he didn't tell her he was eighteen, which he was sure she didn't think he was. He didn't tell her he would be leaving New York in September either. He felt if he told her, she would be mad as hell.

Barbara Traynor made him feel both dumb and smart. Strong and clumsy, wise and silly. The only things he told her about himself were current history, the daily ups and downs of Aubernon and Cagney. She had one piece of advice for everything that took place during the business day: "Screw it."

He had heard cursing before, but never combined with such sophisticated wisdom. He'd never heard anyone express the idea that an account executive who insisted on delivering the sales promotion material to Mr. Aubernon himself instead of entrusting it to Luis was out to "do a number" on him. It was exciting to be molded by her and he began to have the first disloyal thoughts about Mrs. Schwartz, who lived in an unreal world. Barbara lived in the world as it really was.

Washington was filled with crooks and worse, she told him as they watched the television news. What could be worse than crooks? Crooks who were puppets of the Mafia. Everyone in Washington was a puppet of the Mafia? Maybe not Ted Kennedy or Rockefeller. They didn't need the money, but they were dumb, and depended on creeps to tell them what to think. What creeps were those? The intellectuals. Pathetic, homely scroungers. Jews who were Jew haters. Who were out to screw the middle class in the name of liberalism. Who hated the middle class because *they* were hopelessly middle-class themselves.

What's more, the system was breaking down. People

didn't stop for red lights anymore. Car repairmen didn't repair your car. At times, they actually broke it. Doctors didn't cure anything, and god only knew what dentists were doing in those tiny covered-up spaces.

That summer of 1969, on July 20, Neil Armstrong walked on the moon. "Absolutely bloody marvelous," said a London clerk. "It means nothing to me," said Pablo Picasso. "I have no opinion about it, and I don't care." That's what Barbara said, too.

Her cynicism seemed just right for the late 1960s—years in which everything had gone wrong—major assassinations, the *Pueblo*, the suspicion that perhaps America could be ... yes! in the wrong. Then, too, the cynicism didn't affect him. The system she found so loathsome was bending over to befriend him. The last two weeks in July and the first in August seemed like the best weeks of his life. He was relaxed, optimistic and the picture of health. At least once a week, she told him he was the best lay she'd ever had.

He was very interested, although he didn't tell her, in how she took care of herself. Her morning routine: raisin bran, a handful of vitamins, ten sit-ups and twenty-five hip rolls (she sat naked on the rug and waddled across the room on her hips—to keep them from spreading, she claimed). The hip rolls were excruciatingly seductive and he had a feeling she was more faithful to them when he was in the audience.

With mystical attention, he watched her put on makeup.

"Didn't your mother put on makeup?"

"No. My mother put on mentholatum. She put it up her nose and on her throat and dabbed it on her pillow." It was the truth. The idea of taking such care of your body was new to him and he was disappointed in himself for having been so lax. He began doing sit-ups, too. She spent ten minutes every night flossing her teeth, up and down, up and down. Well, so did he. He let her take him to get his hair cut and *shaped* by a short Englishman who brushed it forward like a monk's and let it curl innocently around his temples and face. As sometimes happens, the haircut took him completely out of one category—good-looking, safe, polite—and put him in another—strong-willed, uncommitted, traveling a slightly dangerous path.

When she saw him, his grandmother said, "Ay, ay, ay," as if she were watching something of unendurable suspense.

Oddly, the more he learned from Barbara Traynor, the less he liked her. Her cynicism wore him down. How could everyone be a cheat, a liar, a no-talent coward? She sent food back in restaurants, something he never got used to. She refused wine. It seemed she was singlehand-edly paying back the world for thousands of years of re-pression. Moreover, she was a sexual bully.

"What is this?" she would ask, placing his hand on her lap in some public place.

"You know what it is."

"No, I don't. Tell me." Her voice would get louder in warning that she was quite capable of making a scene.

"It's your . . . awh, come on, Barb."

"Say it." And when he refused: "All right, then, de-scribe it to me."

"Private. Unseen. Mysterious."

"No, no, no. Hot. Wet. Squishy. Squishy right now."

"All right. Hot. Wet. Squishy," he would reply in a cold, dry voice. At such times he felt he had leaped ahead in life experience. He felt like a weary adult dealing with a spoiled child.

"Now," she took a deep breath. "What goes into it?"

It was a never-ending bully game and he was changing. Taking on some of the characteristics of his haircut. Perhaps he was purifying himself for the journey to Princeton, pulling away from all the things that had looked so blessed and glamorous in June. Even Mr. Lande appeared sad in his yellowing tan. Often, he would corner Luis in the hall, study him with narrowed eyes. "You're a good-looking boy," he would muse, as if Luis weren't present. "You'll always have a place here. Always."

He didn't feel flattered by this approval. Mr. Lande didn't know how valuable or worthless he was to the company. "I haven't really done anything," he would protest.

"You will, you will. You're programmed to do okay." He waited to hear from Luis. "I can tell you your future right now. Where are you going off to, Harvard?"

"Princeton."

"Princeton, Harvard, it doesn't matter." He waited again to hear from Luis. "You don't believe me, do you?"

"Yes, sir. No, sir."

"The things you've been told are important aren't that important. And the things you'd think are true aren't always true. Take this building, for example. Now you'd think I'd be able to have my offices in any damn building I liked, right?" Luis nodded. "Not so. I hate this building. I hate the look of it. I hate the windows. They don't open. I feel afraid when I stand at them and look down. It makes my head hurt every time I think of how much rent I pay to have my office in this ugly, useless box. The bank, on the other hand, loves this building. They have their office in one just like it, therefore, it makes me look solid. They lend me millions of dollars because they believe me to be a responsible, forward-looking person. Forward-looking, but not fruity, you understand. If your building is old, with curved lines and windows that open and have proper sills so you can look out without feeling fearful, then you're a fruit or a potential fruit and un-

bankable." He waited a long moment as if he expected
Luis to protest. "Now how does that translate into life?"

"I don't know, sir." He knew. "It's all a game," he finally said. "Is that what you're saying?"

"Precisely," said Mr. Lande. "A very silly game. But,
Luis," Mr. Lande sat up very straight, "it's the only game
we've got so it's still very important, right?"

"Right, sir."

"Good. You come back and work here any summer you
want to. There'll always be a spot for you."

"Thank you, sir." He walked out of the vast office feeling strange. He knew Mr. Lande meant everything he
said, but he also knew that without the huge organization
and wealth to back up his philosophy, Mr. Lande would
sound like the village idiot. You could afford to be cynical
and laugh at success only when you were very, very
successful.

Around the third week in August, he realized that he
might not want to be Barbara's slave forever. Two jobs
that she had worked hard on fell through and her mood
turned foul. She went around the apartment slamming
drawers, cursing and being impatient with her clients
when they called. "How the hell should I know why they
didn't buy it? Everyone's afraid to make a decision so
they'll go with something bland that won't offend, what
can I tell you?"

She was bossy and impatient in bed, too. He didn't like
being on call. What would happen if he said no three
times in a row? On the worst of these nights, he said, "I'm
going to sleep at home tonight. I think you'll be better off
alone."

"Oh, you do, do you? What gave you that idea?"

"You're in a bitchy mood."

"I'm entitled. Grow up, for godsakes. Nobody can be
lah-di-dah all the time. Grown-ups have bitchy moods.
Are you a grown-up?"

"I don't know."

She looked deep into his face. "How old are you, anyway?"

He considered lying but he was tired of being bullied. "Eighteen."

"How old? Come on, come on."

"I'm eighteen. I'm leaving to start at Princeton three weeks from today." Why did he feel the thrill of fear? What could she do to him?

"Jesus. Are you telling the truth?" She stared at him dumbfounded. Then she began to laugh. "Oh, my god. Wait'll they get a load of you at Princeton."

"What the hell is that supposed to mean?"

"Nothing." She flounced around the room coquettishly. "It's just that . . . you know . . . they say 'fatha' and 'motha'. You're not your typical Princetonian." She cocked her head as if trying to picture it all. "Make believe you're Brazilian, they'll have more respect for you, believe me." She was perfectly serious, her old pragmatic self. "You won't go through the minority thing. You can be a rich Brazilian playboy, son of a cattle magnate or is that Venezuela where they raise the cattle?"

"Thanks for your vote of confidence." He was glad she was being so bitchy. It made leaving that much easier and he really felt like getting out of that decorated, scented room.

Two weeks passed during which he put Barbara Traynor out of his mind, although from time to time he felt a twinge of uneasiness. She wasn't the type to let someone else call the shots. Would she let him go, just like that? The first week in September, he met her, at her insistence, at a bleak luncheonette on the corner of 60th and Second Avenue. She was waiting in a booth and looked both tired and pale. He immediately felt sorry for her. Her looks depended heavily on her tan and her energy, both of which had left her. The first sentence out of her mouth didn't cheer him either. "I'm pregnant," she said.

"Pregnant?" It took him a moment to adjust. He looked around the room, which was square, to an old man eating a meat loaf dinner across the aisle from them. "You said you had a loop, remember? The Lippes Loop." He was sure she'd say, "oh, yes," and he'd be relieved. She said nothing. They had joked about it, both proudly reciting Browning's poem about Fra Lippo Lippi. Now she was telling him there was no loop. All that lovemaking, two or three times a night. With no loop? She was a rotten liar.

"It fell out."

"Fell out? How could it fall out?"

"A certain percentage fall out. Mine fell out." She said all this with a cold deliberateness that made his stomach hurt. The old man eating his dinner had false teeth and they didn't fit well. He had to keep retrieving unchewable bits from his mouth. Luis found it hard to look away from him. "Aren't you going to say anything?" she asked.

"I'm sorry."

"*You're sorry?* Oh, god. I'm the only woman dumb enough to get pregnant by a minor. Oh, god," she began to cry with frustration, "a teenage father. I had a baby by a baby. My adopted son is the father of my child." She didn't mean to be funny. She was looking past him as if searching for a more mature, understanding audience. "I had a teenage lover."

"Don't worry," he said impulsively. "Do you want an abortion?" He took one of her hands in his. "I'll help you."

"*Help me?* How can you help me? There are twenty clinics waiting to vacuum-clean my womb. They're overstaffed! They're practically religious about it. One of the men I represent did a magazine picture story on one.

What Happens When You Go to an Abortion Clinic—A Step-by-Step Guide. I don't need your help to get an abortion."
She looked at him contemptuously, as if he had said he would help her to menstruate. Or chew. Or breathe.

"Then what's the problem?" No matter how hard he tried, he couldn't keep his sentences from sounding harsh. He didn't mean them to be harsh. He just couldn't get to the heart of what she wanted from him.

"The problem is I'm thirty-two years old and . . . well . . . I'm not one hundred percent sure I want to give it up." There it was. The bombshell, and it had its full impact on him. He had just decided to forget about Barbara Traynor and her cynicism and prepare himself for the year ahead. He had sighed with relief to be back in apartment 11F, asexual but comforting. Now she was telling him that she wanted to bind him to her forever. A baby. His baby. Out in the world forever. "No, no, no." He could have sworn he didn't say it aloud.

"Look, you," she hissed, "this is just a courtesy, my telling you. You have nothing to say about it. Not one fucking thing."

"Oh, yes, I do. It involves me. And . . . I'm responsible, too. I don't even believe in abortion," he said in the direction of the old man across the aisle. The old man gave him a quizzical look. Barbara picked up her pocketbook and the check and walked out of the booth. He was about to detain her but then realized he had run out of things to say. He couldn't imagine what he had seen in her. Her features looked so coarse. Was it the pregnancy that suddenly made her look so horsey?

The next day he called the Margaret Sanger Clinic—a suggestion made by the New York Health Department. They invited him in for counseling. "I don't need counseling. I just want to know what's involved in getting an abortion."

"You need counseling," they insisted. "Believe us."

On his lunch hour, the next day, walking back to the office, he stopped dead on the sidewalk, making a man behind him curse. Who said it was definitely his baby? It could just as well be someone else's baby. A lot of someone elses. He couldn't wait to find a phone and confront her. He was suddenly furious.

He dialed her number from an outdoor booth and took a deep breath. "How do I know it's mine?"

"What?" She blasted the word into his ear. "You total shit. You think I would say it's yours if I weren't sure?" She slammed the phone down. He continued to the office. He didn't know what to believe. Before he called he had been positive it wasn't his but now . . . well . . . he believed her. Almost.

After work he went to a bar and had six shots of scotch. He sat there watching the Yankees play the Boston Red Sox until eleven o'clock when he decided to go home. When he got into the elevator, there were two young men already waiting whom he had never seen before. The minute he pressed the button for his floor and the doors closed, they began to beat him up. The confines of the elevator worked in their favor. They backed him into a corner and he had no place to go. They punched him needlessly—perhaps his clothes made them angry—and cut him, too, although he wasn't immediately aware of that.

They took his watch and twenty-three dollars but left his wallet. They got out on the seventh floor, leaving him alone. The moment the door closed, he threw up, a severe heaving—he could hear it gurgling in his throat. It was such a shock, he shot to his feet—only surprise could have gotten him to move any one of those throbbing muscles and leave the elevator. He waited until his breathing was calm before knocking. He didn't want to scare his mother to death and there was no possibility that he could fit his key into the lock. When she saw him, she drew in her breath but didn't scream. "*Espere* . . . wait." She put her hand on him as if to root him to the spot, got her pocketbook and pulled him back to the elevator. His vomit was everywhere. "I did that," he said.

"Dun worry. I clean it later."

She took him to the hospital, where they stitched up the gash on the side of his cheek and covered his face with ice packs. It was decided to admit him and see if he showed any signs of concussion or internal injuries. They suspected two ribs were broken and who knew what else. The Darvon began to work. He felt woozy but relatively normal. In the morning, his only thought was to call Barbara. Suppose she tried to reach him? She would think he had run out on her.

At first she didn't believe he was in the hospital, then she insisted on visiting him. "It's probably your fault," she said when he told her what happened. "It's your state of mind that attracts trouble."

She screamed when she saw him. "My god!"

"Maybe you shouldn't be here . . . especially since you're . . . you know." He remembered vaguely something his grandmother had said about a niece who had been frightened while pregnant and the baby had been born deaf.

"What are you going to do?" she asked.

He didn't know whether she meant about her, the baby, his face or his future. He took the easiest one. "You mean about school? I'm going," he said resolutely. "I'm supposed to be there on Wednesday and I'm going to be there on Wednesday. I'm okay—I mean there's nothing major broken or anything. They're not going to keep me out just because of a few bruises." As he said it, a flutter of fear went through his gut. Life changed all the time. Look at what had happened to him in just two days.

8

THAT FALL OF 1972, Harald's course had a new title: Profit Opportunities in a Bear Market. Each day April bought a copy of the *New York Times* and began to read every story on the financial pages. The Schlitz Brewing Company had selected Roy Satchell, the first nonfamily member, to its presidency. A new fabric, Tanera, had been invented that perfectly matched the graininess, suppleness and look of leather; two shoe companies had placed large orders. Robert C. Hollingsworth, a veteran of both Coke and Pepsi, had brought Crown Cola to unprecedented expansion and profits.

For herself, she hadn't regained the twenty-seven pounds dropped since the previous fall, but neither had she lost the additional thirty that the life insurance charts claimed excessive for her frame. Her clothes were better. Everyone was wearing wide-legged pants, which happened to be a good choice for her. She splurged on a well-cut tweed jacket and two pairs of lined woolen slacks with the new flared leg. She had her ears pierced.

Harald looked around nervously that first night, waiting for latecomers and assessing the count of his new class. She waited for him to notice her and say something.

He looked at her from time to time. When he went to open the window, she was certain he had gotten her message subliminally. Marty Bell had told them about the potency of subliminal conditioning, which was now illegal. A man who lives his entire life in the city, playing in the streets, whose only knowledge of a field of grass is Central Park's Sheep Meadow, suddenly buys an expensive tractor. Not only buys it, but anticipates a new lifestyle. Starts wearing jeans and sending for seed catalogues. Such was the potency of subliminal suggestion.

She knew with a cool, distant reasonableness that if life were completely predictable, Harald would marry someone like Faye Dunaway. She was not that someone, yet the depth of her emotion was so strong, it was inconceivable that it wasn't motivated by a larger force that would, sooner or later, bring about its own reward. She felt there was great power in human will and it would work that way for her.

It happened in late November. Not in any way she could anticipate, but it didn't matter. Dr. Leopold Sanders, who had written a book called *The Subconscious Equivalent*, came to their class as a guest lecturer to share his theory that the correct mental attitude was necessary for financial success. After the lecture, he invited them to partake of a mini-version of the expensive weekend program given around the country. He called it a biofeed-in. They all agreed to reconvene at his apartment on Riverside Drive the following week.

The next seven days were unseasonably cold, with the temperature never rising above twenty-five degrees. April arrived late and found a sign on Dr. Sanders's door: REMOVE YOUR SHOES BEFORE ENTERING. She peeled off her boots and walked in, feeling silly. The crowd inside was sitting in a circle on the floor of a room devoid of conventional furniture. At one end, a long pipe rack held coats. At the opposite end, there was a huge copper cymbal hanging sideways from a stand, obviously meant to be struck with the drumstick Dr. Sanders had in his hand. Harald was standing against one wall, the only guest not seated.

"Everyone please get into a comfortable position," said Dr. Sanders. "Close your eyes and when we strike the plate, count each reverberation. As you count, imagine you are going deeper and deeper into your subconscious. I will give you instructions." The room quieted. After a significant pause, Dr. Sanders began speaking again. "Relax, breathe in deeply . . . breathe out. Let us begin." He gave the plate a strong whack and the loud initial response grew fainter and fainter. She forgot to count and found herself longing to open her eyes and look at Harald. She peered through her lashes and saw him picking his way through the bodies to the coatrack and then the door. She rose immediately and followed him out. The people in the room remained stubbornly still, a look of desperate concentration on their faces.

She looked for her boots with exaggerated concern, afraid to face him. He took his shoes and sat against one wall to put them on. She sat on the floor opposite him.

"Did you cease to hear the reverberations?" she asked primly.

"Huh? . . . yes. That's not for me," he said quickly, as if he had a handy list of what was for him and what wasn't. "You going downtown?"

"Yes."

"Want a ride?"

"Okay."

They traversed the park and headed south on Fifth Avenue to 57th Street. "He actually charges two hundred dollars for a weekend of that," said Harald.

"God, that's awful. What a quack." She wished Leopold

Sanders many years of financial success. "I can't believe it."

"It's true. Want to have a cup of coffee?"

"Okay."

He parked on 55th Street and steered her back to 57th to the Mayfair Coffee Shop. The winds were so strong, she had to struggle to stay by his side. When they slid into a booth, her knees brushed against his and her body reacted with amazing speed. She realized she knew very little about him. He had told them he wasn't really a stockbroker. He was a stock specialist but she had no idea what that meant.

"Are you a lawyer?" she finally asked as they waited for the waitress.

"No." He seemed surprised. "I studied to be a lawyer, though, and my father's a judge. Why'd you ask? Do I look like a lawyer?"

"You look responsible and sure of yourself and . . . a criminal would do well to have you represent him." Upon saying this she had the infantile fantasy of being the criminal and having him defend her and fall in love with her for her crime, not despite it. She fantasized that the crime would stimulate him sexually.

He smiled a radiant smile. "I'm a stock specialist."

"You don't buy and sell stocks for people?"

"I buy and sell only two stocks. I'm the specialist in those two stocks."

He had started out to be a lawyer like his father but a summer job in a brokerage firm had given him a taste of a life he liked better. Now he was a floor specialist for two large companies on the New York Exchange. When he explained what he did, it sounded dishonest. He bought his stocks when they were going down so the price remained firm and attracted outside buying. When the price was bid up, he sold his shares at a profit and shorted additional shares (which meant he made money if the price went down, which it did, of course, leaving recent buyers holding a loss).

"Doesn't the government care?" was her first question.

"*The government?* I can assure you I'm not the only person doing it. That's the way the whole thing works. Floor specialists protect the market from its own unruly swings. It's the best way we have for providing for a tidy exchange."

Tidy? Tidily crooked. Still, she was relieved the outcome was in his favor.

"What are your two special stocks? Would they be ones I know?"

"What stocks do you know?" Now he was teasing her.

"I know IBM and General Motors." A gun to her head wouldn't have produced any other names, including the companies in which her own money was invested.

He grunted and smiled. "I'm the floor specialist for ICN Corporation and Lonny Foods." This was as much as he cared to divulge. "What do you do when you're not in my class?" She could see he had decided to find out about her. He was going to file her away in his bank.

"I sort of have a job writing advertising copy."

"Oh . . . ?"

"Well, it's not regular . . . I'm a freelancer. And . . ." she sighed deeply, "I've been reading the financial pages." She said this as if she had done it to please him.

"And what have you learned?"

"Yesterday, I read that the short sellers despaired of pushing gold below $150. I could picture that very clearly . . . these earnest men pushing with all their might but to no avail. Tears streaming down their grimy faces." Her voice grew soft. Her longing flowed out to him like vapor.

"They could have been crying," he said soberly. "There's more crying than anyone would guess."

"Really?"

"Yes."

"Do you ever cry?" She felt momentarily powerful, as if she could ask him anything and he would answer.

"There's no reason. I pay attention and do okay."

"You've never had a loss that brought you to tears?"

"One."

It was a woman, she was certain. She must have died. How else would he ever lose anyone?

As they walked back to his car, the wind was raw and he pulled her protectively to him, his arm around her shoulders. Before they could cross, however, the street was alive with a motorcycle escort surrounding a limousine.

"That's probably Dobrynin," he said, "coming from Lincoln Center. He went to the ballet."

"Did you see the headline in the *News*? 'Our top cop tells off Dobrynin.' His bodyguards wouldn't let the New York cops near him and our cops got miffed. Why do we always end up sounding so childish?"

"Exactly!" His voice was excited as if her astuteness had resolved a nagging problem. She could feel him recomputing her appeal as they walked along. He stopped at a kiosk, bought the *Daily News*, read the headline she had spoken of, turned to the story inside, reading quickly, and then threw the paper away. He held her hand for the rest of the walk to his car.

When they reached her building it looked dirtier and shabbier than she remembered. She saw it through his eyes and was ashamed. He was hesitant to leave her on the street. "Is this your building?"

"Yes."

"You're on the top?"

"The middle." She didn't move away from him. "Leopold Sanders is still whacking his shield, I bet."

"We won't be laughing when they make fortunes."

"Yes. They're all in a trance now . . ." she sounded wistful, "learning how to be rich."

"Sorry you didn't stay?"

"Oh, no. How could I be? It's silly." She looked at him anxiously to see if this is what he wanted to hear.

"Of course. Well . . . "

"Well . . ." She was staring at his lips, trembling with the need to touch them, to caress his face, to put her cheeks against his chest. She couldn't move. He took her face into both his hands and kissed her forehead. She moved upward, tilting her chin and then he put his mouth to hers. It was a sweet brush, followed by slight pressure from her side. It seemed such a frail place to touch. Lips trying to fit themselves to other lips. If she had allowed herself, she would have embraced him tightly and kissed him much harder but she didn't want him to think she was crazy.

"I'll wait till you're in."

"Thank you. I'll call out from the window."

She walked up in a daze of excitement and love. The steps were shifting sand. Nothing seemed real. The apartment door was ajar but even this didn't register in that moment of total excitement. Then she saw it all.

The apartment was a mess. Drawers were open, silverware all over the floor, books pulled from shelves. The small, portable television was near the door. She hurried back down the stairs.

"I don't know what to do," she said simply. "I've been robbed. I've never been robbed before. I'm not even sure what I should feel. It's awful to see your things all over the floor . . . some stranger just going through everything . . . he could have been there . . . maybe he is . . . "

He waited for her to finish. "Is there someplace you can spend the night? I don't think you ought to stay here."

"My parents live in Queens," she looked around and rubbed her fist against her teeth.

"Why don't you stay on my couch for the night? It's so late, there's really nothing you could do tonight anyway. The police wouldn't come for at least two hours and you'd be up all night."

The invitation was so unexpected it left her dazed. Sleep in his house? She wasn't prepared. Everything was moving much faster than she had imagined. The possibility of being near him almost obliterated the shock of the robbery. What a bizarre evening.

As they drove to his apartment, she remained perfectly still. If she breathed too hard, she would break. She looked closely at his profile to see if he suspected anything. Why did she feel so guilty? She *had* been robbed. It *was* too late to go to Queens or to call the police. It was *he*, not she, that had suggested they go to his apartment. She tried to settle down and not act grateful. Dear god, don't let me say anything that sounds grateful.

His apartment was in a very well maintained reddish brown house on East 91st Street between Fifth and Madison. There was an iron grill over the door, the top half of which was made of beautifully etched glass. He had a key for both doors and after he opened them and they stood in the tiny vestibule, he spoke for the first time.

"My roommate might be entertaining someone. I think he mumbled something to that effect this morning. So . . . let's take a deep breath and we'll just go in."

His roommate, Arthur Lewin, was entertaining a tall, giggling strawberry blond. On an ashtray between them was a decorated ceramic, smoldering pipe. The blond was heating up, too. She kept plunging into Arthur Lewin's chest with each renewed wave of the giggles.

"Come on, come on," he urged her in a businesslike voice, "we've got to get a hold of ourselves . . . Oh, hello,

Harald." He tickled the blond under her arms and under
her breasts. With each exuberant movement, the blond's
skirt rode higher on her hips. "Your hair's longer than
your skirt," chastised Arthur Lewin.

"Hello, Harald," mimicked the blond. "Oh, god, look at
me." She was having the time of her life. She rose, turned
her skirt around. "I've got to pee. Where's the john?"

April was surprised this was her first time in the apartment. She seemed so at home. Arthur took her to the
bathroom and returned to stoke his pipe in preparation
for her return. He seemed in no hurry to consummate
anything, as if he were waiting for a boost in energy. He
pushed the pipe toward Harald. With an elaborate sigh,
Harald sank to the floor, folded his legs under him and
reached for the pipe. "It looks as if it's going to be a long
night," he said.

He patted the place beside him on the floor and motioned for April to join him. Then he took a long drag of
the spoon/pipe, closed his eyes and waited. He passed it
to her and she put it to her lips, took a tiny, tentative
drag. She held the smoke in her mouth for a moment
and let it out. Maybe she'd go crazy? The blond was back,
cuddled into Arthur Lewin's chest and it was April's turn
in the bathroom.

After urinating, she inspected his toothpaste—Crest;
his deodorant—Mennen; his remedies—Contac, Buf-
ferin, Robitussin, PedOgene Creme, a fungicide for ath-
lete's foot.

Harald had once again taken possession of the spoon/
pipe and was dragging on its stem. He replaced it on the
dish, stretched out propping his head against a chair and
placed his arm companionably around April. "Don't expect anything normal from those two," he said and closed
his eyes. His fingers were idly massaging her shoulder.
She was almost in his arms. She closed her eyes and
placed her head against him. "'Swonderful," he said.

By the fourth drag, he was moving in slow motion with a dreamy look in his eyes. He traced her face with one finger, around her eyes, down the length of her nose, around her mouth. ". . . crystal streams . . ." he said dreamily as he returned to her eyes. ". . . so clear. I can see way down . . . so far down." From her chin he went to her neck, rubbing the small bones at its base as if they held special meaning for him. Arthur and his date began a wobbly waltz right into the bedroom. When Harald reached her breast, April twitched and began to tremble. "You're cold," he said with extravagant concern, as if someone had died. "Here. I'll warm you." Everything was done in slow motion with a benign smile. After the seventh? eighth? drag, he was in a swoon of desire. She tended his body with total concentration, kissing and caressing it. "Sweet . . ." he repeated as he circled her breasts . . . "so sweet." She opened his pants "Aaaaaaaah. . . ." he said. "That's it." She opened his shirt. He had a small pattern of hair that went from his chest down . . . down.

She had daydreamed everything but his ardent attention to her body. He was totally occupied while she remained vigilant, committing it all to memory. Her inclination was to feel powerful. He had been satisfied, exhausted, spent. He slept peacefully beside her, his gently muscled tennis arm grazing her breast. She was thrilled to guard his sleep until, she, too, succumbed. In the morning, his head looked large on the pillow, his face pale with sleep. She wanted to make a tremendous sacrifice for him. Give up something important, endure pain. Something to show the grandness of her love.

In the days that followed, she knew total happiness and it pushed away everything else. She had been made to love him and the idea that he might begin to love her, too, took her breath and memory away.

Was she supposed to wait for him after class or pretend nothing had happened? During the break, he leaned close to her and whispered, "We'll have a bite at Oviedos, later." She thought of the kisses to come while he explained the mechanics of selling short, puts and calls, commodity futures to his attentive audience.

Oviedos was a small Mexican restaurant on 14th Street that served well-seasoned vegetables and small amounts of meat.

"They use meat as a condiment," he said, as if defending a point. He was against big slabs of meat? Well, so was she. After dinner and two margaritas, which tasted like lighter fluid, he kissed her and held her to him with one arm around her neck. She knew at that moment that it was going to be all right. She didn't move as they sat in the booth side by side. She could smell ironed cotton and new wool and new perspiration. She would remember that smell forever.

When they were studying *Vanity Fair* in high school, April's teacher had told them that a fall or rise in social standing in Europe sometimes occurred in novels as a matter of good or bad luck, something that couldn't happen in America. April disagreed. The luck of being in Harald's class twice each week had a lot to do with his falling in love with her.

If she had gone to a gypsy and begged for the secret to his heart, the gypsy would have said to let him play Svengali and show a willingness to be formed by him. He had a lot to teach her and she was grateful. His parents, while not rich, had made the best choices for their means. All of April's alertness and good sense couldn't substitute for thirty years of soccer camps in Kent, Connecticut, clothes by Brooks for Boys, the right idea of himself, the right mother (trim, gracious, no bad language or bad grammar). Harald still had friends and clothes from college (Dartmouth). He still wore some of his soccer camp shirts and his college pullovers. He knew how to pick good movies and good restaurants. He was very interested in food, and April took a cooking class with two girls from Massachusetts and learned how to do seventeen things to a chicken breast, to stuff a veal shoulder and to make a roux.

"That old Protestant know-how, the luck of the draw, that old Wasp magic." This was Sylvie's assessment when April spent an afternoon with her old friend three weeks before her wedding day. "What about mumsy and daddy?"

"His mother made roast beef *au jus* and carrots julienne, so she can't be totally against me," said April.

"Hmmmmm."

"What does that mean?" She knew what it meant. They were both thinking that her own parents had never invited anyone to dinner who wasn't related. At the dinner table, they didn't discuss news events or politics. They told each other what the druggist said to the woman and what the woman said to the druggist. What dead animals were on the road. Who had their teeth pulled. Harlan and Bernice both used syntax that would now embarrass her: He don't know; he come home; I never heard nothing about it and it don't matter.

"But what's he like? You haven't told me what he's like." Sylvie was leading the conversation to safer ground.

April thought a moment. "If he were in a war," she said carefully, "he'd do the brave thing but he wouldn't get killed. It just wouldn't happen. He would be looked up to by his men and he would personally visit the widows and present them with the flag."

"Sounds a little cold to me," said Sylvie.

"Oh, no. Not cold . . . reserved, maybe."

"It sounds wonderful." Sylvie was uncharacteristically serious. "I wish you the best." She sat back in her chair smoking furiously and squinting at April. "April Taylor finds love in the big city. You owe it all to me, too. Who practically yanked you out of the bowels of Queens, huh?"

There were some things about Harald she decided not to tell Sylvie. He hated bad language. He hated synthetics. And he hated his father. When he told her his father was a judge, he added quickly, "It's not a particularly illustrious place on the bench," lest she become too impressed. Harald's father was a family court judge who, in custody fights, often awarded the children to the father. The most celebrated case involved a lesbian mother who appeared with her lover on Channel 13.

Once, a father in Judge Tierney's court had cried out during the hearing, "You can't deprive my boy of his Daddykins!" When the ruling came down in favor of the emotional father, the press tagged him Judge "Daddykins" Tierney.

Harald's dislike of his father saved them from a large wedding and prenuptial dinner where the inlaws would meet. April was grateful. She knew Harlan and Bernice would feel awkward with the Tierneys. *A judge? My god.*

They were married on the tenth of May. In the two weeks before her wedding, April was too nervous to eat and lost another eight pounds. At 145, she was at the lowest weight of her adult life. Her face was beautiful. Greenish gray eyes had become important in her newly slim face. She appeared taller than her five feet five. Harald chose her wedding dress, a short, silk jersey sheath, simple and dramatic. Her hair was parted in the middle, pulled back severely and covered with a cloche. She looked like a medieval woman of mystery. Another judge, a friend of Harald's father, performed the ceremony in the garden room of his parents' Larchmont home. A string quartet played Bach.

9

THERE WERE THREE WAYS to get to Princeton from New York. A bus from the Port Authority stopped right at the university. Your parents could drive you or you could drive yourself, although it was foolish to bring a car to Princeton. They made it so cumbersome to park that the farthest point to which you would ever drive was probably where they would make you keep the car. The most acceptable way to arrive was on the comfortable Amtrak train out of New York on its way to Washington with a stop at Princeton Junction. Once there, you would transfer to the "dinkey," a shuttle that brought you the rest of the way. If you were an upperclassman assigned to Spellman dorm, the dinkey practically deposited you in your bed.

Luis arrived for orientation week with a black eye, cuts and contusions, and a potential father. His cheekbones were puffed to the color of ripe El Dorado plums. Staring out of that carnage, his blue, innocent eyes now appeared to have seen too much.

He brought his belongings in twin Samsonite two-suiters with elaborate clasps that, according to the ads, could be dropped from airplanes, roll down rocky embankments only to be found safe, locked and unscratched. The color, a cool gray-blue, had appealed to him in the vast luggage department of Macy's.

A self-assured boy with sandy hair and a small boil on his chin introduced himself as Luis's senior advisor. He made a point of not staring at his battered face, gave him a small map of the university, directed him to his room, checked off his name from a list and wished him luck.

Luis's stomach fluttered once or twice as he inhaled the medicinal smell of the halls. The room wasn't spectacular, but neither was there anything specifically wrong with it. It looked out onto a healthy lawn and leafy trees. It was a room for two, not overly large but with an alcove that contained a lamp and worn overstuffed chair. He chose the bed away from the window in a gesture of amiability toward Fred Burdette, who, according to the letter he had received, was the roommate they had chosen for him. He made his bed, put away his things and sat down to wait.

Fred Burdette was of medium height with a round, pudgy face, four or five freckles on his nose and very curly, dirty-blond hair. He wore round, tortoise-shell glasses and looked middle-aged. He slung two canvas laundry bags with the name Exeter stenciled across them onto the empty bed and fell between them with a huge sigh. *"Violà, il commence,"* he whispered wearily, taking a long, careful look at Luis's face. "I hope the other guy looks worse."

"Yeah . . . thanks," said Luis.

"What's your name? I lost my introductory letter."

Luis had taken in the laundry bags, the slim watch, the baggy fawn-colored corduroy slacks and the soft wool sweater, knowing instantly that half of what he had brought, most notably the two heavy suitcases, were hopelessly wrong. He decided his name was wrong as well. "I'm Bob," he said.

"Hullo, Bob." Fred Burdette half rose to reach for his hand but Luis shrank back, struck one fist into the palm of his other hand and groaned in disgust. "It's not Bob."

"It's not Bob," Fred Burdette deadpanned. He looked at Luis solicitously. "Do you wish it were Bob?"

"Not particularly."

They were both silent. "Why so disappointed then?" asked Fred.

Luis smiled ruefully. "I didn't want to tell you my real name."

Fred contemplated this soberly, his hands between his legs. "That's very original. Very original. Do you want to tell me now?"

"Luis."

"*Louise?*" His eyebrows shot up. "That's bad. I can see why you said Bob."

"It's not Louise," he said, laughing.

"That's a relief."

"Oh, god . . ."

"Let's start again. I'm Fred Burdette."

"Luis—that's Lewis to you—O'Neill." He stretched to his full five feet ten inches and extended his hand.

"A pleasure," said Fred.

Princeton provided him with a bed, a dresser, a chair, a desk, three sixty-watt bulbs and arrogant roaches that paraded around looking no more refined than the roaches in the projects. Fred Burdette immediately rented a refrigerator from the refrigerator agency and a telephone from the telephone agency and invited Luis to share both.

Two days after he arrived, Luis went to the employment office. "Any jobs?" he asked of a small, red-haired girl.

"Oh, my god," she said, staring at his face. "How can you take a job?"

"The worst is over," he answered bravely, but that only made her more solicitous.

"What happened?"

"Oh, you know. What always happens. A punch here, a punch there."

"Please . . . sit down. I'll see what's available." She kept glancing his way, looking for signs of an emergency. He noticed that her arms were completely freckled, as was most of her face. She was thin, too, but had lovely green eyes. "Mostly dining room jobs," she said. "In Commons."

"Do I have a choice?"

"Yes. Loading dishwashing machines, removing dishes, replenishing dishes, mopping . . . general work."

"I'll take mopping."

"Say good-bye to your beautiful hands," she gave him an experimental smile.

"Yeah . . . well . . . they'll go nicely with my face."

She turned serious. "I hope . . . I hope everything works out all right."

"Thanks."

As he turned to leave, she called after him. "They're always looking for guys to sell ads for the paper. You could try there if the mopping gets too much for you."

"Thanks, again." He smiled as widely as he could.

"Oh, don't mention it . . . I'm here to help. Come back . . . anytime . . . tomorrow . . ." she giggled nervously. "Ask for Regina Cross." Then she blushed.

"Okay," he waved his hand. Her sincerity touched him. In this supercharged atmosphere, a little friendliness was a valued asset. Maybe he would come back later.

He thought about Regina Cross on and off for the next

few days. The idea that he might impregnate her as he had impregnated Barbara kept him from going to see her. Careless raptures could turn serious. She was probably well off if she was at Princeton. And well bred. It was the latter that made him feel horny. He felt like getting in the sack with a freckle-faced, well-bred girl, but he didn't feel proud of himself for feeling that way.

He remembered Neil Barron from Aubernon and Cagney who once told them that from the day he was sixteen and nine months to the day he was nineteen and six months, he had maintained a bothersome and sometimes humiliating erection. "It just never went down," he said morosely. "Everything made me think of sex. Toothpaste, eggs, light bulbs, red meat, chicken. Traffic lights." Why traffic lights? "Well, they say stop . . . and go." His only thought in those days, he told them, was how he could get laid without waiting and how he could store up potential lays so there was never a day when he might have to do without. Every day, he tried to make a new conquest so he could rotate the women. Every woman he saw was simply a place to park his penis. Their faces all melted into one face. Their conversations were all one conversation—a conversation to be finished so he could take them to the sack. It didn't even have to be the sack. It could be a car, a wall, a chair, a table top.

There were two general reactions to Luis's face. The men averted their eyes and made believe nothing was wrong. The women's faces crumbled and they asked a million questions. He began to believe in the mothering instinct. For Fred Burdette, who knew the truth, it was amusing to watch Luis gain notoriety and a certain rakish status.

"Conjecture is sweeping the campus like a hot August wind," he told Luis with some delight. "The question is:

who beat you up? And why? Was it the Mafia? A jealous lover? You have instant recognition without doing anything."

"You don't consider pain and the fear of being killed anything?" Luis looked indignant. "My ribs are still taped. I can't turn over in bed." He was more than pleased. He needed any edge. You would have had to be made of styrofoam not to be intimidated by Princeton. It was so . . . *old* . . . and traditional . . . and *subdued* and judgmental . . . and *perfect*.

There seemed to be a sub-surface anxiety over who you were, where you had come from and where you were going. It wasn't enough to call the preppies snobs. They were otherworldly beings whose indifference was stunning to anyone with normal ambitions. If you weren't motivated by a desire for money, status or achievement, why do anything? Decent, wholesome people who just two weeks before had considered themselves the cream of the crop were reduced to self-loathing toads.

Luis wasn't worried about his preppie potential. He had real worries. Would his face heal without scarring? Was Barbara really pregnant and, if so, to what extent was he going to provide for her and the baby? He was often preoccupied thinking about the baby. He saw it as a boy with Barbara's wooly, blond hair. He had called twice before leaving but had only reached her answering machine. The message recorded wasn't the message of a desperate or recently weakened individual. "Hello," said the tape in a vigorous voice, "if you hate to talk to this machine, just say your first name. Maybe your last name. How about your initials? Say 'fuck you' if you like. Anything will do. I'm great at recognizing voices."

"Fuck you," he had recorded in a fit of anger. Part of his anger, he knew, was due to the fact that he felt powerless. He didn't want her to have an abortion yet he wasn't willing to give up his rendezvous with Princeton.

Then there was the biggest worry of all. In order not to lose his scholarship, he had to keep his grades up. The idea that by spring he could be out on his ass was unthinkable. The love and pride he felt at being there couldn't be overestimated.

The janitor for his dorm—not like any janitor he ever knew—cleaned the bathroom and not only brought his mail but invited confidences, gave advice, took shoes to be soled, clothes to the cleaner, wanted to serve but wasn't subservient. The janitor called him Mr. O'Neill. "Good morning, Mr. O'Neill." "Good morning, Mr. Kassabian." The civility and grace of this exchange alone would have kept him feverishly loyal to Princeton and all it stood for.

He would get top grades and let his personal style shine through. Let the chips, or the "cheeps," as his mother would say, fall where they may. He wondered why his mother could say "chips" for ships, but insisted on saying "cheeps" for chips.

He chose to underline, not hide, the naggy details of his life, and this attitude gave him a social recklessness that intrigued the very people who might normally ignore him. He became a person about whom people spoke obsessively. Did you hear what he said at dinner last night? Has he told you about his grandmother?

When the once-a-week sit-down dinner included a thin, gruely soup, Luis would detain the waiter. "Uh . . . Bill . . . when my mother ordered soup in a restaurant, she would always tell the waitress to 'dig down and get it thick. You know, from the bottom.' But she didn't say thick, she said, 'teek.' Jew deeg down and get eet teek for me, too, okay Guillermo?" The table was convulsed with laughter but there was always the occasional stage whisper: Is it any wonder they're overrepresented on the relief rolls?

The blessings and friendship of Fred Burdette, whose father, Lionel, was chairman and chief stockholder of the

Burdette chain of department stores added about ten pounds of charm to the things Luis was known for. The assumption was that Luis was devoted to Fred and Fred found Luis diverting. In fact, it was the opposite. Fred was devoted to Luis and Luis, because the devotion was diverting, couldn't really see what Fred was all about. In any case, they had a talkative relationship that passed for intimacy.

During his fourth week at school he received a postcard from Barbara Traynor that must have straightened Mr. Kassabian's curly hair. "This is to let you know I've had the abortion. He or she is now lying in some garbage dump or floating in some sewer—wherever they throw such things away. Warm regards, you shit."

That day he went back to see Regina Cross. "Ah, you're here," she screeched. She wasn't exactly one to play her cards close to her chest.

"I wanted to thank you for the two jobs." *I wanted to fuck you.* "I'm mopping and selling ads. If I sell a lot of ads, I'll give up the mopping."

"You'll be terrific." She sounded like the stage manager bolstering the understudy who has to go on suddenly.

"Want to have a cup of coffee?"

"Sure."

That night, he made love to Regina Cross and found that her freckles stopped at her breasts, which were white and smooth. It was hard to believe she was nineteen years old. She had the figure of a twelve-year-old. Her face looked frightened all the time but she was surprisingly passionate.

"I'm on the pill," she had whispered, which he took as a request. He hadn't planned to really screw her, merely grope. But after that stark, bold confidence, what else could he do? I'm on the pill translated into I don't know what you're here for but I'm ready and willing to fuck.

"Want to do sixty-nine?" she said when they were well under way.

"Sixty-nine?"

"Yes, you know. You eat me and I'll eat you."

He knew what it was but the casualness of the request almost knocked him off her narrow bed.

Regina Cross's father was a surgeon and her mother was an amateur golfer of some renown. Regina was an only child, squeezed into the life of two overburdened careerists. She wanted to be a doctor, too.

None of this interested Luis. He couldn't feel any sense of responsibility for her waiflike, bereft look. It wasn't his fault her parents had been too busy to make her feel secure. What was he supposed to do? If he didn't screw her, she'd look elsewhere.

"If you're looking for a stable relationship with warmth and attention, you're in the wrong place." He said it in a joking manner on their first evening together, but it was still a warning. "I've got to keep my grades up and I've got to work. That doesn't leave much time for anything else."

"I know," she said.

She had beautiful, springy, gleaming red pubic hair, her sole sexual advantage. Still, he liked to make love to her, although he found it difficult to listen to her plaintive cheerfulness whenever he said good-bye. At Thanksgiving, he stopped screwing Regina Cross. No matter how he tried to rationalize it, he did feel responsible and he knew he would never love her.

Within a week, he was in a new bed with a new girl.

"Tell me about yourself," she said.

"What's there to tell? I'm here."

"Oh." She looked understanding. "What you're trying to say is that it doesn't matter what happened before."

"Sort of."

The second girl didn't last more than two weeks and then there were others. He told them all what kind of person he was. "I'm always broke. I have two jobs. I have to keep my grades up. I come from a poor family. Worse than poor." The blacker the picture he painted, the more he screwed. That first year at Princeton, he screwed his brains out. There was always a bed, a car, a secluded spot. The girls were clever and audacious about finding a place to do it. They *wanted* to arrange it. They wanted to prove how resourceful they were. And they were. They were anxious for experience and experience to them meant sex.

Later, when he tried to remember those years, he couldn't think of a single name or reconstruct any of their faces except for Regina. She stayed with him, and thinking about her always made him sad.

10

In September of 1976, Sylvie married a lawyer ten years her senior and went to live in Ardsley-on-the-Hudson. She said her mother didn't mind that Spencer was an Episcopalian. Sylvie was a new woman. She had straightened her frizzy hair and wore it pinned in the back in an untidy knot. She dressed in the kind of reversible skirts and jumpers advertised in the back of the *New York Times Magazine.* It was as if she'd become a nun without taking the vows of chastity or poverty. Spencer Straight was loaded.

April had been married three years and found it was a full-time job being Harald's wife. She took a current events course at NYU from Imre Nagy's cousin and learned about Red China and the Middle East. She was able to contribute provocative sum-ups that spiced conversation. The Soviet Union would one day come to the support of Israel, she told the lawyers and brokers who came to dinner. Red China would court the U.S. and then use it shamelessly for its own purposes.

Marty Bell continued to give her work, entrusting her to conceive and write a complete campaign for paper plates and cups that looked like real china. Her first ad in the series—*Wedgwood Paper Dinnerware, including a great little cup that keeps cold things cold and hot, hot*—improved sales by eleven percent.

On days that she went into the offices of Bell and Adonesio, Harald brought home two portions of the *plat du jour* from Stella and Stanley, a tiny catering shop near their apartment: stuffed cabbage or veal marsala or filet of sole véronique. He also made the salad and set the table and they mentioned this proudly to their friends.

Everything seemed joyful that third year but then, without warning, the bad news began piling up. At the end of June, April's mother went to the hospital to have her gall bladder removed. After the operation, Bernice looked awful and had no strength. The doctor assured them it was a normal aftermath. He was the philosophical type. "Such an assault on the body," he said. "Cutting, invading." On the fourth day, a Dr. Greef called at one o'clock in the morning and told April he had very bad news. She thought it was a crank call. A joke. The doctor said he didn't want to call her father who was at home alone but he would tell her because someone was with her. Her mother had died. He said her heartbeat had become incompatible with life. She knew then he was telling the truth. No prankster would say a thing like that. Besides the flood of grief and regrets, April was left with persistent, irrational fears—that others would die around her, that more unspeakable bad news was right around the corner.

It was just a few weeks afterward that Harald's father, Judge Tierney, again hit the newspapers. It was a custody fight for two small children, between an exotically beautiful young mother and her estranged husband, an indicted felon awaiting trial. With any other judge presiding, there wouldn't have been a public hearing. Who would favor a felon over a decent mother? In Judge Tierney's court, however, anything could happen.

The young, beautiful mother appeared in some part of the newspaper almost daily. Harald refused to discuss the case and April didn't bring it up. She wasn't outraged by the idea of giving the children to the father, not because he deserved them but because the mother wasn't what she appeared. Somewhere in her heart, April had special information about Melissa Montini. She didn't really love or want her children. She loved the drama of having the world watch her lose them.

In a decision that brought an audible gasp in the room, Judge Tierney awarded the children to the father. "I have seen these men carrying their children on their shoulders," he read from his decision. "I have seen them struggling with galosh buckles and tiny buttons."

"The bastard never struggled with my tiny buttons," said Harald, breaking his silence on the case.

The *Daily News* and the *New York Post* devoted two full pages of pictures to the story showing the mother, the children, the father, the lawyers and the maternal grandmother holding a Snoopy dog and a G.I. Joe doll while trying to blow her nose.

News reporters brought up all of the judge's previous controversial decisions—the lesbian mother, the man who had said his boy needed his Daddykins. They mentioned the judge's only son, Harald, an investment analyst who resided in New York City. Yes, the judge answered when asked, if he had been faced with divorce, he would have fought vigorously for custody of his son. The statement enraged Harald who remembered a very different relationship.

The most remarkable picture of the trial was of Melissa Montini pounding the walls of the judge's private chambers insisting that he couldn't take her children away.

"Why does he want to do this dreadful thing to me?" she cried helplessly to the reporters. "I've never done anything to him."

A week later, as April and Harald were watching "Laugh-In," the telephone rang but there was no one on the line. This happened repeatedly over the next few days.

Two weeks later, there was a knock at their door and April found a woman there with long, silky Oriental-looking hair and a startlingly beautiful face.

"Please, may I come in? I'm here to see Harald Tierney." Her voice became more aggressive. She had no interest in April.

"Whom shall I say is here?"

"I would prefer not to say." She folded her arms in front of her and looked sideways down the hall.

"Well, come in. Come in." April saw how silly it was to continue to stand in the open doorway. They entered the living room together and it came to April who the woman was. Her face and expression were so familiar after the many weeks of the trial. "You're Melissa Montini." It came out as an accusation.

The woman glared at her. "Is Harald Tierney here?"

"Yes, yes, he is. I'm Mrs. Tierney," she said unconvincingly. "Harald," she called out. "There's someone here to see you."

Harald came to the living room in his stocking feet. He looked at both of them and then exclusively at Melissa Montini. April didn't blame him. It was hard not to look at her. She had lips that were full and lusciously red, like the lips in ads that sell cosmetics.

"I'm Melissa Montini," said the woman to Harald. "Your father took my children away. I've tried and tried to see him. I've written him every day since the trial but he doesn't answer my letters or my telephone calls." Her voice trembled and her chin began to quiver. "If I don't talk to someone, I'll go crazy." Two tears (fat and full like her lips) rolled down her cheeks. "The press is no help either." She didn't try to stop her tears as most criers do. They rolled single file down her cheeks, which in itself was riveting. She told them that she had tracked Harald down to his Wall Street office and then to the apartment.

"What do you hope to gain from seeing me?" asked Harald in a cold but civil voice.

"I don't want to gain anything from you," she said. "But I needed to find you. You see," her eyes became round and moist, "I have trouble sleeping. I keep seeing my little ones' faces, especially the baby girl. She's only four and we were very close. She couldn't go to sleep without saying good night to me. We would cuddle together on the bed and I'd kiss her tiny dimpled hands and her arm. I'd make believe I was eating her plump, little arm. As if I was a hungry giant and couldn't help myself. She would giggle and say, 'Go ahead, Mr. Giant, eat the other one.'"

"Maybe you frightened her by doing that," said Harald.

"What do you mean?"

"Well, children can be frightened and still giggle but if you listen carefully, it's not a particularly joyous giggle. Sometimes they don't like those games."

She looked at him as if he were insane. As if she now could understand the father. "She was crazy about that game, mister."

April, too, was surprised to hear him say this. She had not thought that he had such definite ideas about children. It made her wish they had a child. She felt suddenly sad and filled with a terrible loss.

The more she thought about what Harald had said, the more agitated Melissa became. "What kind of a crack is that, anyway? You're just like your father. Why do you both want to punish me?" Her voice broke and she began crying for the third time but this time she began also to pummel Harald's chest. "I want my babies! I want my babies! I can't live! Why did he take my babies?" She sobbed as if her heart were broken. April didn't believe her heart was broken but was riveted to the scene. Harald led her to the couch. April seemed to have no part to play.

Melissa sobbed into a handkerchief. "What kind of a woman was your mother?" she asked Harald, gulping for air.

"Is my mother," corrected Harald.

"Is your mother," she said obediently.

"Very nice. Not so affectionate but nice . . . nice to my friends. A good cook. Always visited at camp. Always made the extra effort to do the right thing for me." He was glad to distract her and tried to weave an interesting story. "She's not a woman who wants to be correct to impress people. She just takes pride in doing the right thing. She's a very happy person."

"And your father?"

"I haven't always agreed with my father," said Harald carefully.

"That's a relief," said Melissa.

"My father wasn't good to me as a child," said Harald unexpectedly. "He never played with me or read to me. He never carried me on his shoulders. When I was in my teens, I was unable to call him father. For four years I never called him anything. I would touch his arm to get his attention or make a noise in the room. I became very inventive about not having to call him. It became an elaborate game with one player—me."

April sat motionless. Harald had never told her any of these things. What's more, his eyes seemed locked on Melissa's face.

"I'm sorry," said Melissa. "I'm truly sorry."

"And I'm sorry for you," he answered. "I can imagine it must be hell for you."

April decided this would be a good time to give them both a drink. "I drink my brandy neat," Melissa said. "Neat," she repeated. "No ice."

In the kitchen she made a decision. She would give Harald the high sign. One drink and she had to go.

Melissa took the drink, sipped it quickly, as though drinking dubious medicine, stood up, straightened her skirt, blew her nose and said good-bye.

The next night, about nine, Harald said: "This is about the time she showed up last night." That was precisely what April was thinking but she was disappointed that Harald was thinking of it, too. The doorbell rang.

"I hope you don't mind," she apologized, entering the room as if she already knew it by heart, "I've been thinking . . . what you said about your father never carrying you on his shoulders." Her beauty gave her great freedom to say and do as she liked.

"Well, there are worse things, I suppose," said Harald. He seemed satisfied that someone had finally understood the depth of his deprivation.

April thought of all the things she would have preferred that he say: *What? You here again? You can't keep coming here.* Instead he seemed happy to see her.

April had a chance to study their guest. Today, her hair was curled at the edges, which coarsened rather than sweetened her looks. Her conversation was crammed with facts, it was hard not to listen to her. Despite herself, April hung on every word.

"It really helps me to talk like this," she told them with a dreamy, innocent look. "I mean, this man I've never met does this terrible thing to my children and now . . . I get to know his son. It satisfies me somehow. The other way, it was just too cold . . . too impersonal. He changed my whole life and I wasn't going to see him again. He wasn't going to see me either, but now . . . "

April left the room and went into the kitchen. She stood at the sink letting cold water run on her wrists as Harlan had taught her to do when she was too hot. "It cools all the blood running through there, and pretty soon it cools all of you." She stayed there with her arms in the sink until she heard Melissa leave.

The visits continued. Many nights, April turned on herself for not putting her foot down. She fought for righteous anger and set the scene for a confrontation but couldn't bring it off. Melissa or any number of ills were what she had in store—an inevitable outcome because she had been dumb about her life. She could appreciate the irony involved and was surprised that such an uneducated woman could do such a complicated thing.

11

APRIL SEEMED TO NEED more food to keep her satisfied. She wasn't sleeping well and being tired made her hungrier. She craved sweets and began buying chocolate bars, something she hadn't done since her marriage. She also craved salt, and at times, when she went to the kitchen, she would eat half a bag of Fritos or potato chips before coming out. After that, she needed something wet and squishy and she would stir herself a fruit-flavored Dannon yogurt which she ate in the living room.

Within a week she had gained four pounds. Within two weeks it was nine. It was not happy eating.

There was less and less to do during the day. She had completed a campaign for Marty Bell and decided against taking on any new work. "We're going away for a month," she told him so he would not urge work on her. It was too hard to think about the product he had assigned to her. It was shampoo. Shampoo that was especially formulated to leave the scalp with a healthy acid mantle of protection. She couldn't think about that. She could think only about Melissa Montini and her visits. What could protect her against that?

Harald was willing to let her visits continue. He said it was the least they could do. He was afraid she might commit suicide if they refused her. He said the visits were a good way of defusing a potentially dangerous situation. April didn't think she would commit suicide.

She was surprised that he couldn't see through Melissa. Perhaps what they both saw through was herself. She watched them in the living room as if she were watching a foreign film, where people waste no time with courtship but get right to it.

Many times it crossed her mind that Melissa Montini reminded her of Bernice. In some ways, one was an emotional deadringer for the other. Made only to entice and bedevil men. But then she wept for putting her dead mother in such a bad light.

Harald became moody and silent, answering all questions with a yes, no, I don't know.

"Is something wrong?"

"No."

"Are you hungry?"

"No."

"Should I fix dinner?"

"I don't know."

It was so quiet in the apartment, it gave April the creeps. Any noise she made was intrusive. The normal use of dishes and pots and pans made a tremendous clatter.

There were days when she was certain that her marriage was threatened, that Harald was waiting for a good time to tell her. Other times, they would go to the movies or have another couple to dinner and she would tell herself it was all in her imagination. The whole episode was something to relate with careful understatement at a dull dinner.

The private moments between herself and Harald told a less cheerful story. During four years of marriage, they had nurtured their intimacy. She had learned to be provocative in innocent ways . . . nightgowns that didn't always contain her breasts. She knew how to be still in the mornings until he awoke to find her disheveled, exposed, touchable. He was continually aroused by her unexpected nakedness. Sometimes she lay there so long and so still and so desirous, she almost came waiting for him and had to calm herself to keep from slamming his hand down over her.

These days he rose quickly in the mornings, showered and left without eating. If she rose with him and made coffee, he was silent and moody. "I've got a lot of paper work to catch up on," was the password out of the apartment. Out on the street and out of her sight. It was such an unimaginative excuse. The worst of it was that it was probably true yet paper work had never driven him out early before.

On these mornings, she would eat nothing until ten or eleven. Then, in a fit of hunger, she would stand in her nightgown at the open refrigerator and look for the most satisfying easy food. Usually something sweet. Leftover dessert. But that made her hungrier.

She would return to the refrigerator several times, searching for something else to haul back to bed. This would go on until midafternoon—hopping in and out of bed with portable food. Sometimes, she ended up by heating the leftover rice and bits of meat from the previous night's meal. After a while, she realized it was useless to cook because Harald was seldom hungry. "I had a big lunch," he would say. "It's not healthy to eat two big meals."

"What about one long, continuous meal?"

"What?"

"Nothing."

At her slimmest, April was twenty pounds over her ideal weight. Now, within four weeks, she gained twenty more. One night after Melissa's visit, she heard the front door close. She knew Harald was out in the hall, too, because both had walked to the door and no one had walked back into the room. She surmised he was kissing her. She had felt his desire and could see the tortured, stolen kiss as if she were directing it. He looked ill and feverish. He was on fire for Melissa Montini, who, with consummate skill, appeared totally innocent of her effect on him.

She quickly ate two chocolate bars and drank a glass of milk. The candy was cold and tasteless and did nothing to make her feel less hungry. She drank another glass of milk. She heard the door open and close and footsteps to the couch.

She experienced an agonizing need to expel gas. In the deathly quiet, it was not some small, indefinite noise that could have been the scrape of a chair or the systematic ripping of paper. It could only have been what it was—a long, noisy fart. She was sure Harald had heard it. They probably heard it in the next apartment. They probably heard it across the river in Hoboken.

When she came into the room, he was looking out the window the way people do when they are grief-stricken or restless.

The potential danger in the air made her feel heroic. She sat down on the sofa—would he sit down beside her? No. He chose the chair and stared at her feet which were bare.

"Look at your ankles," he said with total dismay. "And your feet. How swollen they are." Nothing could have hurt her more. Silent tears rolled down her cheeks. She knew it was not going to be a quickie fight. The cold, desperate look in his eyes told her he had shaped and saved his words like huge wads of gum. "I know your hurt silence," he said, as if warning her that it was a useless tactic now. "Your philosophical silence." She was amazed at his finesse. "Look at your knees . . . and your eyes . . . you look like a stranger. I can't live with it."

She noticed that his shirt was showing a little under his vest, punctuating the slope of his hips. She had ironed that shirt many times because it was his favorite and he feared the laundry would be too harsh with it. She could not have foretold the sense of relief at hearing him spell it out. Concrete terrors are better than those imagined. Relief was followed by a suffocating fear. "I'm pregnant," she shouted impulsively. Nothing could have been farther from the truth. She was in the midst of one of her heaviest menstruations. He looked so horrified she couldn't continue. "No, no. I'm not."

Many days after that she would lie on the couch, shading her eyes from the sunshine she had once thought cheerful. She could get up and close the drapes but it was too much of an effort and there was something gratifying about being uncomfortable. It kept her from giving full attention to the problem of what she should do with the rest of her life. It never occurred to her that she could keep the apartment.

She thought a lot about where she would go. Not that she had a place in mind, but it comforted her to think about the kind of place she'd like to have. Clean, comfortable, small.

Sylvie had always not so secretly suspected she didn't deserve Harald and now she would be proven right. She invented things that Sylvie might say, playing the scene a dozen ways. She wondered if Sylvie would feel any satisfaction.

She wept for all the babies she might have had. That would have made it real. Her stupidity had been in not getting pregnant. Men strayed all the time but they always came back to their wife *and children*. She could not believe how stupid she had been. She deserved this arid, hopeless life.

For some, when they picture perfect happiness or freedom, they picture themselves dancing or jumping. Jumping for joy. Not so with April. She had always felt the moment of greatest happiness would be perfectly still, a moment of exquisite finesse between lovers, when their minds and spirits meshed. When their every move and word is of compelling interest to the other. She couldn't convince herself that there would be anyone or anything that would hold her interest again as Harald had done. She knew more about him than she knew about herself. She had watched over him for five years, taking in facts and hammering them like tiny nails into her memory. The loss was immeasurable. She felt her heart physically sinking over and over.

Her refuge was food. What was there to do but eat?

The official parting was remarkably simple. She received a lump settlement of fifteen thousand dollars as well as her stock portfolio, and was lucky to find an inexpensive studio apartment in the thirties. A few days after she moved in, her telephone rang.

"Mrs. Tierney?" asked an official-sounding voice.

"Yes."

"This is Randolph Tobias of Bear Stearns. We have purchased a Ginny Mae which yields effectively nine and one eighth annual percent which you may buy into for twelve thousand dollars."

"I'm totally illiquid," she said quickly. "I'm not a good bet for you." It ended almost exactly as it had begun— with an investment offer.

12

Luis had been at Burdie's Atlanta for six weeks and he had learned a lot. Ninety percent of what there was to know about buying sheets, towels, quilts and tablecloths could be summed up in three words: "white sales" and "seconds." White sales, traditionally a January event, now were scheduled several times a year for the simple reason that they tripled traffic in the department. Seconds—merchandise that was less than perfect and sold at reduced prices—were now programmed into production by every mill. Women liked the idea of paying less. It made them feel astute and thrifty and the flaws in the merchandise were many times undetectable.

As assistant buyer, Luis bought budget sheets, comforters and kitchen linens. He spent a great deal of time on the selling floor listening to what women wanted and looking at how they made decisions. He found quickly that women liked to sleep on flowers more than on stripes and geometrics. And they liked small pink, yellow or white flowers more than blue, orange or green ones. They liked prints that reminded them of colonial America, by far the favored period of decor.

The women who liked stylized cucumbers and squash on their potholders and kitchen towels were usually bookish types with small breasts. The majority favored roosters, on or off weathervanes. Mushrooms were second in popularity. Not realistic edible mushrooms, but cheerful mushrooms that sheltered elves.

Luis resisted the temptation to buy mill overruns and closeouts which he could sell as special purchases. He made a decision to buy the merchandise women wanted most and sell it at regular price. The strategy paid off. In a recession year, when better linens and domestics lost ground, his department showed a respectable ten percent rise over the previous year. Within thirteen months he was promoted to a full buyer and transferred to Burdie's, Chicago, the flagship store of the Illinois chain.

In this large, complex and partly affluent city, his strategy changed. He wanted to raise the consciousness of every woman whose linen closet harbored a mishmash of sale merchandise that she'd be happy to throw out. Chicago in winter was depressing. The wind never stopped blowing. He could picture winter-roughened skin being dried with limp, faded towels while he had shelves and shelves of thick, thirsty terry; winter-weary bodies lying down to sleep—one third of life—on worn-out, ugly, mismatched sheets, while he was stocked to the rafters with lustrous, comforting percales. He shared his insights with the women of Chicago in a full-page ad in the *Chicago Sun-Times* and the *Chicago Tribune: Mrs. Georgia Wilson sleeps on ugly sheets she bought on sale in 1967. What are you sleeping on?*

The gist of his message was: saving a dollar or two on something you would be living with for years was a false saving. You deserve better than that. The women took a good look at their beds and had to agree with him. The excellent response to the ad prompted the store to run a series that began with the running header *O'Neill's Law:*

The uglier the towel, the longer it lasts. Sleep on skimpy pillowcase, wake up with feathers in mouth.

Sales in the department went up twenty-five percent in the first six months. He urged his customers to complain and tell him what they wanted that was not available. To his surprise, he discovered a sizable market that yearned for the return of the all-cotton sheet and towel; it prompted him to run a promotion that had a historic response and made his name known to the powers that be at the Burdette Corporation. The campaign struck at the heart of every woman's desire to be taken seriously. To have her small requests honored and to be admired for her common sense. The first ad read:

Jane Ferrar doesn't like the squeak that her polyester sheets make in the summer when it's hot!

What's more, she doesn't like the feel of polyester against her body. "Who's going to take the small annoyance of a housewife seriously?" asks Mrs. Ferrar. Burdie's. We want Mrs. Ferrar to feel good at night and we've asked a renowned manufacturer of luxury linen to make us our own, Burdie's label, all-cotton percale sheets. But not at his usual price, which would put most of us out of the market. He says he will have to call them seconds. We said, call them anything you like. We all know what seconds are— they're firsts to the naked eye.

The response was extraordinary. They sold out most of their stock and received future orders for merchandise when it came in. One day, a woman shopper mentioned in passing, "Now if you'd only bring back my mother's mangle, I could iron my cotton sheets in no time flat." Luis agreed. He made a deal with a manufacturer of commercial mangles for a smaller model and ran a mangle ad: *Burdie's leaps into the past.* He had a week-long demonstration in which it was proven that you could iron a king-size sheet in ninety seconds.

Luis loved retailing. He ran a lively department with special events and guest decorators. He loved the idea of direct results for known efforts and he seemed to have an instinct for merchandising. Women wanted to be understood and comforted and encouraged in their special view of things. Luis did this and he prospered. By 1978, three years after joining the Burdette chain, he was made merchandise manager for soft goods, a post he held for two years. By January of 1980, in an unprecedented leap, he was named president of Burdie's New Jersey. As exciting as this was, it was far from his final goal. In his mind, New Jersey would be a brief stop. He chose to live in Manhattan and commuted to Newark by train and limousine. The real apple of his eye was Burdie's New York, the shining jewel in the Burdie's crown.

The other advantage of living in Manhattan was the availability of women. He had never lacked for companions but now it seemed he was in the hot, white center of the new, take-charge woman.

The first woman he went to see upon returning to New York was his mother in the projects. He showed her the business page of the *New York Times* with his picture.

"Jew're the president?" she asked with proper awe.

"Yes, I am."

"Berry good," she said.

13

WITH HER FIFTEEN THOUSAND dollars and her cozy, dark apartment, April felt temporarily safe. She didn't have to think about anyone hating her.

Many days, she would grab her coat and run into the street, walking briskly as if to some important destination. Then, realizing she had no place to go, she would stand in the middle of the sidewalk, men cursing her stupidity for blocking their path.

It was a remarkable winter. Bright and cheerful with many days of blue skies and brilliant sunshine. It snowed frequently and the light reflecting off the snow added to the brightness. She didn't go out much and the sunshine was a reproach. To be indoors on a sunny day in America was worse than Communism.

Every day she awoke with the resolve to *do* something. Today would be the day she would begin eating sensibly. She would even start out the day by cutting up a bagful of carrots and celery sticks to munch on when her habits got the better of her. By eleven o'clock, she had begun nibbling. First a piece of toast with cottage cheese. That was wholesome. Commendable. She dribbled a smidgen of honey over the cheese so she wouldn't be left with a cheesy taste in her mouth. Still, okay.

Ten minutes after the toast and cheese and the smidgen of honey, she was back in the pullman kitchen. She felt like something juicy. A ripe pear or an apple and while she was there a few peanuts—a nice complementary taste and texture. Thirst took over but the idea of water alone wasn't appealing. Perhaps a milk shake, something frothy and sweet. She had kept the Waring blender.

Her jaws ached and her head buzzed. She could feel the chemical changes taking place inside her, the crossed signals, the weariness, the torpor and ultimately, about four o'clock in the afternoon—which began the loneliest time of the day—a stonelike immobility. She would sit there in her giant club chair, unable to move or think. She did this almost every day for the next eight months.

One morning she awoke after sleeping fourteen hours and didn't know what day of the week it was or what hour of the day. She went into the bathroom, returned to bed and flipped on the television. Stanley Siegel was interviewing a black woman who had given birth to Siamese twins who had been successfully separated. It was a poignant story but after listening for one or two minutes, April heard only gibberish. She tried to concentrate but all she got was a garbled sound.

Her first desire was to leave the apartment. It was claustrophobic. She had been alone for four days and wanted to be surrounded by people. She put on a dress— a pretty print made of a cheap synthetic picked up in Gimbel's basement. It was cut on the bias and had once fit well. Now it bunched up in the back above the hips and was indecently short. She put on a raincoat to hide the shortness. It was too warm for a raincoat. It was the perfect season for a suit. She had always admired women who wore well-cut suits with ironed dimity blouses that buttoned up the back. Sara Davis's mother had worn suits all through school and was now a lawyer. She had gone back to school—Harvard or Yale or some other big deal school.

In her dress and raincoat and sneakers without socks, she walked from the Thirties to Fifth Avenue and then to 50th Street. It was close enough to lunchtime to make the sidewalks crowded. The sun really hurt her eyes and made her want to close them but she couldn't just stand on a busy sidewalk with her eyes closed. First she fished into her large shoulder-strap bag for sunglasses but her eyes still hurt so she stepped into Saks Fifth Avenue where it was cool and dim. She would look around at the merchandise until she felt like going home again.

It was 12:30 on a Thursday afternoon and she had all the time in the world. She wasn't especially clean but her hair was pulled away from her face with two barettes. She couldn't remember if she had lipstick on or not and decided to put some on with her pinkie from the freebies on the cosmetic counters.

She had entered from a side door and was in the men's department. It was so cool and softly lit, she didn't want to leave right away although a salesman behind the underwear counter gave her the once-over. He was staring at her sneakers and bare legs. It was too cold for bare legs. She moved to another counter and picked up some sale pajamas that were strewn about. As she was standing there, she looked up and noticed a middle-aged man—a customer with thinning, well-combed hair—staring at her. He was holding a sports jacket on a hanger in one hand and had a quizzical look on his face. He wasn't just looking out into the air, he was definitely staring at her. He began to walk in her direction.

"Pardon me," he said. He was still holding the jacket. "I can't quite see in this light. Is this green in the tweed or blue? I need green but not blue. I don't think any good Harris tweed would be blue, do you?"

"I don't know," she said.

"Would you mind looking at it?"

"No." She took off her glasses, remembering about the lipstick. She hadn't washed her face either. "It's definitely green," she said and put her sunglasses back on. He was about forty-eight or fifty, with gray at the temples and quite young looking except for a waddle under his jowls.

"Could I ask you one more favor?" He tried to get her to look at him. "Could you come with me to the sports jackets and look at one other one?"

"All right."

He kept looking back to see if she was following him and gave her a shameful little smile. As if he really were sorry to involve her like this.

He took off his own jacket and placed it on a chair while looking through the rack. She noticed he had the slightest roll around his waist. On his wrist was one of those thin watches whose faces were made of lapis or jade. She wondered how he told the time. It wasn't the sort of watch a really mature person would buy. The ads for them said something snobby like: *Only twelve people on this planet can own one of these for Christmas.* Yeah, she had always answered aloud, twelve jerks.

Now she was face to face with one of the jerks. But he was rich. He selected a jacket off the rack. "What color is this?"

"Yellow," she said.

"Last fall, I bought a jacket here," he was trying to explain his dilemma, "and when I got it home it was all the wrong colors. I didn't have any shirts that really looked well with it. I don't want that to happen again. Am I keeping you from something?"

"No. I have some time to kill." She was immediately sorry she'd said that. Perhaps he thought she had been waiting for someone to pick her up. "Actually," she added quickly, "I've got to go. It's later than I thought."

"What time did you think it was?"

He was trying to trap her. She didn't know what time it was. "It doesn't matter," she said curtly. "I've got to go."

"Of course," he said gently, "I've got to go, too. I'll save this for another time. Are you going downtown? Maybe we could walk a few blocks together." Tiny spikes of terror shot through her chest. Since she had gained all this weight, the least little thing made her heart beat like crazy.

"Just a block or two."

"Of course." He gave her a warm, reassuring smile and walked as if protecting her from the crowds. He held the door and when she was safely out, maneuvered to the outer edge of the street, the perfect gentleman.

"Going back to work?"

"No." Now she didn't want him to leave so quickly. After all, he was kind and treated her well. He wasn't a bum or anything like that. She would really have liked to sit down and have a drink with him or something. "Just home."

"But you said you had to go."

"That salesman kept staring at me. I didn't want to stay." Whatever he had thought of her before, now he thought something worse.

"Of course. Want to stop somewhere and have a drink?"

"All right."

He turned left on 48th Street and found a small restaurant with a bar. "Maybe you'd like lunch," he said.

"No. A drink . . . wine will be fine." They sat at the bar. "You on your lunch hour?"

"So to speak. I don't have a lunch hour *per se.*"

"The boss, eh?" she said, surprising herself with this sudden gaiety.

"Yes. De Boss." He chuckled. She chuckled back. The bartender asked for their order. "Two wines. White."

They concentrated on sipping their wine, holding the glasses between their hands. It was noisy at the bar and difficult to hear. When they were about halfway through he asked her if she wanted another.

"Oh, no. This is fine."

"Well, then maybe we should think about leaving then. Too bad. I've enjoyed the company. I'll give you a lift home in a cab." He gulped down the rest of his wine.

If he was having such a good time, why did he finish half his wine in one gulp? "That would be fine." Now she was furious with herself. She didn't want a lift from him.

The cab was cozy and she became less furious. There was something reassuring about driving through the streets with someone by her side who felt kindly toward her and who could afford drinks and a cab. He dismissed the cab at her door and walked in with her. Inside the door, he kissed her on the mouth. "Don't worry," he said. "I'm not going to attack you, if that's what you're thinking. It's just very pleasant, following an instinct like this. Just letting things take their own course without squelching every urge. It's very nice. I get a nice feeling from you." His hands had strayed under her raincoat, around her back and then to the front. "Why were you prowling around the men's department though?"

There it was. He *did* think she was a pick-up. "The sun was hurting my eyes so I went in to rest and waste some time, too. But not to pick up anyone." She walked away from him and went into the bathroom to see what she looked like. It wasn't good. Her eyes had dark circles around them. Her hair was showing signs of the greasies. She brushed her teeth. He must be a pervert to want her when she looked like this. He looked so clean himself.

When she came out, he was sitting on the couch with

his legs crossed. He looked up at her and smiled. She sat down beside him.

"Well . . ."

"Well . . ." His hand strayed toward her arm and traced one of her veins from the crease of her elbow to her wrist. Then he traced the palm of her hand, around and around. She felt both sexy and fearful. Maybe it was just fearful and not sexy, it was difficult to tell. He came closer and outlined her breast in the same silent way. He took off his jacket and half reclined on the couch. Then he pulled her on top of him, kissed her and kneaded her breasts very hard. He was wild about her thighs when he saw them. "Oh, lordy," he said.

He came before he entered her but he made sure she came, too. "Was it okay?" She nodded. "Listen," he said, "I've really got to go. It was wonderful. Spontaneous and wonderful." As he walked out the door, he handed her a fifty-dollar bill. "Buy yourself a great pair of shoes or something. Please. And let's see a smile before I leave." She widened her lips, and he touched two fingers to his as if he were blowing her a kiss and left.

Ten minutes later, she couldn't believe what she had done. She was so upset by it she wrote it all out on a piece of paper: "Today, April Taylor went into Saks Fifth Avenue and was enticed by a kind, rich man to have sex with him."

Today, April Taylor went into Saks Fifth Avenue, looking god-awful. Her hair was greasy, her dress too short, her raincoat dirty, no stockings on her feet (not even the queen size fit anymore). She stood in the store staring at men's pajamas like a mental defective until she enticed an old man—old enough to be her father—to buy her a drink and screw her.

Today, April Taylor picked up an old man and let him screw her for money.

She burned all three papers. Someone on a talk show

had offered this as an effective way of getting rid of something that was really bothering you. Still, it was several days before she could get the picture of that man and his stupid watch out of her mind.

A few days later, she awoke in the middle of the night in a cold sweat and feeling sick to her stomach. There was an acrid smell in the room, something was fermenting inside her. The blood was rushing to and from her tingling skin, her head was starved for oxygen. She realized she hadn't really tasted anything in days. The craving for particular tastes and textures was gone. The desire for chocolate or Fritos or meat or ice cream or peanut butter, bread and butter, things frosty or succulent or mealy or crusty was gone. She had a vision of fat skimming along her bloodstream like soup gone cold. Her body was struggling to carry its burden of food. The food was fermenting along the way.

She knew that it would be impossible to continue in the way she had been living. She had to change her life. She had to find a job. A real job. Someplace to go besides this dark apartment.

Even with this firm resolve, her mind and will moved so slowly, it took her two weeks more to mobilize herself for the ten-block trip to the Top of the Line Employment Agency where a reluctant Sondra Greene finally connected her to Burdie's.

14

"This is what the American woman will be wearing on her feet this fall." Martin Guttenplan, the better shoe buyer, held up a beige wedgie to the circle gathered in the merchandise manager's office for the Monday morning ad meeting. The shoe had a dark toe that dissolved into a lighter shade, as if it had been rescued from a fire. "Wedgies are the thing." He looked meaningfully toward Erica, the copy chief and April's immediate boss. Erica was tall and big-boned and had worked out a set of diminutive movements to minimize her size. She was not unattractive, and April suspected that naked she was a knockout.

"*That's* the fashion story?" Erica was incredulous. "*Wedgies?* That's not news. There's got to be something else."

"There's nothing else. It's a nice looking shoe." Martin Guttenplan folded his arms in front of him meekly.

"We can't say, 'Come and buy our nice-looking shoe,' Martin. What's it made of? Is it leather? Is it comfortable? Maybe we can call it the eighteen-hour shoe, like the eighteen-hour bra."

"At $17.95, you know it can't be leather," said Martin smugly. "It just looks like it."

"Then *that's* the story." Erica wrote busily in her notebook. "The look and feel of leather at half the price. . . . Okay, Martin, give me the shoe."

April wrote busily in her notebook, too, lest she miss the one advertisable difference in each piece of merchandise. She alternately thought about getting down the facts and keeping her knees covered. Today, all the seats on the couch had been taken and she had been forced to take a wooden chair facing the merchandise manager, Alan Leeds. The seat was high. Her skirt didn't quite cover her knees, which she considered the most embarrassing part of her body.

Each day, Burdie's was more familiar. She became used to the lights, the vignettes of summer-to-come, shoppers taking the escalator steps two at a time, a mannequin family of happy campers smiling nonstop at the hot dogs on their propane stove. Her spare time was spent sleeping off the weariness of a round trip to Newark and finding something suitable to wear each day. One night on a talk show, a diet doctor asked the audience to hold one of their shoes out at arm's length for five minutes. After one minute, all but a few arms were down in weariness. "That," he said, "is how much energy it takes to carry around one extra pound of body weight. Now multiply by ten or twenty and you'll see why you're so tired." April saw. She had to multiply by sixty.

Each Monday, she, along with Erica and three other writers, went to Alan Leeds's office to view the "hot" soft goods items for the week—the stars that would pull in the customers who would then impulse-buy all the other merchandise.

Soft goods were things that weren't hard—among them dresses, coats, children's clothes. Some soft goods were hard—shoes and handbags. And some hard goods were soft—tablecloths and sheets. But mostly, hard goods were very hard—washing machines, televisions and furniture.

The hottest item of the week for April was the soft goods merchandise manager, Alan Leeds. From the first day she had seen him, he had made her remember sex and how it felt to want it, although she didn't particularly like him. He was clean and healthy-looking. His nose was peeling, making him appear boyish and innocent. Reddish hair peeked out of his immaculate cuffs. She often fantasized that he was fondling her in the office. He didn't know she was alive.

"We're having a fur sale in time for Easter." Ralph Schildkraut was holding a pale beige mink stole on a curved, padded hanger. He looked exactly like Franklin Roosevelt.

"So what else is new?" said Erica.

"Stoles," said Ralph, ignoring her. "Male skins, fully let out. Hush-hush designer."

"Why is it always all male skins?" Erica was irritated. "Female skins are no good?"

"No." Ralph looked puzzled. "They're good."

"Then why don't they ever say all female skins?"

"I don't know. It's always been male skins, fully let out."

"So what's so special about the stoles?" She was poised with her pencil.

"They're designer stoles."

"What designer?"

"We can't say."

"Oh, Cassini again?"

"No. Not Cassini."

"Then who?"

"Schiaparelli."

"Yeah . . . so why can't we say Schiaparelli? Isn't he dead?"

"It's a she."

"Isn't she dead?"

"I don't know. But we're selling them at well below retail so we can't mention the name. That's the deal."

"We can't say it rhymes with Chantilly?"

"That's confusing."

"So what do we say? Hush-hush designer stoles, well below her usual price?"

"Doesn't sound strong enough."

"At this ridiculous price, we had to cut out the label— but you can sew it back on at home."

"Hey, that's good. That's good. I like that."

"Wonderful."

April looked at Erica with awe. She was a walking headline machine.

In between presentations, Alan Leeds stared at Susan Scott, the stylist who chose the accessories for the ads and managed the photography sessions. Susan was always exquisitely coiffed and dressed. On warm days, she wore pleated batiste shirtwaists with baby tucks and linen coats. Her makeup was always fresh. She was self-centered but not mean or rude. The men all wanted her. They wanted to take her to dinner and to parties because she looked good on a man's arm.

"Whose dress is that?" asked Alan, examining Susan's chocolate brown dirndl-skirted sheath.

"It's mine." She blinked and bobbed a headful of curls.

"You know what I mean." Alan's smile was out of all proportion to the joke. He played it gruff but you could see his hunger for her mounting.

April countered this rebuff with a fantasy that Alan Leeds was fondling her breasts while dictating a letter into a machine. He had one big clean hand inside her dress while the other held the mike. "Doris, take a letter to Joe Greenberg at White Stag," he said into the mike. "'Dear Joe: are you aware that we're not getting our orders within the time promised?'" (Well-padded fingers would be searching out well-padded spots.) "'The whole shipment of jogging shorts and tank tops missed our peak week.'" (He was pointing with the mike to his own throbbing organ and she got busy.)

His boyishness prompted her to give him boyish dialogue: Could I park my car in your garage? Could I put my bread in your box? Could I put my hot dog in your bun?

Her reverie was interrupted by Lorenzo Bucci, the budget coat buyer, who was next in line. Lorenzo was radically thin. He looked like the poor relative of the main gangster, taken in out of family loyalty.

"What have you got, Lorenzo?" asked Alan.

"Let me say this," Lorenzo stood over Erica but spoke to Alan, "if the ad doesn't say sale, sale, sale, you can forget about it."

"Lorenzo, we're not going to say sale, sale, sale," said Erica drily.

"No, of course not. You might sell something." Again he turned to Alan. "You wanna write poetry or you wanna sell coats?"

"We're not writing poetry," replied Erica calmly. She began to inspect the stitching on the coat Lorenzo held up. "We can say something interesting."

"What interesting? They're the same coats I bought last year and the same coats I'll buy next year. They're coats. Wool coats. Lightweight wool coats with three buttons down the front and a modified balmacaan sleeve. The same women will buy them, too. Not the women who bought one last year but the women who bought one two years ago."

Erica was not listening. "Just the coats you want for spring," she said, as if reading it off the ceiling. "Lightweight. Three-button closing. Flattering balmacaan sleeve. Would you believe only thirty-nine dollars?"

"I don't want to say that," said Lorenzo.

"Well, that's what we're going to say," hummed Erica. "Or something like that."

"Alan, for crissakes. It's my ass if they don't sell."

"How can you sell wool coats for thirty-nine dollars?" Alan brought his chair and body upright.

"I got a deal with Royce."

"What's the deal, Royce stole them from somebody?"

"You know me better than that."

"You can't sell honest wool coats for thirty-nine dollars."

"They're reprocessed wool."

"It's not virgin wool?" Alan's eyebrows went up.

"Virgin? Virgin?" Lorenzo's look was contemptuous and impatient. "No such thing anymore. You know any virgins, girlie?" He turned to April and she turned to jelly. He was going to say something about her weight. He was going to say something about her genitals. She folded her hands in her lap and looked down at them. Mercifully, he looked away. "Look, you wanna sell coats or you want to wait until the niggers get restless during the summer . . . no offense," he turned to Selma, a black girl who wrote for children's wear, "and come looting and burning?" The picture he painted made him angry. "You know what you are? You're Doctor No. No, you can't say this. No, you can't say that. This isn't Saks Fifth Avenue, you know. This isn't Bonwit Teller. This is Burdie's." He waved his arms, like a conductor asking for a large sound. "And you," he turned to Erica with particular contempt, "you're Nurse No."

No one had considered Burdie's any less dignified than
the other stores but Lorenzo's performance made them
feel uninformed. April admired him for turning the
meeting around to suit him.

"We'll put the word sale in the ad," said Alan soberly.

"In twelve-point type?"

"Eight."

"Make it ten," said Lorenzo.

"Out," Alan rose from his chair. "Out . . ."

"Okay, okay." He left quickly, dragging his reprocessed
wool coat behind him.

"Is he trying to tell us something?" Erica asked.

"Of course not. We just opened two new stores." His
brow remained furrowed, however, and he didn't tilt his
chair back in the same careless way.

15

It took her three weeks to settle in. To stop gnawing pencils each time she placed a piece of copy on Erica's desk for approval. During the third week, Erica sent her back five times to rewrite an ad for a bathing suit sale. She had written fifteen variations on the theme of maillots riding high on bare, tan thighs; cutouts showing more than ever before.

In the end, the huge, double-page ad had read: *20% to 30% off every swimsuit in our stock.* She knew that was the best thing they could say about those damn swimsuits. Erica had been right.

It took her three weeks also to take the commute in her stride. There were a variety of trains that stopped in Newark and continued to New York. There was the Metroliner from Washington. The train from Chicago. The trains whose final destination was New York and those that continued north or south. Each had its own debris and strange newspapers.

The second week at Burdie's a photograph taken on her first day appeared on a stand in front of the executive cafeteria—everyone in advertising was an executive—

with the words NEW FACES under it and her name. The
fourth day it was there, someone had written in front of
her name THE TWO AND ONLY.

Don Loren, the display manager, who seemed in a
position to know, said it was the photographer himself
who had done it. "It's that Nazi, Dennis," he announced
at lunch. "Who else would do a thing like that?"

"Can you confront him?" asked Erica.

"Huh? Not me, honey. He's rough." No one knew what
Don meant. No one wanted to know.

For April, the graffiti wasn't the worst thing. The worst
thing was the way she looked. The photographer had
caught her too glad face, startled, open, puffy. She could
have been a man or woman or a gruesome child. Every
time she went to lunch and got a glimpse of the photograph, her stomach muscles—wherever they were—
bunched together in a knot of humiliation.

Don Loren was responsible for windows and in-store
displays. He dressed the mannequins and chose the
motifs. He looked like a well-dressed mannequin, too.
Tall, slim, straight spine and distant. Twice a week, April
met him in his workroom to get the information for writing display copy.

The first time she walked into his large, cluttered room
he was systematically chipping away at the plaster face of
a male mannequin on an ironing board. He looked up
briefly when April entered. "The only way I can get them
to buy new ones is to destroy the old ones."

"Why do you want new ones?"

"Well, just look at these! Look at the wigs! Look at the
faces. Look at the bodies. No breasts. No contours. The
makeup is all wrong." He stopped. "You here for the
window copy?"

"I'm April from advertising."

"April, huh? Why April?"

"I was born in April so they named me April."

"Veeery imaginative." He looked her over quickly. "I used to be with Oleg Cassini," he said immediately.

"Oh . . ."

"I was his draper."

"Draper?"

"Fabrics have to be draped. You have to see how everything is going to hang."

"What happened?"

"What happened with what?"

"Oleg Cassini?"

"Oh . . . *that*. What *always* happens." He said it archly, implying things too personal to mention. Still, April was impressed. His clothes looked as if they were pressed hourly, while he was in them. They were the most beautiful, well-fitting clothes she had ever seen on man or woman. Everything shone with the faint gleam of good silk. His hair was exquisitely cut, perfectly framing his large eyes, the broad nose, the full lips. He was one swell black.

"Your clothes are beautiful." She couldn't hold back.

"I spray-starch everything." Now he was taking her in slowly, head to toe. "Give me your blouse, I'll show you a trick." April was appalled and hugged herself stubbornly.

"Don't be ridiculous," he said. "I don't like women."

"That's not the point."

"Come on," he said impatiently, "take it off. You can go behind that screen."

She took off her blouse, which was off-white with a Nehru collar and a small string tie, and handed it to him, peeking anxiously from behind the screen to see who was going to walk in and see what was going on. Don was like a magician with his iron which he held in one hand while he wafted a mist of spray starch from high above with the other. He could have been conducting the Philharmonic.

When he finished, her plain, cotton Lady Manhattan stood at attention.

When she put it back on, he stood back to admire his work. "There, you see? Isn't that better?"

"Yes. It's beautiful." She adjusted her clothes and picked up her pad and pencil. "I should be getting back. They'll be wondering what happened to me."

"Who's going to be wondering?" he looked annoyed. He began tossing the limbs of the mannequins into a pile in the corner.

"Erica."

"She's a coward underneath. Like any bully."

"Who said she was a bully?"

"Then why are you afraid of her?"

"I'm not afraid of her. I've got a job for which I'm getting paid."

"Not enough either. They can't pay you enough to work in Newark." He tossed the last hand into the pile and gave her his full attention. "What do you think Erica will do to you?"

"I have no idea. She might just ask me where I've been."

"Tell her it's none of her business."

"It is her business. Why should I be angry?"

He threw up his hands as if the whole thing were self-evident. "I just hate to see another victim."

"I'm not a victim."

"Hah!"

"What's that supposed to mean?"

"Take it for what it's worth."

"It isn't worth a damn thing." Now she was annoyed.

"Look, don't get mad at me because you work for some crazy bitch." His face became contemplative. "Maybe you're right. You're the only one you've really got to answer to."

"You mean you—everyone you—or me?"

"Everyone you, but yes, you especially."

"Why me especially?"

"Well, just look at you. Repression is written all over your body."

She didn't know what to say. She was sure he didn't mean to be insulting. Why would he have ironed her blouse if he was going to send her away angry? No, it was something else. Some people were analytical. "I'm not going to ask what you mean by that." She poised her pencil over her pad to show him she was ready to get the information for which she had come.

"Suit yourself." He went to stand by his pile of mannequins and sighed deeply. "This week we have a public service window for . . . are you ready? The Leprosy Foundation." He cackled uproariously. "Aren't the mannequins just perfect . . . all those little chips and crumbling limbs." When she didn't laugh, he pursed his lips and went to a pipe rack with blazers and pleated skirts. "It's the same old, spring story—same as every year—red, white and blue separates in synthetic blends."

"Would you say," asked April, imitating Erica, "old standards in new, easy-care fabrics?"

He inspected the buttons and lining of one of the jackets. "What would *I* say? I would say it's all crapola. The fabric is craperoo and the finishing details are craperoo. But you have to do what you have to do. Soooo, if you want to call them old standards in new easy-care fabrics, go right ahead."

"Okay, so long," she rose to leave.

"Ta ta."

He was obviously a pain in the ass. Childish. Immature and annoyingly candid. Compulsively honest. So why did she like him so much?

16

Luis had decided there were cycles to his life. Not the biblical seven years of fat and lean. His were more like four or five. Princeton was definitely the fat, then came the lean. When he had gone to Atlanta as an assistant buyer at little more than half his previous salary, there had been a spurt of hopefulness that generated constant energy. Psychic income, they called it—when a job made you happy and healthier. There was no psychic income in New Jersey. Often he felt depressed and with a growing uneasiness that stumped him. He was more a delegator now, although his input had made some of the merchandising gimmicks work better.

The lines for Burdie's two midnight sales had choked the streets and wrapped around the block as everyone waited for the doors to open. The police had come, as had the television cameras. The event made all three network news shows. He had set a time limit—ninety minutes—and had a prize drawing on each floor. There had been a buying frenzy that was contagious. A woman went into labor. People were sure it was the chance of a lifetime.

When he had been at Burdie's New Jersey for three months, his grandmother had a stroke that affected the left side of her face and her left arm. Her mouth turned down as if she was purposely trying to look grotesque. It made him feel so helpless, he found it hard to visit. He offered to move them out of the projects but his mother insisted it was the best place for them, so he offered to send them on a vacation to Puerto Rico, which sent them into a fit of ready-making that belied their casual acceptance. As the time neared, his mother dyed the gray out of her hair and had a permanent. He thought of the similarities between them. They were both cunning enough to assume the virtues they needed to survive, she was a loner of sorts and so was he.

For a while, he thought his depression was due to lack of a continuing love. He needed someone to love over the long haul. He needed a background and a sense of continuity instead of just waking up every morning alone in his beige apartment. Yet when he looked around at the married couples who invited him to their perfect apartments and wicker-choked summer homes, there was no couple he envied.

Alan Leeds, his merchandise manager for soft goods, and Merlow Hess, the manager of the Short Hills store— which was the largest of the eight-store chain—were his closest friends, and they urged him to speculate in the stock market. They were making handsome profits and, seeing how it excited them, he joined in. "It's better than sex," said Merlow. Within three weeks, he lost five thousand dollars and that ended his speculating. He took up jogging, running two or three miles along the East River before taking the train to Newark. The jogging made him feel good, his mind raced with ideas, but it didn't replace the optimism he felt seeping out of him.

The second quarter earnings, reflecting his tenure, were very good considering that interest rates had climbed to thirteen percent and business in general was in a slump. Burdie's New Jersey was the only unit in the corporation that showed a double digit percentage increase.

The quarterly report wasn't yet in type before two executive search firms contacted him. The overtures were conducted with such elaborate secrecy, he thought it was a joke. Five years ago he had walked into Burdette's headquarters on Sixth Avenue and filled out a job application for the executive training program. Now he was such a hot property, his movements had to be protected.

The man from the search firm who sounded the least demented convinced him to listen to the offer over lunch. He looked like the model for Paul Erdman's financial musclemen who control the currency fluctuations of the universe. Luis felt very much on his guard. "I've been in New Jersey six months," he told his contact. "Anybody who's grabbing at a six-month record is not in a stable situation."

"Perhaps it will appear more stable when you hear their terms," said the man quietly. "Double your present salary . . ." he put out his hand as Luis began to interrupt ". . . they know what it is. They also know about the stock options and they have a similar compensation."

"That's ridiculous," said Luis, determined to keep the upper hand. There was something sinister about the whole business, and it crossed his mind that the Burdette Corporation might be testing his loyalty and there was no real offer at all. "It isn't that I'm not worth it, but the deal is *too* spectacular. I would say the answer is no."

"Think about it for two days," said the man. His air of interested disinterest was not altered. "Then say no. I'll call you."

"Suit yourself," said Luis.

A case of expensive wine arrived at his apartment by evening. A note from his contact was nestled amid the bottles. "This is in appreciation of your time and consideration." It happened to be a wine he liked a lot. Was it coincidence or did they know everything about him?

Two days passed without a call. If it was a tactical maneuver, it worked. Luis felt anxious and unsettled. On the morning of the third day, his contact called to say they had added fifty thousand to the per annum salary and, since this was virtually a new offer, he prevailed on Luis to take another forty-eight hours before saying no. This time, Luis didn't protest.

Despite his public disdain, he thought of little else but the possibility of making two hundred and fifty thousand dollars. He felt as if he already made that much and could do the things such a person could do. He looked in the paper for summer homes in the Hamptons. He looked at Mercedes automobiles with a proprietary air. The possibility of being rich made him warm and happy in the center of his chest.

When the time came to give his answer, he said no again without any immediate regrets. Such a leap in salary would psych him out. And, suppose it didn't work out? Who would pay him such a salary again? He didn't even use the situation to get more money out of Burdie's, feeling that he would have more clout in a year's time. The high-mindedness didn't last, however. Within a week, he had turned on himself as the real drawback. Perhaps, it was his own deficiencies that had clouded the issue. Perhaps he was a fool. Now, after it was too late to do anything about, he felt that he had missed the point.

17

"ARE YOU DOING ANYTHING about your life?" It was Sylvie on the phone from Ardsley, a small bedroom community in Westchester where she and Spencer Straight had settled with their son, Bradford, who, Sylvie said, was a big boy now.

"He's almost four," she explained crossly when April asked if he talked yet. "He's learning to ice skate in preparation for playing ice hockey. He takes violin lessons."

"Violin lessons? Can he hold it with his chin and everything?"

"He doesn't hold it *yet*. It's the Japanese method. He plays on a Cracker Jack box glued to a stick. Just until he gets the feeling of the bowing."

"Does he read music?" April was in uncharted territory. She would have accepted that Bradford did brain surgery on the side.

"Of course not. He'll play by imitating the sounds. He listens to his record every night before he goes to sleep."

Bradford's nonstop life was making her feel depressed. She wanted to get off the phone and wash her hair. Her

146

left eye felt as if something were in it. "Does he ever play with toys?"

"What kind of a crack is that?"

"Sylvie, I'm not trying to discredit you. Honestly, you sound so defensive."

"Of course, I'm defensive. You're asking if my child speaks yet when he reads all of the Sam and Sally books. Doesn't that sound hostile to you?"

"Yes, it does. Stupid more than hostile. And thoughtless. I'm sorry." She felt saddened that she had not been to see Bradford and bounced him on her lap. He was practically her nephew. Now it was too late. He was beyond cuddling and bouncing. She wouldn't have minded seeing Sylvie, too, but Sylvie would be distraught at the sight of her. How could you have done this to yourself, she would ask and April would not have an answer. She feared most someone asking her why she had let herself go. Something inside her *had* let go.

"This conversation is supposed to be about you, remember?" Sylvie's voice was conciliatory. "How *you're* doing with your life." She made life sound like a metaphor for knitting.

"My life? Well, now, let's see. I'm working." She stopped to let this positive fact sink in. "For a department store."

"I'm afraid to ask, are you selling?"

"Oh, no. I work behind the scenes, so to speak. For a chain of stores in New Jersey. I work in Newark."

"*Newark?* You go to *Newark every day?*" She could feel Sylvie turn anxious. She was afraid that April's life was settling into some bizarre pattern that wasn't reversible.

"Yes."

"Why, for godsakes?"

"A very good reason. That's where the job is."

"What kind of job?"

"Writing ads. I'm the advertising writer for soft goods.

It's an executive position. I get a discount on everything. Except sale items, of course."

"Oh." There was an upbeat pause. "That's not *so* bad."

"It's part of the Burdette chain. Eight stores just in New Jersey."

"Oh. Can you be transferred to another city?"

"I hadn't thought of it, but I guess I could."

"Oh, well. It's an investment in time. That's not *so* bad. Not when it's going to lead to a decent career."

When she hung up, April was amazed that she hadn't thought about her job in just that way. She hadn't considered her trek to Newark each day as an investment which would earn her interest in the advertising world. It had taken efficient, pragmatic Sylvie to see that the job at Burdie's put her in the most advantageous position she had ever been in to create a niche for herself in the business world. And she would do it, too. She would definitely do it.

18

*YOUR FRIENDS WILL THINK You Struck It
Rich!* The thought was gross but perfect for the job. She
wrote a couple of variations to convince herself. *That
Sinking Feeling. Get It With Plushtron Four. Frankly, This Is
Carpeting to Show Off!*

The carpeting was at least three inches deep. It would
hoard dirt like crazy. It would be difficult to walk on. Nobody would buy it to do the things carpets were supposed
to do—cover floors and add coziness to a room. This carpet was purchased as a Dun and Bradstreet on your life.
We've got so much, we feel like wasting some of it.

She stared across the aisle to the window wall and contemplated the gray April morning as if Newark's
nouveaux riches would form themselves out of the ether
and reveal their weaknesses to her. The sample square
had a bald spot in the center where Frank DiMaio, the
carpet buyer, had put a match to it to show its resistance
to fire. "It's right behind wool in flame retardancy,"
Frank had said smugly. "You should play that up."

Erica had put her hand on her hip, reminding April of

Alice Kramden on "The Honeymooners." "You mean it doesn't burn?"

"Of course, it burns. Everything burns sometime." He held a lighted match to the fiber and it began to turn into a black gooey mess. "It melts," he said, astonished.

"And throws off toxic fumes that kill instantly," said Selma.

"What are you? A friend of the earth?" Frank was once again the buyer. "Any synthetic melts. This one melts slower."

"So what should we say?" asked Erica. "Buy this carpeting, it melts slower?"

"Awh, come on. This is luxury carpeting."

April inspected the tall, squiggly fibers surrounding the melted spot. "You could lose your shoe in it."

"Hey. Maybe that's what we should say." Erica stared into the distance. "Carpeting so thick . . . so plush . . . you could lose your shoe in it."

"No, you can't say that. These are down to earth people who want a little luxury. They won't understand."

"It's all yours." Erica handed the sample to April.

She decided to go with *Your Friends Will Think You Struck It Rich!* Anybody could understand that. She was about to begin the body copy when Missy came down the aisle alerting them of an impromptu meeting on the tenth floor. The president wanted to see them—the entire copy and art departments, some thirty-odd people.

The president had never spoken to them before. He usually spoke to the vice president in charge of advertising and sales promotion, who then spoke to Missy, who then spoke to the art and copy chiefs, who then spoke to the artists and writers. But this time, there was a new president and he wanted to talk directly to them.

"Something big is up," said Erica.

"Or something small," said Selma, who, among all of them, had been there the longest.

As she rose to leave, April tripped on an open drawer, bumping her knee smartly and tearing her stockings. She joined the others as they trudged up to the tenth floor in a straggly, balky line. It was ten o'clock in the morning and they wanted to have their coffee and read the paper. April particularly didn't want to go. Her knee was throbbing and Patrick Linn had snuck a late ad into the schedule which meant she had to finish the Plushtron ad and then do a quarter-page on Supp-Hose which Patrick had decided to put on sale after Easter.

She wasn't even looking when he came in. She was thinking of how best to punch up Supp-Hose's unique assets. *A thousand little hardworking fingers . . . supporting you. Supp-Hose, it's like having a mother for your legs.* Too long. Too complicated. She could feel a hard lump beginning to form on her knee. Maybe it was a blood clot? She would have to be rushed out of this meeting on a stretcher and taken to . . . Newark General Hospital? Was there a hospital in Newark? *A thousand magic fingers put your legs on easy street. Now . . . 20% off.* The lump had burst through the hole in her stocking and bulged out angrily. She should get up and put some ice on it but a man had come in. *20% off on your favorite support hose. All the fashion shades.* Stock up now, you fool.

She was surprised to see him. Everyone was. You thought of a president, you thought of gray at the temples, maybe horn-rimmed glasses, a pin-striped suit. But here was this—*kid!* Not a kid exactly but this—*guy!*

My god, she *knew* this guy—from the airport. She opened her wallet and looked at the paper with his name on it, as if that would confirm it. It was weird—one of her daydreams had gone too far. She felt light-headed and happy and couldn't look at him hard enough.

His suit wasn't pin-striped. It was an oatmeal "crash"

linen which, she had learned only last week, was the most desirable linen and came from Italy. Erica had assumed she meant crushed linen and rejected the ad. "No," April had insisted, "the buyer says those who can afford it know what 'crash' linen is." "There are certain things that are the best in their category. Santa Clara prunes are the best prunes. Kadota is the premier name in figs. Beluga caviar, Sèvres china. And now, 'crash' linen. Crash as in fashion POW! At one time only the pope's summer vestments were made of this treasured fabric."

"Is this true? About the pope?" Erica had asked.

"I don't know."

"We can't say it's true if it's not true."

"What do you think," said the buyer, "there's a Vatican consumer advocate in Newark?"

The guy—president—introduced himself quickly and said he was glad for this opportunity to meet them. He turned deliberately and nodded to Susan Scott who had on an outfit from mainland China. A silk turquoise wrap with a wide sash that made her look delicate and mysterious. He had already found the best-looking woman in the store.

He was so attractive, it was difficult to listen to what he was saying. His hair was parted in the middle and brushed back diagonally in a slight roll that seemed impossible to maintain, yet it fell into memory layers that moved in concert as he turned his head. He exuded health. He *was* health. She could see his heart pumping rich, nutrient-laden blood throughout his body. There would be no plaque on his teeth, his small and large intestines were in perfect order, his eyes were clear, the white almost blue and the blue, very blue. A small vein at his temple, throbbing gently, bore testimony to his supercharged metabolism. He was at the peak of his power and

April felt it as a reproach. Her stomach sent its signals wide and desolate. As if it had tastebuds. As if it had tasted cold metal. She slunk in her seat, wanting to become invisible.

He was pinning two ads to a bulletin board, taking his time and pushing the pins in securely. "I want to read these two headlines to you," he said turning to the ads. "The one on the right is for a foundation cream and it says, *'He'll boast to his friends that you never wear makeup.'*" He paused and looked around the room. "Would you like to comment? What is this saying to you?" He nodded to Selma.

"The foundation is so sheer and light, as far as the guy's concerned, she's not wearing makeup at all."

"And you think that's a plus for her. That she's fooled him?"

"Let me put it this way. The ad did very well."

He smiled as if her answer was exactly the one he wanted. He turned to the other ad, for a perfume, and read the headline in a flat voice. *"'Finale. Very expensive. But then so is being single.'"* This time he nodded to Erica, who became defensive.

"We all know what it implies."

"What does it imply?" he asked quickly.

"The perfume is going to mesmerize the man into committing a rash act."

"You mean marriage."

There was general laughter.

"There's no guarantee, of course. It's only a provocative line. It's a little tough. A little ironic. And a little funny. Just like Finale itself." Erica spoke in headlines. Instead of answering his question, she had written another Finale ad. He saw it, too.

"I wish you'd written that instead."

"Why?" Erica was really surprised. "That ad did fine.

Better than fine. Besides, it was a co-op ad. We only paid for half of it."

"We're going to pay again," he said ruefully. He was powerful but vulnerable. He had regrets, which doubled his appeal. "Both headlines work on the idea that the women who are buying these products are out to pull a fast one on the men they love most in the world." He let his words sink in. "In the first ad, the man is led to believe he has Rebecca of Sunnybrook Farm on his arm when, in reality, he has a normal person who needs foundation cover-up to look her best. In the second ad, a man is bewitched by a smell—and it must be quite a smell—into thinking he's found the only possible mother for his children, when he might just have a so-so lady who's been priced out of the apartment market."

A few people laughed—but not the president, who, while not exactly grim, was not smiling. "I'm not the only one who's caught the underlying message in these ads," he added solemnly. "One of them is being reproduced in *Ms.* magazine as an example of advertising that humiliates women. I don't think it does much for men, either." He took down the ads and replaced the pushpins in the board. His voice was conciliatory. "The ads did well. Pulled in customers and sold their products . . . but we've got to change our emphasis. Women are what Burdie's is all about. We don't want to alienate anyone or perpetuate old stereotypes."

"What's all the fuss about?" said Selma with the emphasis only she could give it. "Women are doing what they always did. Whatever it takes to get what they want."

The president smiled good-naturedly. "You know more about that than I do."

"I sure do," said Selma.

He was gone even before Selma had stopped laughing. They were left staring at the spot he had occupied so vigorously just seconds before.

"Quel hunk-o," said Selma, jabbing April in the ribs.

"He's all right."

"What's the matter, you don't like perfect?"

April smiled. Her knee had stopped hurting.

One day, Missy told April that her work was being noticed and approved of. As a reward they let her write an institutional ad—one of two or three poetic ads that ran each year: *Burdie's cares about you and your dreams; Burdie's salutes the moon walk; Burdie's wishes the hostages a Merry Christmas.* When her ad appeared, Luis O'Neill called her on the telephone to tell her he liked it. After she hung up she had to go to the ladies' room and hold her wrists under the cold water. Suppose he had called her to his office and she had had to walk straight toward him wearing this poly/cotton-blend bibbed tent in the fake patchwork print, size 18½?

She had an abject fear of being seen, really seen, by someone she admired. Sitting down was okay. Dim light was better than bright. Outdoors was better than in. A frontal view was better than a back view. Waist up was better than waist down. But the absolute worst, and she could remember this since high school when she had to go up a center aisle to get her diploma, was walking alone in empty space while others had nothing to do but watch you.

However, the phone call was fine. She had been natural and thanked him in an offhand way. "I'm glad you liked it and thanks for calling to say so." One run-on sentence in an unalarmed voice.

That night she walked home via 37th Street which had three brownstones she particularly liked. The window boxes were spilling over with red and pink geraniums. The knockers on the doors were polished, the windows washed. A beautiful girl in jeans was walking a large dog.

The dog was pulling her along and the girl was laughing as if this were the happiest moment of her life. She had tied her shirt above her waist, showing an inch or two of downy concave stomach. April stared in admiration. She felt happy, too, and filled with hope.

When she got home, she washed her hair, watered her three plants and cleaned the burners on the range. She wanted to see how long she could go without eating. At quarter to nine, she had three peaches and a bunch of about twenty grapes. At nine, she added a peanut butter sandwich and a milk shake made with vanilla ice cream, nutmeg, milk, frozen strawberries and seltzer in a blender. After eating the peanut butter sandwich, she saw there were eggs and cottage cheese in the refrigerator. She could have eaten an omelette which would have been better and not made her so thirsty.

At quarter to ten, while watching a rerun of "Upstairs, Downstairs," she had no recollection of having made the milk shake or deciding to make it or even drinking it. But there was the glass with half an inch of liquid left and she felt very full.

The episode of "Upstairs, Downstairs" was a sad one. Hazel, the commoner, who had married James, the blueblood, dies. Even though she had seen it before, and knew it was coming, April cried. Hazel had been treated badly by James. She had been treated very badly by the butler. Nobody cared much when she died. She probably died of a broken heart.

Besides Hazel's death, April was upset that she had made up her mind not to eat and then ended up eating mindlessly, without really being hungry, without even being desperate to eat.

She turned off the television, went to the bathroom and sat on the edge of the tub. Maybe she should try to throw up. She had read that models did that regularly to keep thin. They ate everything they wanted and then quickly went and threw it up before it began to digest. One had described it graphically. Run cold water over your tallest finger—Mr. Tall Man they called it in kindergarten. Then stick it down your throat as far as it will go. Keep sort of tickling around the area and pretty soon, it's barf city. The model was gorgeous, with milky skin and no sign of shadows under her eyes.

April ran cold water over Mr. Tall Man and knelt over the toilet. She put her finger down her throat twice but nothing happened. She didn't feel like throwing up but she did manage to raise some acidy secretion that made her throat burn. She brushed her teeth, washed up and went to bed.

The following day, after work, she stopped on the main floor to see how her closeout ad for men's shirts had pulled. She would have liked to have seen an empty counter with a sign: *All Gone*. The headline she'd written had made the men's shirt buyer grudgingly content. *Hush, hush! We've left just a smidgen of the label to give you a clue to the famous maker!*

The shirts were by Hathaway and the body copy, while not mentioning the name, was nauseatingly studded with cute clues. *"We pirated these shirts from their famous maker at this tiny price. Nobody hath a way with shirts like he does. Sizes and colors aren't patchy either. There's a full selection—even difficult-to-find sizes in one hundred percent pima cotton. Remember cotton? Remember the* Queen Mary? *Remember luxury? Hurry!"*

Harald had always worn cotton shirts. He had said that synthetics gave him a headache. She had been only too glad to scour the city and find them at a time when manufacturers seemed wedded to blends. She had also found a tailor who tapered them to fit as if custom-made. Harald told her she had solved a problem that had plagued him all of his adult life—the shirts that fit his arms and neck were voluminous around his chest and waist. She had become obsessive about it—as if finding the scarce shirts would prove her resourcefulness, even make her a little magical.

The counter before her was piled high with shirts that would have made Harald very happy. Blues, oatmeals, pencil stripes. A wretched, hollow loneliness manifested itself between her ribs. She began to forage in the pile looking for his size.

"What size are you looking for, maybe we can help each other?" Don Loren was at her side. "I'm looking for 15½, 33. What's yours?"

"16, 35."

Don raised an eyebrow. "A big man," he said respectfully.

"He's not *that* big . . . not very big." She was defensive. "Just has long arms."

"Touchy," Don muttered under his breath and began flipping through the stacks. "Here." He handed her a button-down with thin raspberry stripes against off-white. "It'll go beautifully with gray flannel. Does he own a gray flannel?"

"Yes. As a matter of fact, he does." Harald had two gray flannel suits. A good ten years' investment, he had told her. They typified his success, his love of order and his optimism for the future.

"You're not looking for my size."

"You're right." She busied herself in the pile but there were no size 15½, 33's. "There aren't any. I'm sorry."

"I'll take these anyway." He picked up a medium blue oxford cloth and a brown with a white collar. "They're a little big, but I'll taper them myself. Everything's made for the big American gut. Ooooops . . . sorry."

She looked down at her hands. He took his shirts to a cash register and she followed. When he paid, he turned to look for her. "Aren't you going to take your shirt?"

"I don't think so."

"Why not? It's a great shirt."

"It is. It's beautiful. But . . . well . . . he doesn't exist anymore."

"*He's dead?* Oh, no. I can't take it."

"He's not dead. We're divorced." It was the first time she had said that. It sounded strange and a little glamorous. Don surveyed the length of the main floor. A long, empty gaze.

"You're pretending to buy shirts for a guy you're divorced from?" He saw that she, too, was distressed by her behavior. "Don't worry. I've heard of much sicker things than that. I knew a woman once who *wore* her husband's clothes, after he died. Jockey shorts, neckties, pajamas, everything." Her expression didn't change. "Why don't you come and have a drink with my friend and me? Have dinner. Have my friend, ha ha. Come on. If we hurry, we can catch the Metroliner instead of that smelly shuttle. *Newark!*" He grunted in disgust as if April's regrets had touched off a few of his own. "How the hell did I end up in Newark? I used to be with Oleg Cassini, for godsakes."

They didn't get the Metroliner but an Amcoach called The Patriot that rocked wildly from side to side as if it would fall off the tracks.

When she saw where Don lived, she knew why he was so resentful of working in Newark. His apartment—a floor-through on the main floor of a wide brownstone on East 18th Street—was as smooth and comforting as Newark was scarred and unsettling. He hustled her through the rooms to a small bricked garden with a wide border of plantings now barely in bloom. He insisted on naming everything.

"That's impatiens . . . see how plump and dense." He put up his arms like a conductor. "Thrive, you gaudy things! I can't stand the color fuchsia. They all came out fuchsia. Over there . . . painted daisies. Parsley, of course. Arugula—*très* chic . . . *très* bitter. I won't waste space on *that* again. Basil for pesto but I'm sure you've heard *that* before. Mention basil without yelling pesto and people think you're just in from Teaneck. I'm going to get away from that. I'm definitely going to get away from *that*." He passed a hand over his brow.

The room inside was as neat as its owner. Two plump love seats and two armless sectionals made a pleasant square inside of which was a square, bleached oak coffee table. On it were four magazines—*The Nation, Architectural Digest, Window Design Digest* and *The Nation's Baker*—as well as the *Times*. A copper bowl held a pot of pink begonias. A deep blue paper with tiny white flowers covered the walls to the wainscoting which was painted white.

She thought a long time before commenting. "It's like walking into a small country cottage in Provence. But it doesn't look premeditated or false." She had never been in Provence but it seemed a tasteful thing to say.

"What do you mean by premeditated or false?"

"Well, you know how people sometimes fix up their basements to look like a fishing village?"

"Oh, yeah. I see what you mean."

"Well, this doesn't look like that."

"Good."

Pierre emerged from the kitchen with a carafe of wine and three glasses. He was a fragile, smiling, thirtyish man with sparse reddish ringlets framing a bony white face. He was unperturbed by her sudden appearance. "Hallo. Ees cooler inside, no?"

"Pierre, this is April. Avril to you. Avril is the cruelest month. Anyway, she needs a drink."

"Moi aussi." He put the tray on the table and his hands to his temples. "I too. The kitchen was terrible."

"Pierre is the pastry chef at Le Canard d'Or."

"I saw a documentary film called *The Kitchen,*" said April. "It showed what went on during a busy lunch hour. The chefs were lunatics. They threatened each other with carving knives. After they served lunch, they all calmed down and went home."

"Authentique. Ees true." He turned to Don and patted him

on the back. "*Alors, j'ai faim.* You want *chinoise?* I order and we stay here, okay?"

"Fine with me," said April.

"Anything," said Don, tickling Pierre in the ribs. "Chinese, Hungarian, Mandarin, Korean, who cares."

"I do," said Pierre seriously. "And April, too, no?"

"Yes," said April. "And tell them not to put MSG in it, please."

"Oh, sure," said Don. "Then they'll urinate in the soup. They just love all that holistic crapola."

"What is urinate?" asked Pierre.

"Pee pee."

"Ees true?" He turned to April for corroboration. "Pee pee in zee soup? Pigs."

"Orientals are very hostile," said Don, pouring himself a glass of wine. "Scratch that gorgeous poreless skin and you'll find the most hostile people on earth."

"You cannot make ziss blanket statement."

Don winked at April. "Pierre also believes in G-O-D."

"*Mon dieu!*"

"You see?"

"No, no. About ziss you cannot be comic."

Pierre meant business and a look of anxiety appeared on Don's face. "All right, all right." He picked at the slub of his linen pants. "I take it back." Pierre was on the other side of the room looking out of the window. "Come on, Pierre, I won't do it anymore. Don't be mad."

April looked for a place to sit and walked to a small armless side chair. It had a petit point seat with the likeness of a lion. "Don't sit on *that,*" shrieked Don from across the room. She jumped away. "It's not strong enough."

A look of misery invaded Pierre's face. "You have no thought for her feelings? *Sauvage.*"

"She'd feel a lot worse if she sat on it and it broke," said Don with renewed spirit.

"Don," Pierre came and stood next to April, "I am insulted for her. Please, apologize."

"I'm sorry. I really am."

"There's nothing to apologize for." There's plenty to apologize for. "At least you're not asking me why I'm so fat." There was a deadly silence. Now why had she said that? It was just the opening Don, the demonic truth seeker, would love.

"Would it be so bad to ask you why you're so fat?" he said immediately."

"Yes."

"Why?"

"Because I don't talk about it."

"Oh."

Pierre disappeared to phone for the food and returned with a generous wedge of Brie and a strange lump of bread. "Ziss bread ees wizzout flour," he said proudly. "I bake eet for Don becauzze he ees allergic to zee flour." She was impressed. It tasted okay and looked only slightly misshapen.

Don, who had left to change, returned in creased jeans and a knit shirt. She looked at her jumper and twisted it around where it had shifted. Don took his wine and sat on the couch with a heavy sigh. He opened the *Times,* which was lying on the coffee table.

"Look," he said after a while, "only Jews got married today. Here are three announcements right on the television page . . . Carolyn Schwartz, a stockbroker, married David Gribbin, a dental student at NYU. They'll reside in San Francisco. Anita Diamont, a graduate student at Columbia, married Alan Green, a systems analyst—what's a systems analyst?" April and Pierre shrugged. "And," Don continued, "Dorothea Smulovitz—I'm not making this up, it's really Smulovitz—married . . . oh, no, she went from Smulovitz to Smuck, she married Steven Smuck, president of ABC Rentals. They must all be very happy. They have their announcements right on the television page where everyone is sure to see them. You see how life works out, you never know." He said this as if life had not yet worked out for April and Pierre.

"Eet says they are Jewish?" asked Pierre. He pronounced it djewish. "Prejudice, no? In France, we don't do ziss."

"Pierre, calm down. It doesn't say they're Jewish." Don pulled him onto the couch to show him the paper. "But the ceremonies were performed by a rabbi, except for the Smucks who were married by a judge, but what else could they be? Smuck-Smulovitz, it's gotta be Jewish, no?"

April listened to this back-and-forth totally absorbed. Pierre really approved of Don. He hung on the words. With a sigh, he rose and set the table with beautiful china. White fluted plates with a delicate border of freesia. He made a small bouquet from a few clippings of English ivy. The food came.

"So how long are you going to mourn your divorce?" asked Don casually while helping himself to Moo Goo Gai Pan. "Uh, I don't want to be indelicate but were you f-a-t when you were married to 16, 35?"

She turned white. She couldn't get used to people mentioning her weight. It made her anxious and unfocused. Don was so casual, it should have made it easier. "No."

"You were thin?"

"No."

"You were medium to heavy?"

"Yes."

"All the time?"

"Until the end." She finished what was in her mouth. "Then I shot up to my worst. I stayed in bed all day and ate. I ate cold food that should have been hot. I ate packaged food. Take-out food. Canned food. Frozen food. I was crazy. Really crazy. I was disoriented. I had lost the best thing that had ever been in my life. I thought it was my own fault. That I should have been more canny. Sophisticated. Knowing. Bitchy. I really don't know what." She was surprised at her own sudden chattiness. She felt dispassionate, as if she were discussing a movie.

"What happened?" asked Pierre.

"A woman came to our house and stole his heart. Really. A woman we had never met before just showed up at our door." She told them the story of Judge Tierney and the Montini children and the beautiful Melissa. Even Don shut up. "It had the ingredients of great drama: injustice, irony, sex and a certain startling reversal. The man, who was smart, acted in a dumb way. And the woman, who was dumb, acted in a smart way."

"*Mon dieu!* Ees like movie, no?"

"Yes. Like movie. When the story hit the papers—and it did—a man from Warner Communications asked if we were interested in selling the movie rights."

"*Quel sauvage.*"

The evening *chez* Don was a big success. She felt as if she were at the very center of the modern world. They became slightly drunk and kissed all around when she left. She crossed Lexington Avenue to take the northbound bus, then decided to walk, hoping to find an open grocery. The Chinese food hadn't filled her but she only felt it now, out in the fresh air. She stopped at a deli on 24th Street and picked up a loaf of French bread, choosing the darkest one.

When she got home she took her time, opened a can of Bumble Bee Chunk Light Tuna, chopped some green pepper and celery into it, smoothed in plenty of mayonnaise to bind it together. She slit her bread lengthwise to make a flap, scooped out some of the soft middle and packed in the tuna mixture. She closed the loaf and cut it crosswise at two-inch intervals. It made a pretty pattern of lusty, colorful salad amidst the innocent halo of white. There were eleven two-inch rounds.

She sat down with two of the rounds to watch *Mother Wore Tights* with Betty Grable and Dan Dailey. She spread a small towel on her lap, feeling happy and lighthearted. She felt . . . *with it,* a tired but accurate description of her progress.

On the way home on the train, Don had made an observation about Lorenzo, the budget coat buyer. "He's on good terms with his asshole," Don had said. She had blanched, not even certain what he meant, but knowing it was accurate. No matter how indelicate or unflattering, Don was always accurate. She knew also that Lorenzo would have no trouble referring to Don as a fag. He would say, "That fag, what does he know?" Or he might say, "That fucking fag," which reflected a frustrated, unfocused anger. Don, on the other hand, was sinister and imaginative and scathing, which reflected a cold but fully vented disdain.

When the movie was over, she was surprised to see that she had finished all eleven of her tuna rounds. She couldn't remember eating them all and the happy, satisfied feeling was gone. She felt full, dazed and uncomfortable. She went to the bathroom to brush her teeth. When she came out, the telephone rang. It was Don.

"Pierre and I have a bet," he said. "I said you were probably eating right this minute or very recently and that you probably ate more than you ate with us. Pierre says no. Who's right?"

She felt trapped and angry with him for making her feel that way. What an insulting, mean bastard. The tuna rumbled in her stomach. "Well, is it true? Am I right?"

"It's true," she said in a whisper, "but what made you think that?"

"Fat people always eat in private. They eat normal portions in public and then pig out in private. It's not exactly my theory. Or very new. It's a well-known fact."

"I see." There was a dull, awful buzzing in her head. She longed to hang up. On the other hand, she didn't want Don to know he'd upset her. "Okay, you won. Was there anything else?"

"Yes. Pierre is crazy about you. He wants to save you. Make you over. More precisely, he wants *me* to save you."

"Yeah, well, I guess his mind isn't challenged making éclairs and mousses."

"That's not a very nice crack."

"Huh? Is it the pot calling the kettle black?" *Oh my god, he was black!*

"I'll pretend I didn't hear that," he said prissily. "And I'm still glad you got home without being accosted."

"Ta ta," she said and hung up.

19

AFTER A COOL, WET spring, June of 1980 turned unseasonably hot. Terrible storms and tornadoes battered the Midwest. Cuban refugees were pouring into Key West. The Indian Look and the Western Look vied for fashion silliness. Headbands and faded denim clothes that might have been thrown out the year before were the uniform of the trendy.

Alan Leeds, Merlow Hess and Jack Tobias, the furniture buyer, had rented a house on Fire Island at Ocean Bay Park, which was next to the more conservative Point O' Woods where Fred Burdette was going to spend the summer. In early June, Luis was a guest at both houses during ninety-degree weekends.

On June 15th, he accompanied Fred to a Family of Man testimonial dinner and dance where Fred's father, Lionel, was to receive an award for endowing a rehabilitation center for teenage drug addicts.

At their table was Harry (Buzz) Gargan, brigadier general and head of Fort Laughton, Texas, also being received into the family of man. Sitting next to Buzz Gargan—beauty and the beast—was his daughter,

Lisanne, a spectacularly wholesome young woman with unretouched blond hair, light lashes, little makeup and a togalike gown that exposed one dazzling shoulder.

She asked Luis to dance and Luis, ignoring Buzz Gargan's immediate and disapproving frown, expressed delight and led her out onto the floor. She looked vaguely familiar, and after a few minutes Luis realized she was the girl in the Mike perfume commercials. His interest cooled. He loathed the Mike commercials. *Mike, for the outspoken woman. Confident. Devastatingly feminine.* They should have added: *Brash. Cruel. Devastatingly hyper.* In the commercial, the woman walks briskly in a park with a man who is having the tiniest struggle keeping up. Suddenly, in a moment of total surprise, she whirls around and plants a kiss on his mouth. It's not a tender kiss. It's a smug, I'm-calling-the-shots kiss.

"Mike," Luis whispered into her ear, "for the out-spoken woman who is her own person. Are you your own person?" *Or Daddy's girl?*

"I wouldn't mind being your person," she said audaciously. Then she giggled. "Is that too brazen?"

"Not at all," he assured her lamely. "It's very . . . very Mike." Her nervous, girlish giggle rekindled his interest, which was eighty percent physical. She had an electric effect on him, something that wasn't automatic. Maybe it was the thrill of rousing the wrath of Buzz the Beefy.

When Buzz Gargan wanted to leave, his daughter revealed that she preferred to stay. Father was suspicious. He stared at Luis with the look he might have perfected for commie-pinkos and asked, "Are you a fairy?"

"No, sir."

"Good." He turned to his daughter. "Lisanne, come home this weekend. It's your mother's birthday." When he walked away, Luis was happy to see that he limped.

Meeting Lisanne Gargan definitely turned him around.

Right away he began to regain his old energy and cheeriness. As to why she had this effect on him, it was hard to say. Their conversations were so insubstantial it amazed him. How could he contemplate an ongoing relationship with a woman with whom he couldn't have a meaningful conversation? He even wondered whether he wasn't unconsciously following some macho Mediterranean code of coupling with a soft, uncomplicated woman who would be devoted to his happiness. She was handy in the kitchen—a no-no to most single women—and wrapped all kitchen refuse neatly in paper towels, a wastefulness he found endearing.

She wasn't dumb either, although the speech patterns of eastern Texas, unfamiliar to Easterners, sounded dumb. She made as much money as he and had already invested in real estate—a ski condominium in Vermont—that had doubled in value while he had lost five thousand dollars. Like the army brat she was, she had an extraordinary sense of duty and did volunteer work on Tuesday nights—running the movie projector at the veterans' hospital—and Saturday mornings—taking toddlers from the St. Christopher's Foundling Home for outings.

"Do the veterans ask you out?" he wanted to know.

"Oh, no. I never get chummy with them. I keep it general."

"And they never ask you personal questions?"

"Sure. They ask me if I have a boyfriend and I say 'yes.'"

"That's it? Just 'yes'?"

"I change the subject or ask if they want me to write letters for them or to get a book from the library wagon."

"What about the babies? Don't you get attached to the babies?"

"Not so that I think about them after I leave. I'm involved with them all the time I'm there, but once I leave, I'm gone. Thinking about *you* . . . or work. What's wrong with that?"

"Nothing. Your attitude's very healthy. Very realistic." He admired her lack of false sentimentality. Obviously she cared or she wouldn't go in the first place.

"It's better not to get too deep," she sighed and stuck her hand under his shirt. "That doesn't include you, buddy. I want to get very deep with you."

"Good."

She appealed to him on a level that was new to him. Maybe it was her lack of vulnerability. She didn't have that crushing fear of separation that paralyzed many women he knew. A week of no calls could change a pretty, intelligent woman into a fretful, anxious one. They took it personally. It didn't make him feel powerful. It made him feel sad and determined not to raise expectations he couldn't fulfill. He had the distinct feeling that Lisanne would be sad for an hour, tops, if they parted forever.

Many evenings she sat on the floor working on hobbies with yarn and needles. Her blond hair would fall over her face and she'd tuck it behind her ears over and over, like a careless child. He would sit on the floor with her, slip his hand up her fine, long legs, nuzzle her ears and neck. "Oh, bunny"—during amorous moments she called him bunny—"do you feel like it?" she would ask in surprise. And here is where the relationship deviated from the simple. What she meant by "it" wasn't what he meant by "it," because although she allowed herself to be fondled in the most lascivious way, she wouldn't consent to actual intercourse. "I just can't, bunny."

"What are you going to do when you get married?"

"Then, of course, I'll do it."

"Are you trying to blackmail me into marrying you?"

"No. I'm too young to get married. Daddy says I shouldn't get married until I'm twenty-eight." And when she saw his chagrin: "I know it's silly. It doesn't make any sense because I've let you do all sorts of things that are sexier than putting it in, but . . . well, it's the way I was brought up. I just can't do it. Can't you understand?"

"Yes. Of course, I understand," he lied. In the back of his mind he was sure that at one time or another, he would convince her and win over Buzz Gargan.

But she didn't relent. Many nights he had lain on top of her, crazed with lust, and begged her to open her legs. "Lisanne, we're two adults. I'm going to go blind from coming on your stomach. It's bad for you, too. You'll get gum disease. Gingivitis comes from lack of vaginal penetration. It really does."

"Just don't put it in, bunny. Do whatever else you want, but please don't put it in." On a really desperate night, when he was sure he'd won, she said, "I don't want you to invade my body with your invading rod." After that, he kept his invading rod to himself for an entire week.

Her reticence worked on him in two ways. He began to regard her vagina on a par with the Holy Grail. To invade it was a Holy Quest. He knew with certainty that the moment she was Lisanne O'Neill, she would open her legs as wide as the Grand Canyon. Oddly this appealed to him, too. Her high-mindedness.

Then there developed yet another wrinkle. Maybe she didn't want sex at all. When she asked, "Oh, bunny, do you feel like it?" and he replied, "Yes, I feel like it," she would kiss him on the lips and say, "Then I feel like it, too." He wondered if this quick response had been learned at her mother's knee. When Buzz Gargan came home from maneuvers and wanted it, did Mrs. Gargan immediately decide that she wanted it, too?

"How do you feel?" he would question her. "Tell me how you really feel."

"I feel like being close to you."

"And . . . ?" He wanted some admission of lust.

"And . . . doing it."

"All right, then," he would say, exasperated, "take off those ridiculous shorts and we'll do it."

"You're angry."

"No, I'm not. I'm ready for love," he would reply grimly.

"You don't like my answer."

"I love your answer." The crazy thing was, he *was* ready for love. No amount of love talk or handling would have made him hornier than Lisanne's compliant "If you want to do it, I want to do it, too."

He couldn't even share the irony of it with her because she had no sense of irony. What she had was a strong sense of duty and he knew, as if he were plotting a campaign, that a sense of duty and lots of energy would, in the long run, make for a better relationship than an ironic sense of humor. There was a lot to be said for her sunny, uncomplicated disposition. He had had liaisons with many women who didn't know how to be cheerful. They were passionately involved in one thing or another. One wanted to dance. Only to dance. Another potted. There were somber, glazed containers all over her apartment. Lisanne was not like that. Her work was only something to do until she got married.

So. If he was so happy with her, why didn't he just marry her and get it over with? He didn't know why except that he felt it would be better to marry during one of his uptick periods. Another year in New Jersey and then he'd marry her.

20

ONE NIGHT IN LATE April, the telephone rang and a voice she had never heard, high but self-assured, asked if she was April Taylor. "Speaking."

"My name is Bob Waller." There was a moment of silence. "I'm calling at Sylvie's suggestion. I'm recently separated and she said you were in the same boat." Again a long silence which she didn't feel obligated to fill. "Hello . . . are you there?"

"Yes." Another silence.

"Well, are you?"

"Am I what?"

"In the same boat?"

She had a vivid picture of herself and Bob Waller in a flimsy rowboat, in the middle of the ocean, wearing business clothes. Yet she felt no responsibility to be friendly and helpful. Sylvie had no idea how fat she'd become. This man would show up at her door and faint. What could she tell him, I'm very fat, can you take it? "I guess," she finally answered.

"I have a little boy who spends the weekends with me. How about you?"

"How about me what?"

"Do you have children?" He asked it hopefully. He would be disappointed if she were any less emotionally stranded than he.

"No."

That made him thoughtful. And silent. So what? He was the one who wanted to row out of the harbor of loneliness into the port of togetherness. She considered offering him this metaphor but decided against it because she could feel herself seething with anger. Why? What did she have against this stranger?

"Well . . . uh, I was wondering if maybe we could go out or something." Her slow, dim-witted delivery had appealed to him. She could hear the eagerness in his voice.

"I don't know." She wound the cord around her wrist.

"I know it'll be awkward, but you've got to start somewhere."

You don't have to start with me. "How long have you been separated?"

"Three months."

"That recent?" It was just something to say but he took it as a criticism.

"You think that's too recent. It seems kind of long to me. How long have you been separated?"

"I'm divorced. I've been divorced for seven months but I haven't been living with my husband for fourteen months."

Long silence. "Well, what do you think? You think we can go out and see what turns up? Come on, it'll be good for you. I know it'll be good for me."

"I'm not in such great shape."

"Who is?"

"It's been a long time. Don't expect much."

"I won't."

"I mean *really* don't expect much. Dating is the last

thing on my mind. . . . Look, if you just want someone to talk to, we can talk on the phone."

"Stop worrying . . . it'll be all right. We're two adults, two battered adults. We know what the score is."

For a moment, she wanted to go. He was patient and kind. "All right."

"Sylvie said you were a lot of fun." He waited for her to confirm this. "Are you a lot of fun?"

"Oh, sure. A laugh a minute."

"So how about tomorrow night?"

"Okay."

She gave him the address and hung up. Right away she was sorry she'd said yes. Which one did she hate more, Sylvie or Bob Waller? Why did Sylvie still consider her a friend? They hadn't seen each other for two years. Sylvie, with all her reversible clothes from Talbot's, was a stranger. Now she was going out with a stranger, as a favor to another stranger. He would fall down the stairs and kill himself when he saw her. It would serve them both right.

After the call, she was starving. She opened a can of Old El Paso tamales. She was crazy for the taste of corn. Doritos, Fritos, all those corn-y snacks were high on her list. The tamales were standing erect in their corn husk envelopes, five stiff soldiers. She fished one out, shook off the sauce and ate it in two bites. Bits of reddish fat clung to her fingers and she decided to heat the rest. When she finished the tamales, she wished there were more and debated whether it was worth going out to get another couple of cans. No. Her ribs hurt, something new that had cropped up. There was a bursting, wrenching pain that began when she sat on a soft chair or slept on her side. She got up to bind herself with a scarf and stubbed her

toe. She cursed, brushed her teeth twice to get rid of the
sauce taste which clung to her mouth and went to bed.

That night she dreamt she had a new apartment in an
Art Deco building. She kept finding new hidden spaces
that she hadn't been aware of before. The apartment was
empty and she was anticipating the fun of furnishing it
from scratch when she noticed a huge, old couch, hogging almost all the space.

Either out of nervousness or momentary blindness, or
because he was still in shock from having his wife walk
out on him, Bob Waller didn't show by word or expression that there was anything unusual in his blind date.
She wore a silk look-alike shirtwaist in size 20 with a self
sash that she considered leaving off. It was colored in
what the fashion world called ice-cream stripes. At the
last minute she added hoop earrings. She had blow-dried
her hair into a careless, no-part disarray of waves and
curls. Her green eyes looked restless and feverish because
of a light tan acquired on the previous weekend. If you
didn't stray below the neck, she looked pretty.

He appeared to have planned and timed the evening
and picked her up at 7:00 for a 7:30 dinner reservation
at a restaurant on the West Side.

As they walked along 34th Street, looking for a cab, she
realized he was trying to look at her when he thought she
wasn't looking at him. But that was crazy. She was an expert in pretending not to be looking when she knew people were looking at her.

She found Bob Waller handsome in a babyish way, with
round cheeks, round eyes and a heavy, labored gait that
didn't go with his slim, tall body. She said as little as possible, waiting for the more relaxed atmosphere of a dimly
lit restaurant to get acquainted.

The Café Lyon was small and narrow and cozy, accom-

modating about twenty-five tables. "They serve everything on one plate here. Very unpretentious," he said
with the proprietary air of a longtime customer. "The
food's terrific. I always drink the house wine. It's Sebas-
tiani. See that woman, she's the manager. The French
make good businesswomen. Tough as nails, but very
proud. They use the best ingredients and if you complain, they get very angry."

"How do you know? Did you complain?"

"Me? No, I love everything. There was a man who sent
back a lamb chop because it was too pink and she had a
fit. He said he had asked for it medium and she said that
was medium, and in any case, the meat was choice and
the chop would be ruined if it was put back in the fire. It
would dry out and be tasteless. Then she said a lot of
other angry things in French to the waiter."

"What happened to the idea that the customer is always
right?"

"Oh, she was right. Don't you think?"

"No. The man should have walked out. And maybe
tossed the lamb chop around a little."

He was disappointed and she saw him reassessing the
evening. Might she throw something around? She made a
conciliatory gesture. "Why don't you tell me about your
marriage?" After all, he was spending good money to
take her to dinner.

He perked up at once and motioned the waiter and
asked for some wine while they decided what to order.
"Is white wine all right?"

"Fine."

As the waiter was leaving, he changed his mind. "Uh
. . . make that a vodka gimlet." The waiter looked ques-
tioningly to April.

"I'll stick with the wine," she said.

"My wife was a very pretty woman," he said by way of a
preamble. "She was the sort of person who had to always

be going someplace where she could put her prettiness to work. You know what I mean?" April did and nodded. He had described his wife very concisely. "Well, after a while, a marriage settles in. You can't always be going places. Anyway, she became restless. Very restless. She used to tap her fingernails on any surface. Tap, tap, tap, while she was waiting for the bacon to cook for my son and me. Or while she was waiting to add the softener to the wash cycle. Tap, tap, tap. She was very edgy, but I never dreamed she would leave. She walked out . . . just like Joanna Kramer."

"Joanna Kramer?"

"Yes. Ted Kramer's wife. You know that book *Kramer vs. Kramer*? Well, it was just like that with me. I could be Ted Kramer except that my wife took the kid with her. Also, I'm not in advertising. Also, I'm not the Class A jerk that Ted Kramer was. I didn't neglect my wife or work long hours, but it was the same basic situation. I married a girl who was too pretty for me and she got restless. There was no place for her to put her prettiness to work and she was afraid it would all be gone and she'd have nothing to show for it."

April was surprised at her lack of sympathy. "What was your wife's name?"

"Why do you ask?"

"Why do *you* ask everything in that suspicious tone of voice? It's not information I can sell or anything like that. I just want to picture the woman you're talking about. This callous, adventurous woman. Is it Ramona Waller or Elizabeth Waller or Cynthia? It helps to know." Actually she thought Mrs. Waller was smart and brave.

"Samantha."

"Oooooh, Samantha." She bobbed her head up and down as if she now understood everything. "There were a few years where everyone was naming their children Samantha after Katharine Hepburn in some movie. Her parents must have been high-class." Why had she said that? She really didn't think so.

"Yes. Yes, they were." He was appreciative of her deductive powers.

"But how can you compare your life to a movie? *Kramer vs. Kramer* was full of shit. Just good old Hollywood craperoo." She knew that was not herself talking. It was Don. She was talking and behaving like Don.

"Why do you say that?" He was startled by her language.

"Why do I say that? Because there's no way Dustin Hoffman could have a kid that looked like the kid in the movie. Even with a mother like Meryl Streep. And, for another thing, he was too frenetic. The first fifteen minutes of that movie, where he tries to make French toast and does everything wrong . . . how could you believe anything after that? I was glad she left him."

Bob Waller looked at her in a funny way. As if she might be glad his wife had left him, too. As if he were taking out the enemy instead of someone who could offer him succor. Fortunately, the waiter showed up and they ordered the food.

"My quarrel with Ted Kramer was that he treated Joanna like a piece of furniture. He marries this gorgeous superior person and then expects her to be satisfied to wash his socks."

"That's not so hard to understand," said April. "My husband thought I was born to wash his socks, and you know what? I did, too. My husband was perfect. A perfect person." Right after she said that, she realized for the first time that Harald was not perfect. That she might not even choose him again even if she could. This sudden reversal so engaged her, she wanted to stop talking and think about it. Bob Waller looked bored. He didn't want to hear about her marriage.

"Look," he said, pointing to the end of the bar where

the lady manager was sitting on a stool, "that man. I think
he's her boyfriend. When he shows up, she shuts up."
The man was leafing through the receipts in a surly way.

"Maybe he's the manager."

"No. He might own it, but she runs the show."

There was nothing for her to say. He seemed to get a
second wind and told her about his childhood. He had
been an altar boy at St. Thomas the Apostle Church. He
was originally from Boston. Boylston Street. Georgetown
University was his college. Then he, too, was at the end of
his vivaciousness and looked nervously around the small
room. Their food came and they ate it. April said it was
delicious. She was tired of acting like Don. "Where do
you work?" she asked. A guarded look came over his
face, as if she was going to show up at his office and call
him sweetie. It was true. When you were fat, people expected underhanded behavior. If you were capable of
being fat, you were capable of anything.

Her feet were beginning to tingle, as were parts of her
thighs. Of late, she had been losing sensation in different
parts of her body, as if they were going to sleep or the
blood supply couldn't penetrate all the fat. When she
thought her circulation was about to give up, she became
alarmed. She bought a detailed body atlas put out by
Hammond, the map people, so she could see how it all
worked. She often studied it, tracing her own blood out
of the heart, into the lungs, back to the heart, out the
arteries, to the capillaries where the nutrients were extracted, drained by the veins and then, the used, tired
blood going back to the heart to be replenished again. It
was the used, tired blood part that got her. Was it too
used and too tired to take the journey again?

The ice cream had separated in her dish. Bob Waller
looked tired. Little beads of perspiration had formed on
his upper lip. There was a pointlessness to the evening
that gave her a headache. She felt more sorry for him

than for herself. Did he know as an altar boy in Boston that his life would take such a turn? As he was learning his ethics from the Jesuits, did he suspect he would have to cope with the faithless Samantha and then attempt to lift the leaden stone of rejection off his chest by calling a faceless stranger connected to him by the fragile thread of coincidence and Sylvie Straight, nee Beck? Sylvie, who now wore wraparound skirts and short-sleeve cotton lisle shirts with a repeating pattern of strawberries or smiling frogs, who had been elected treasurer of the Episcopal Women of Ardsley, New York. *Oy vay.*

She decided to go to the bathroom. It would give her legs and feet something to do. It would give Bob Waller some privacy to fall apart and it would give her a chance to pee, which she badly needed to do.

The bathroom was small and not altogether clean, with a hook latch that rattled when anyone walked by. She looked for a place to hang her pocketbook and finally placed it in the sink. She sat down on the toilet. Immediately there was a loud snapping sound. *My god, what was that?* The seat had broken. She jumped, startled, and the sudden release of pressure on the seat made the two pieces come together again, catching the flesh of her underthigh. Now the pieces felt cemented together with the glue of her blood and skin. Some blood began to collect on the dirty white tile floor. She let out a cry of pain and fear.

"You've got to unlock the door," said a voice from the other side. "Are you all right?"

"No."

"What do you mean, no?"

"Who are you?"

"Myrna. The waitress."

"I'm not all right. I need a towel, a piece of cloth . . . something to stop the bleeding."

"*Bleeding?* Let me in there."

She rose to unlock the door and the seat finally gave way.

"You're having a miss," said Myrna when she saw the blood. "Is that it? Oh, my god, you're having a miss."

"No," said April. "I'm bleeding."

"A miscarriage . . ."

"Oh, no. I cut myself on the seat. See, it broke and I cut myself."

"What's going on in there?" It was a man's voice. The man who had been annoyed with the night's receipts.

"It's a long complicated story," said Myrna. "Get me a clean dish towel."

"Don't give me that crap." He thought she was being perverse. "I've got a dining room full of people."

"She broke the toilet seat and her thigh got caught in it. She's got a bad cut."

"You mean the fat one? I saw her go in. Oh, my god, she broke the seat? I'll get a cab. She can go to St. Vincent's. St. Vincent's is the closest."

"First get me a clean dish towel."

Myrna the waitress pulled her underpants gently over the cut, bandaged her thigh, slung her pocketbook securely over her shoulder and told her to have St. Vincent's send the bill to Martin Lord, who was the owner of the restaurant. "Let him pay it," she whispered. "He's lucky you don't sue. Come on," she led April out, "you can go through the kitchen. I'll tell your boyfriend."

For the first time she thought of Bob Waller. The urge to laugh was so strong, she had to bite on a paper towel. What would he tell Sylvie? It was a moment of exquisite humiliation. It affected her hearing. Her ears seemed stopped with blood, her face, too. Engorged. Too much blood rushing to all those emotional centers, plus an iciness that stopped digestion. She was in turn very hot and very cold.

"This is a new one," said the intern at St. Vincent's

while the night surgeon sewed seventeen stitches into her thigh. He said it was a messy, ragged cut. She asked them to call Don and Pierre and then was sure they would not come. Why should they come? She hardly knew them. She didn't even know why she needed anyone to come. A cab could take her home.

Food is love. That was the thought that floated across as she lay recovering in a cubicle. Mother love. But she had stubbornly decided long ago that Bernice was okay. Better than a mother who smothered you with kisses but screeched if you dropped crumbs on the floor. Bernice had never screeched. She wasn't a big talker but she wasn't introspective either. And as for love? Who knew what Bernice had loved? She had loved the radio. Little Richard and the Four Freshmen. But she wasn't dumb. It was Harlan who was dumb and a bully. He was service manager for a major appliance corporation. He loved to scare people with the size of their repair bill. "Oh, that's going to cost you some money, yes sir. We're talking about big money here."

She had always been afraid of Harlan. Once he had come into her bedroom with a sticker in his hand which he placed on the window. She was certain it was a mark for something sinister even though he explained it was a Totfinder, a sign to alert firemen where a child was. Whenever she awoke and looked at that sign, she never liked it.

They had moved her to a stretcher in the hall when Don and Pierre walked in, immaculate, pressed, brushed. Tears came to her eyes. "Over here," she said. They had given her a shot of Demerol, so the story was patchy but they got the main points.

"Poor bastard," said Don, referring to Bob Waller.

"Bizarre," said Pierre.

The wound healed surprisingly fast. The only discomfort was in sitting. She had to sit on the edge of her seat and sleep on her side. The surgeon assured her the scar would be slight. A lawyer came to see how she was and she signed a letter saying she would not sue.

"My god," breathed Sylvie into the phone. "What happened?"

"What did Mr. Waller say happened?"

"He was incoherent. He said it was the third worst day of his life."

"I think he was being modest. What were the other two?"

"The day his mother died and the day his wife left him." She could hear Sylvie's voice building up to an accusation. "April . . . how *could* you?"

"How could I what?"

"Ruin a perfectly viable situation."

"Sylvie, I've got to hang up now. I can't talk anymore . . . it's . . . it's just too much to explain." She put the phone in its cradle and felt an enormous sense of relief.

21

Suit-O-Rama, said the window sign.

"Crap-O-Rama," said Don with contempt. He held up a chartreuse and pink checked suit with large pearl buttons. "What would you turn down in favor of *this*?" He turned to April, who had arrived to get information for window signs. "What would make you wear this suit?"

"The Boston Strangler."

"Oh, please, don't kill me. I'll wear it." He looked at the suit once again. "On the other hand, go right ahead and kill me."

There were only three months of the year that Lorenzo didn't sell his awful budget coats. During April, May and June, he sold his awful budget suits and his awful budget raincoats. The raincoats weren't putty or beige or gray, but a pinkish gray/beige or a sick iridescent green.

"Why do they have to be this awful color?" asked Erica each time he presented them at a merchandise meeting.

"What's wrong with the color?"

"It's awful. Why can't they be a nice putty or tan? As long as you're starting from scratch every year, why can't you make them in a nice color?"

"Look, girlie, I've been selling these raincoats in this store, in this color, for twenty years. They march right out of the store."

It was true. The raincoats marched right out of the store like the rats of Hamelin. It was the price. People loved Lorenzo's $18.99 raincoats. And every spring, when his two-page Suit-O-Rama ad ran, his suits—at $24.95—marched right out, too.

April agreed with Don, there was little on earth worse than a cheap suit. A cheap suit was indicative of everything that's wrong with life: gaudy, insubstantial, no attention to detail, unreliable. The lapels are too stiff, the skirt seams not always straight. Too little interfacing, the colors garish. The blues not true blues, the reds with too much purple. The greens with too much blue. The checks much too large.

THE SUITS OF SPRING. A suit event that's a New Jersey tradition. Tell your mother. Tell your grandmother. The Suits of Spring are here. Would you believe checks? Right now when you need them most. The new longer skirt (a year late), the double-breasted jacket (fake double-breasted with dummy buttons), the wide lapel, tailored to fit (tailored to bind and pucker), all the newest colors (the same dreary colors we had last year). At one unbelievable price. Yes. This was true: $24.95 was an unbelievable price. They were waiting for the doors to open when Lorenzo's suit event started. She and Don with all their snide remarks couldn't top that.

Don worked silently, pinning suits on two mannequins. How well his own clothes fit. How tastefully he dressed. This morning, he had on a putty shirt with matching pants in cotton hopsack, slightly gathered in front, European style. His tie was lemon yellow organdy lined with silk. She looked down at her own drawstring pants of heavy cotton. They gathered between her legs, making the inner seams shorter than the outer ones. She had on her black, low-heeled shoes that needed reheeling.

He watched her looking at herself. "This little number comes in size 20 if you change your mind." He held up the pink and chartreuse suit.

"What are we playing, get the writer?"

He folded his arms across his chest. "Is there any way of bringing up your weight so it doesn't make you angry?"

"No."

"So we can't *ever* talk about it?"

"What is there to talk about?"

"What is there to talk about?" He walked around in a circle, a deer stunned by automobile lights. "To begin with, there are fifty or sixty pounds to talk about. Each one weighs as much as"—he picked up a mannequin's foot—"this. Feel it. Sixty of those all over your body. Think of what that's doing to your liver and your pancreas."

She knew he knew absolutely nothing about her liver or her pancreas. He was trying to scare her. Well, she could scare him by pointing out what drugs did to his system, not to mention his brain. "Then, of course," he continued, "there is your l-i-f-e. Are you satisfied to live out your days without s-e-x-u-a-l attention?" She flinched but said nothing. "Thirdly, there is the waaaaste of it." He wrenched three syllables out of the word waste. "The waste of your face."

"Such a pretty face," she mimicked.

"Joke about it if you want to, but it isn't funny. There's nothing that's harder to come by than beauty. There was a survey and they found out that beautiful people were considered more honest, more reliable, more intelligent, than the ugly ones. It was in the *New York Times*. The Science Section. It said beautiful people were hired faster, married younger, made more money at their jobs and were treated better by salespeople and waiters."

"That's awful."

"Unless you're the pretty one, which you are." He rubbed her cheek. "Gorgeous skin."

"You just like it because it's white." It gave her a little fearful thrill to joke about his being black.

"Hmmm. You think. Your skin is not found every day of the week." She was amazed how this pleased her. She wanted him to do ten minutes on her skin.

"Yeah?" She looked at herself in a nearby mirror. "You really think so?" Then, seeing she was playing right into his hands, she took up her pencil. "Did the article say beautiful people also get their hearts broken?"

"Huh? You think you have the franchise on heart-break?" He said it in a way that invited questions. "You're not the first or the last to have someone walk right over your body."

"You?"

"Yes, of course, me. There'll never be anything like *that* again. Well . . . I'm too old now anyway. Those things only count when you don't have line one, or sag one, you know what I mean?"

"No. You look perfect to me."

He arched an eyebrow. "Perfect? No. Far from it. Well-groomed? Yes. Exercised? Yes. But perfect? No. Things happen to the old bod." He was silent a moment. "*He,* on the other hand, was *perfection.* The first time I saw him my heart skipped a beat. Literally. I was having an irregular heartbeat. I thought I was going to die right there. It was awful. I told him everything. I said, I can't walk out of here and out of your life. I'm wildly interested in you—that was putting it mildly. Do whatever you want because I'm not leaving your side. You know what he said to me? You want to know what Lucrezia Borgia said to me?"

"What?"

"He said, and I quote, 'Aw, shaddup,' with this bored wave of the hand. He sounded like a young Bette Davis. 'Aw shaddup.'"

"And then what happened?"

"I stayed, of course. All he had was a face but that was enough. One look and you gave him anything he wanted. His face was his brain."

"And you loved him?"

"Loved him?" He looked at her as if she were stupid. "He was my life. I would have breathed for him if he'd asked. Let me tell you, he wasn't beyond it. I fed him. I, who had never lifted a spatula in my life, learned to use a whisk to beat the eggs for his omelettes and a mallet to tenderize his veal. And this vicious little chopper in a jar to mince the parsley that decorated his plate. Many nights, he would look at me over a candlelight dinner and whisper: 'Whaddja put in this stuff anyway . . . I can't tell whad I'm eating.'

"One day, this hunk—his IQ would have had to go in parentheses—says to me, 'Our script needs a rewrite.' Our script? I said. What script? 'Our script. You know, it's a metaphor for our life. Our relationship.' I played for time. Something was fishy. Someone had put all those new words in his mouth. Someone from California. It sounded definitely like West Coast crapola.

"You think our relationship needs a rewrite? 'That's right.' He was tugging at his Eisenhower jacket and buffing his nails on his pants. In what way? 'Oh, in every way. I want to go to California.' Aha. There it was. I told him I couldn't go to California. I was just getting started in the fashion business. I couldn't just pick up and go. He said, 'It's either your career or me.' I thought he was joking so I said, If that's the way you want it, ta ta."

"What happened?"

"He left." Don's eyes got wider in his face. He looked miserable. "The next day, he packed his clothes and left."

"My god, just like that?"

"No. He left me with a two hundred dollar phone bill and intestinal parasites."

"My god. How?"

"Don't ask. It's too gruesome. It's my own fault. Instead of going to a gay doctor who would have seen immediately what was what, I went to a jerk who treated me with enemas. *Enemas*. That only gave the darlings an elevator ride home."

"I can't take this," said April, shaking her head. "I just . . . it's too much."

"You said it," said Don. "It's too fucking much."

"You have Pierre."

"True. But I'm very mean to Pierre. The only time I'm really nice to Pierre and stop hassling him is when I'm on hash. Then I'd be nice to my dead dog."

"Are you on hash a lot?"

"Don't ask."

"But you do love Pierre?"

"Don't ask."

She turned all this information over in her mind. Not that she could do anything about any of it. "Do you think I could change? Do you think I could be normal again . . . I mean lose the weight and everything?" She hadn't known she was going to say that.

He looked surprised and his face took on a childlike excitement. "Jesus, I think so. Why not? Imagine a thin little thing stepping out of you. Oh, I can't stand it. Be still, my heart. You'd be gorgeous." He said it again as if the idea was blazing in his mind. "You know . . . you'd be gorgeous."

22

ON MAY 7TH, 1980, at 8:00 A.M., two hours before they had to be at their desks, Don and April arrived on the roof of Burdie's. The space was impressive, easily the size of half a city block. Natural light filtered in through huge arched windows softening the relentlessly green indoor/outdoor carpeting. A quarter-mile jogging track was outlined on the parameter of the room with thick white lines to separate two lanes.

In the center of the room was a Universal exercise machine—the Rolls-Royce of the muscle builders, according to Don. Farrah Fawcett had one in her luxe home gym. It looked like a square metal donut. Each side had graduated slots where you increased resistance by inserting metal wedges. There were benches, trapeze bars, rings, handles to push or pull with your feet and hands.

Terry Bleicher, assistant buyer for housewares, was lying on his stomach on a skinny leatherette bench pushing a bar with his heels.

"What does that do?" asked Don.

"It strengthens these muscles." Terry pointed to the back of his thighs under his buttocks. It already looked

perfect and, in any case, was not a major part of his body.
Yet Terry appeared gratified that he was doing something of value.

Beyond the jogging track, there were Jacuzzis and
showers and a multitiered sauna. In a far corner, there
were two less serious machines: a rotating cylinder made
of spaced wooden rollers that rolled bulges away and a
wide fabric belt that vibrated wildly against parts of your
body. It was now vibrating against Mary Fiduccia's left
thigh (she was a cashier in the executive dining room)
while she read *Princess Daisy*.

Burdie's management had been one of the first to
provide a health break facility for employees. Yellowing
clippings were tacked to a bulletin board. "Burdie's Built-
in Health Break Brings a Bonanza of Benefits," said the
Nation's Retailer.

April felt self-conscious, stupid and headed down a
wrong road where no good thing awaited her. She hadn't
been able to find large enough jogging shorts—Don insisted she wear shorts for shock value, and he had finally
sewn a pair out of a huge bath towel, on a machine he
kept at home. She looked awful and felt awful. The terry
rubbed painfully between her legs. The tank top outlined
the bulk of her arms, shoulders and back. She had
pinned her hair back in a sloppy ponytail and it made her
face look hard and aggressive. She was a solid block of
flesh. A Sherman tank. The only thing that looked nice
were her feet in brand new, baby blue jogging shoes and
white socks with ridiculous pom-poms bouncing at her
heels.

If she had seen someone like herself in a like outfit, she
would have considered it hopeless. She looked at Don
who was trim and fastidious in a beige Head jogging suit
with matching Adidas running shoes and . . . yes! ter-

rycloth head and wrist bands to contain his perspiration. "What now?" she asked.

He opened a soft-sided briefcase and took out *Miss Craig's 21-Day Shape-Up Program*. "If it's good enough for Elizabeth Arden, it's good enough for us." April looked at the title page: A Plan of Natural Movement Exercises for Anyone in Search of a Trim and Healthy Body. It sounded so innocent for what they had in mind.

They both lay down on green mats and began. They did the right, left and center neck roll, five times each. The full body stretch, the opposite arm and leg touch and the side stretch five times. April couldn't complete the fifth exercise, called the Figure Eight. It called for bringing your knees together over your chest and then rolling them to each side, ending with a smart smack on the floor while keeping your shoulders and waist pinned to the mat. Don told her to do as much as she could. She got her knees over her buttocks and rotated them two or three inches to each side.

When he was satisfied that she was stretched and limber, he led her in a fast walk twice around the track. It was a very precise walk with a deliberate roll of the foot, an energetic swing to bent arms and an exaggerated thrust of the hips from side to side. "What is this?" She thought he had to be kidding but there was no air of mirth within ten miles of that room.

"It's called wogging."

"Did you make it up?"

"I didn't, but what if I did," he asked indignantly. "You'd trust some mediocre quack who's getting paid off by The Heart Fund to pass off all kinds of crapola about cholesterol before you'd trust me?"

"No." She wogged vigorously for twenty seconds. Four times she had to stop wogging and hold on to the wall. Her heart was beating maniacally and she couldn't get a breath of air that satisfied her. Her lungs burned. "Maybe we're doing too much," she gasped.

"Keep going," he called back, passing her on the track. "Crawl if you have to." When she finished the half mile, the perspiration rolled off her head onto her cheeks, off her nose onto her lips, off her back down into her underpants, between her legs, down the back of her legs into her socks. Sweat was everywhere. Don insisted on a four-minute sauna followed by a cold shower. Even after the cold shower, April continued to perspire. It was as if her body had been perforated like one of those garden hoses they lay between rows in a vegetable garden. She needed to drink.

They headed for a lunch counter that was just opening on the third floor and he ordered three glasses of water and a lemon. He proceeded to squeeze the lemon evenly into the three glasses. "Drink these."

"I can't drink water. I've never been able to drink just water."

"Drink it anyway."

"Why?"

"Because it'll clean out your liver."

"From what? I haven't eaten anything."

"From twenty-eight years of overeating. You're filled with toxins. Everybody is. Water and lemon helps to clean you out. I heard it from a dentist on the radio."

"A dentist?"

"A holistic dentist. He said if people had bad teeth, you could be sure they had bad bodies, too. Now, drink the water. You have to drink at least eight glasses a day. These are just a start. Come on, you can take as long as you like, but I don't have all day. Sip, sip, sip." While she sipped, he opened his briefcase and took out a supersized grapefruit. "You owe me thirty-five cents," he said, "unless you want to take turns bringing in the grapefruit. Be sure to pick one with mottled skin . . . see," he turned the fruit to show her. "The skin's very thin which means it's juicier."

She was too exhausted to respond and too busy dabbing at her upper lip and temples to blot the continuing perspiration. She ate her half of the grapefruit slowly and thoughtfully, savoring the wetness. She took her cue from Don who chewed carefully and didn't place another segment into his mouth until he had thoroughly disposed of the previous one. When they were finished, he took out two hard-boiled eggs and handed one to her. "Here's your protein. That's it until 12:45, so eat it slowly."

She made four trips to the bathroom before ten o'clock and peed torrents. It was a satisfying feeling, as if all that lemon water had sought out every crevice inside her body and nudged out the impurities. Each time she came out of the bathroom, she drank three small paper cups of water. She felt smug until eleven o'clock when a blinding headache came on. She walked by the vending machines three times, eyeing a display window with an individual pack of Wise potato chips. She knew the size and plumpness was a come-on. It held 1.3 ounces, a mouthful. She'd have to eat five or six packs. The thought of all that salt mixing with all that water inside her made her turn resolutely back to her desk.

She dialed Don's extension. "I can't take it."

"You can't take what?"

"It. IT! You know what I mean. I'm starving. My head hurts. I can't do my work."

"Oh, that. This is only the first day. Wait'll you starve yourself for a week and find you've gained a pound. *Then,* talk to me about not being able to take it." He hung up.

Lunch didn't go well. Don insisted the waitress bring them whole lettuce leaves, a whole tomato and half a portion of cottage cheese.

"The lettuce is cut up for salads," said the waitress.

"What about the lettuce you put under the tuna and egg plate?"

"That's Boston lettuce. We don't use that for salad."

"Good. Because I don't want a salad. So bring me about ten or twelve leaves of Boston lettuce." The waitress stared across the room and pursed her lips. "Just hold the tuna and egg and we'll pay for the whole plate." She still didn't respond. "You'll make money on the deal. Tuna is seventy-nine cents a can, what can the lettuce cost?"

April didn't want to pay for the whole plate if she was just going to eat lettuce, but she said nothing.

"All right," said the waitress, "if I can get you the lettuce—and I mean *if*—what do you want with it?"

"A whole tomato and half a scoop of cottage cheese."

"The tomatoes come sliced."

"Well, bring me one before they slice it. I'll save you the trouble." He let her finish writing. "Now, for myself, I'll have the king crab salad on whole wheat."

When the waitress left, April waited for an explanation, but none was offered. "All right," she said, "why the big fuss over the lettuce?"

There was that familiar look of indignation. "Lettuce for salads is cut up in that big salad bar in the sky and shipped all over the country in Baggies. They must put embalming fluid on it to keep it from turning brown." She must have looked skeptical because his tone turned scornful. "You think all those luncheonettes that advertise bottomless salad bowls sit around cutting lettuce and washing lettuce from scratch? Not on your life. It's cut up by machines in some godforsaken place. It could even come from Chile. You'd be surprised how much food we get from Chile. Ask Pierre."

For dinner, he took her home and Pierre, in celebration of her first day, steamed large portions of broccoli, cauliflower and carrots. He added strips of steamed chicken breast and stir-fried it quickly in a lemony soy sauce.

Don took all but three slivers of carrots off her plate. "Carrots are a trick. The worst diet fallacy. They're loaded with sugar."

It was a large plate of food, very crunchy. It took a long time to chew. The color was spectacular—rich orange, deep green against the snowy whiteness of the cauliflower. Dessert was one giant strawberry—the size of a small orange.

"They cost fifty cents each at the robber on Third Avenue," said Don. Pierre winced.

After dinner, they measured every part of her body. Bosom, 44; waist, 35; hips, 44; each upper thigh, 24; each upper arm, 13. After each measurement, Don whistled in disbelief. When the next measurement came, April clamped her hand over his mouth. "You don't have to whistle anymore," she said sarcastically. "We all understand that you're flabbergasted."

He shrugged and looked at his watch. "It's nine. By the time you walk home and brush your teeth, it'll be 9:30. That leaves you two hours to resist temptation." She drank two glasses of water when she reached her apartment and was in bed by 10:30. She was asleep in moments. Don called at eleven to warn her of all the terrible things that would happen if she put anything into her mouth before he saw her again. She dreamt of Harald and Sylvie, they were making love on a slim, narrow table but didn't have any trouble staying on and appeared perfectly comfortable.

The first three days passed quickly and were exhilarating. She had an image—silly but satisfying—of all the water washing away terrible moments of humiliation that had got stuck inside her. Her anxiety lessened.

"Don't you dare weigh yourself," Don cautioned. "The minute you see a big loss, you'll head straight for the refrigerator."

"How are you so sure? Don't you think I have a stake in all of this?"

"Not just you. Anybody. A big loss equals permission to eat. Or even worse, that little voice that hates you will say 'you *deserve* to eat because you've been so *gooood.*' Well, you haven't been *that* good. Don't go near a scale."

On the fifth day, the euphoria left. It was then that she realized what an enormous commitment she had made and the fear of failure loomed high. Besides the hunger pangs, now she was dizzy and felt light-headed from time to time. When she was alone, she despaired. How could she ever melt away those hundreds of inches that separated her from her bones? Perversely, the weight she'd lost left her feeling so empty and small, she was afraid of losing all of her substance. Could she live with herself sixty pounds lighter? Her identity was closely tied to the solidity of her flesh, the strong pull of her arms and chest. Many nights, she was sure she was meant to be fat. The feelings of despair settled in her chest, making her feel bound and hollow at the same time.

Each morning, however, the telephone rang. "And how is Raquel today?" Don would ask.

Within a week, she was doing ten neck rolls, ten full body stretches, ten opposite arm and leg touches and ten side stretches. She could complete the first movement of the Figure Eight and do three of Number Six, biking side by side, done half reclining on your side, biking with your legs as the thigh was massaged by the floor. Number

Seven, the leg crossover, was a loss. She couldn't touch her leg to her opposite outstretched arm. Don told her to skip to the "hip walk" which she did very well. The hip walk was like wogging with your buttocks on the floor. Upright, she had increased her wogging by another quarter mile and some of that time, she shuffled along in a near jog.

The morning menu remained the same: half a grapefruit, pulp and all, one hard-boiled egg and as much lemon water as she desired beyond the mandatory three glasses. She could also have tea and diet ginger ale. He let her have as much lettuce, tomatoes, celery, cauliflower, broccoli, green beans, peppers, cabbage and parsley as she liked, but weighed and measured portions of salmon, cottage cheese and chicken breast on a small yellow kitchen scale he made her carry in her pocketbook.

As ten days passed, she didn't need a scale to tell her the good news. Her clothes weren't constricting, even her shoes were loose. She saw things better and heard more clearly.

"That's because you're on the edge of starvation," said Don triumphantly. "A hungry rat is a very alert rat. Sharp as a tack in case any food passes by."

"Thanks a lot."

The chronic fatigue that always plagued her lessened. She regularly walked home from the train because it was good daydreaming time. She had an insatiable need to daydream, as if there was a backlog of happy images that had been put in cold storage. She hadn't daydreamed since before she married Harald. Many times her daydreams centered around Luis O'Neill. Why not? He was there, he was attractive and she had glimpses of him from time to time. It didn't bother her that he wasn't likely to fulfill any of her fantasies.

Every evening for a month now, she had sat behind him on the train home. A limousine brought him to the station but then he boarded the 6:03 from Philadelphia with two stops in Newark. She always sat behind him, staring at his tan, healthy neck. Occasionally he caressed his neck or ran his fingers quickly through his hair. She watched him read the *New York Times*. He folded it neatly, turning to the Op-Ed page, reading Lewis and then Safire. She sometimes saw him clamp his lips together in annoyance. When he was finished with the editorials, he put the paper on the seat beside him and looked around at his fellow passengers. He never saw her. There was never a chance meeting, she made sure of that. She waited until he was safely off the train before she got up.

One evening, she got on the train first; it was very crowded and she knew it would be pointless to wait for him. As they were pulling out, he slid in beside her and she almost fainted with nervousness. Her heart felt like a cartoon heart, beating right out of her chest. If she put her hand over it, it would begin to push out somewhere else like the hearts on "Tom and Jerry."

He was reading the *Newark Evening News,* looking at the Burdie's ads, reading her ad for John Kloss nightgowns. *So Beautiful—Dare You Wear Them Dancing?*

What was she to do, poke him with her elbow? Betcha don't know who you're sitting next to. He wouldn't appreciate an opening like that and what would it accomplish? Would he ask her to dinner, pinch her bottom? Of course not. He would be polite: I recognize you, how is everything? He would wish he were in another seat so he could read his paper in peace. Who wanted politeness?

After three weeks on the regime—an hour of serious exercise, 800 to 900 calories a day, a half gallon of water, plus at least two miles of incidental walking—she had not seriously cheated. Once she had chewed a handful of raisins but then spit them out before swallowing and brushed her teeth. Several Triscuits had been chewed briskly *and* swallowed, but then the box had been put in the sink and drowned.

One day on the way home, she entered a candy/tobacco shop and bought four Mounds bars. She ate two of them on the street and the other two sitting on the couch, her shoulderbag still strapped around her. She could have done a lot of things to keep herself from eating the candy: jumped rope, masturbated (Don said masturbation was the greatest aid to reducing, it took your mind off eating for that crucial moment). But she didn't want to distract herself. She wanted to eat. She went to the D'Agostino market around the corner and bought half a gallon of Heavenly Hash ice cream, a package of pita bread, a pound of hamburger, a jar of Aunt Millie's marinara sauce, Corona red pepper flakes and six ounces of mild cheddar cheese.

She browned the meat, added the marinara sauce and red pepper, stuffed three of the pita pockets, added a generous amount of the grated cheese and ate all three quickly and silently. After that she had the ice cream. Two bowls.

For about fifteen minutes, she felt as if she were going to suffocate. Nausea overtook her. She tried to quiet her stomach by lying down but it didn't help, and half an hour after her last spoonful of Heavenly Hash, it all came up.

After that, she felt fine and brushed her teeth, took a long cool shower—sitting in the tub and letting the water beat on her head. She changed her sheets, put on a thin cotton nightgown and went to bed. She was happy that none of that godawful stuff had stayed in her body. When she considered how carefully she had taken care of herself over the past weeks, the idea of going back to what she had been frightened her.

She thought of all the things she was afraid of: being a

quadriplegic and having to write with her mouth. Having her period oozing through her skirt and being unaware of it. Being finally caught after an exhausting chase by some man following her out of the subway. Losing her eyesight. Now she was also afraid of eating.

"God, everything's wrong." She was sitting with Don on the exercise mats looking at the little pouch on the inside of her leg, right above the knee.

"Not really. You could have angry pustules fighting for space on your cheeks."

"Don't say that."

"Well, you *could*." He looked her over, head to toe. "There's nothing here that's not fixable. At least I don't think so," he teased. "We'll know more later. Now, come on, get a hold of a good hunk of your thigh. Right above your knee, there . . . where it bunches up. Take it in both hands and twist part of it one way and part of it the opposite way." She did so and tears came to her eyes.

"What's wrong?"

"It hurts."

"Of course, it hurts. Life hurts. Love hurts. Don't do it so hard. Bonnie Prudden says this is the only way to break down the hardest fat. Slabs of it. He held his hands apart to indicate how thick and hard the slabs above her knees were. "You've got to break that stuff down. Soften it up and it will pour right out of you . . . well, maybe it won't *pour* exactly, but it's a nice image."

"You're sure this is the way to do it?"

"Yes." He was already doing push-ups, having no slabs of his own to twist and pull.

She had stopped asking how he knew so much. The things he said were true had proven to be true. Her skin had never looked so clear since she had begun with his three lemon cocktails each morning and five additional glasses of water during the day. Her skin had a finer texture, too, a beautiful opaqueness. He had also advised her to scrub every inch of her body with a forty-nine cent nylon Scrubee that housewives used to clean their precious Teflon cookware. He said the little rectangle of abrasive nylon was cheaper and better than a loofah. By increasing the pressure, you could peel away several layers of dead, useless cells while stimulating those that were still alive.

"You're exercising your skin," he exclaimed, as if the thought had just originated in his head.

As for her hair, he advised her to pull it. "You've got to get the blood up there. Blood, blood, blood," he sing-songed, "three ways to a prettier you. Dangle your head over the side of the bed and pull your hair."

"Pull it?"

"That's right. Take little clumps of it tight in your fist, very close to the scalp and pull for all you're worth. It should take at least twenty minutes. Take special care with the hair around your forehead. Most people's foreheads are so tight, blood never visits."

His final admonition was that she must consciously relax her forehead, her eyelids and the muscles around her lips at least ten times a day. "All that loathsome eagerness to please, the self-hate, it all shows up around the mouth. Relax your mouth, and the world will kiss your ass."

When she balked at the idea that *her* forehead, eyelids and mouth were tense, he told her to put them in what seemed to her a comfortable, relaxed position. Then he told her to deliberately relax the muscles around her mouth in ever widening circles, beginning with her lips. She did so. "See. Did you feel how tight you had been holding them?" She did. It felt as if she had put down a burden. "Now relax your forehead muscles." That, too, felt like a major undoing. The eyelids proved to be very taut as well.

"Now tell me," he said, "when you relax your forehead, eyelids and mouth, how do you feel about yourself?"

"Satisfied."

"Precisely. You're satisfied, which translates into exciting."

23

It was early June of 1980. The hostages were still in captivity although Ramsey Clark had defied the president and traveled to Iran, offering himself in exchange for "fifty-three innocent Americans." In a full-page Memorial Day ad, Burdie's assured the hostages they were remembered. On television, the show "Dallas" had left everyone with the hottest cliffhanger since the *Perils of Pauline*—who shot J.R.? In politics, Jimmy Carter won the Ohio primary, clinching the Democratic nomination.

Don and Pierre decided to take April's measurements and found she had lost four inches from the bosom and waist, three around the hips, one and a half around the upper arms and two around each upper thigh. She had to buy a few new things to wear during the transition. Her hair had grown out and was grazing her shoulders. Don urged her to bleach 'sun' streaks into it, but she resisted.

Lorenzo kept giving her looks during the Monday

morning merchandise meetings. One day, in the corridor behind the selling floor, he took her arm and propelled her into the notions buyer's office. "Well, if it isn't Hemingway," he said and put his arm around her shoulders. She tried to shrink out of his hold. There was no one in the room. The desk was littered with thimbles, shoulder pads and odd stuffed forms for ironing sleeves.

"Hey, don't squirm away from me." The palm of his bony hand grazed her left breast and she went rigid with confusion and anger. "Take your hand off me or I'm going to scream!"

"You want a coat?" he asked impatiently.

"What?"

"A cashmere coat."

"You're crazy." He still had his hand on her arm.

"With a mink trim."

"Just shut up and let go of me." She slammed her elbow into his pathetic, hollow chest. Someone would burst in at any moment.

"They're nice coats," he said, ever the salesman and took his hand away.

She walked unsteadily out of the office and toward the advertising department. The whole beige/pink shipment of Lorenzo's budget cashmeres came to mind and all the tired, overweight women who would buy them. *The cashmere clutch coat you've always wanted*—a headline she'd written herself.

> *Would you believe cashmere this luxe?*
> *Would you believe cashmere on sale?*
> *Would you believe only $89?*

The first person she saw when she reached her desk was Susan Scott, cool and confident. "You're just the person I'm looking for," she said.

April didn't want to be the person she was looking for. She was still shaken and anxious to be left alone. "Yeah?"

"You want a share in a house at Fire Island for July and August?"

"I don't know. I've never been to Fire Island."

"You'll love it. There aren't any cars, just beach and sun. The house we're renting is right on the bay. We . . . you and I . . . would go out every other weekend, including Labor Day."

"I don't think so."

"What'll you do all summer? You'll suffocate."

"I've managed before."

"It'll be fun. Everyone just sort of . . . hangs out together." She threw her hands wide from the center to simulate a human jumble of togetherness.

April wanted to ask exactly when all this hanging out took place. Did it, for instance, start right away, after breakfast? And would it start out for Susan before it started out for April? "Do I get a room alone?"

"You can room with me."

"I'll think about it." Susan had men swarming over her. The overflow might spill over on her. It was something to consider.

"I have to know by Tuesday."

"You'll know by Tuesday."

She sat at the typewriter to do an ad on a skirt that was hanging on the wall. It was made of polyester and would probably start pilling after one sitting. She was furious about Lorenzo and wondered if she should tell someone. Don would kill him. Pierre would go berserk. *Eight artful gores,* she pounded on her Royal. *Slim where you're slim, flare where you flare.* Maybe she could meet some decent men on Fire Island.

That night, she dreamt she lived in a very tiny house— so tiny she could touch the walls with her arms outstretched. Then she could touch the walls with her arms at her sides. The idea of such close quarters scared her to death. In the morning, she decided to take the share in the house with Susan Scott. She needed a more wholesome life. She should be getting out into the world. Besides, she could wear a bathing suit. Almost. The swimming would be good exercise. She could jog on the beach.

During the third week in June, she awoke early one morning and while contemplating the rise and fall of her chest, realized with a start that she had never had any adult to adult emotion with Harald. She had never revealed herself to him or he to her. They had had sex, talked, held hands, bought furniture and put up bookshelves. She had handed him the hammer and held the molly screws which puffed out in the hollow walls. They thought that was closeness when it was nothing but a skittish playacting.

That morning, Don put her on the Universal Gym. "Your stomach muscles—they're orphaned children. No one has asked anything of them." He could have been talking about some terrible, senseless crime. His voice was sad. She wanted to ask if anything was wrong, but felt too sad herself. She had gone through her marriage to Harald holding her breath. She couldn't remember one thing about herself during those years.

Don placed her on the bench and secured her feet under a strap. He held her feet and supported her knees in a half bent position. With great effort, she did two situps. They had already done their limbering and stretching and she had hip-walked twice the width of the exercise area. All that was left was the wogging, which was now three quarters jogging. She had been doing a mile now for a week, but because he seemed sad, she kept going and did a mile and a half. If he noticed, he didn't comment.

They finished up early that day and the store was still

dark. "Watch out," said Don, menacingly, "the K-9 force is still around."

"What's the K-9 force?"

"K-9 as in canine. Dogs. Get it?"

"Dogs? They let dogs roam through the store at night?"

"In case anyone stays in to rob the place. They would sniff you out and tear you apart."

"Really?"

"Really." He threw up his hands. "I don't know. What else would they do? These people trained in detective work are vicious. They don't see men, women, nephews, veterans and widows. To them, everyone is a potential thief, felon, murderer."

She knew they placed ordinary-looking people throughout the store as plainclothespersons. At her heaviest, she suspected one of them was watching her. They watched the fat ones, thinking part of their heft was a clever coat with built-in pockets to receive merchandise.

"They caught a woman," Selma had told her, "she looked like she weighed four hundred pounds but then they opened her coat and she had a toaster, a facial sauna, a waffle iron, a Waring blender, two curling irons and assorted men's sweaters all fitted snugly in the lining of her coat." She also told her about two men who walked out with a piano. They put a SOLD tag on it and carried it out. No one said a word. This sent her into a fit of laughter. "They *held* the doors for them."

She told all this to Don in an effort to cheer him up. He was only half listening and after a while she gave up and ate her grapefruit and hard-boiled egg in silence.

She didn't see him for the next three days. When she called his apartment, Pierre said he was too sick to come to the phone. The day he returned his eyes looked sunken and his hands weren't the steadiest thing she had ever seen as he held his Styrofoam cup of coffee. "This is poison," he said, "but there's nothing like it for opening the old beepers."

"Are you all right?"

"Don't ask."

"You look pale. You're the only black person I know who can look pale."

"You know you're funny," he said without smiling. "Now that you're not so fat, you're getting funny."

She didn't feel funny. She felt like crying. She knew Don felt he had missed his chance in life but he had decided to live with it, cushioned with his cynicism and a few snorts of whatever was handy. He never talked about the specifics but what did it matter? What could she do even if she knew the specifics?

That was the day, too, that Luis O'Neill came down, strolling through the narrow aisle of the advertising department to look around.

"Hello." She was so startled to look up and see him, she didn't answer right away. He looked at the ad pinned to her board. It was for culottes. It showed three girls jumping in the air. *It's time to spring for some real fashion sense.*

"What does that mean?" he asked.

"They look like a skirt but . . . they're sensibly . . . sensibly comfortable."

"Not my favorite fashion," he said. His right arm was propped over the partition of her cubby. He looked as if he were going to settle in for a chat but Missy came down the aisle and pulled him away. April was relieved she had washed her hair the night before. And she had on her brown blusher that Don had told her to use to punch up her cheekbones.

"They're not my favorite fashion, either," she said after he was gone.

24

BY THE TIME APRIL spent her first weekend on Fire Island in early July, she had lost thirty-two pounds. Her loyalty to the Universal Gym and Miss Craig's exercises had firmed her stomach and thighs. She insisted Don needn't come with her in the mornings, but he still did most of the time. Her breasts and stomach were separated by an indented, if not totally flat, midriff. She bought two black one-piece bathing suits cut high on the thigh in the season's style. This gave her an impressive expanse of leg, smooth and glowing from her daily buffing with the Scrubee pad. Her saddlebags had been twisted and pummeled into submission and only a manageable ripple remained. The sun had begun to streak her hair with red and gold. Stretched out on the beach with her slinky maillot and oversized sunglasses, she was noticed.

Jogging on the beach in the early morning, she met a social studies teacher from Philadelphia, her first admirer as the new April. They talked a couple of times and he said: "I like you because you're not hungry." Unfortunately, she wasn't hungry for him, but it was nice to be pursued.

The house Susan Scott had rented was a modern one-story box with many skylights. The Sunday supplement would have said: Unexpected light makes this modest row house a triumph of originality. Its best feature was a square, ground level deck just steps from the bay. Its second best feature was the house next door occupied by ten male lawyers who also alternated weekends.

Susan's other recruits for the even weekends were Lana and Tina, college students from wealthy families who lived in Short Hills. Lana and Tina were buxom and energetic. Before long, they had collected a directory of men and came home only to change and shower.

By the beginning of August, each of the lawyers next door had been to bed with at least one of the girls from next door. Two of the lawyers had had more than one of the girls and one of the lawyers had had three of the girls. April fell into the third category, having succumbed to George Tandy, a personal injury expert whose divorce wasn't final. April came after Lana but before Tina, which was a compliment of sorts. Considering the circumstances, it was not a bad experience and George had hung around her all the next day smoothing suntan lotion on her back and generally behaving as if he wouldn't mind repeating his performance.

"Do you realize those louses have screwed all of us?" said Lana.

"Look at it this way," said April. "We've screwed all of them and we're going to keep doing it until they get it right."

"Hey, that's good," said Lana. She had found a point of view she could live with and was off again.

As for April, she didn't feel used. George Tandy, a

teddy bear of a man, was likable and a good neighbor. She was grateful that he had sprung her from two years of celibacy without trauma.

In early August, April's father unexpectedly married a woman he had met only six weeks before. The wedding took place at the Marble Collegiate Church where the woman was a parishioner. April wore a silk, Victorian-collared dress and had her hair wound into a French braid. At the reception, held in a restaurant, Harlan kept looking at her as if she might do something to embarrass him. It was the hairdo, she decided. It was definitely not a Queens hairdo.

That was the month, too, that Sylvie gave birth to her second child, a little girl, at Lenox Hill Hospital. "I'm a multipara now," she said over the phone. April visited twice to see the little bundle, but Sylvie was far more interested in staring at April, fascinated by her emerging figure and admiring her harem style polished cotton slacks with the matching boat-necked top in coffee brown.

"I think central casting sent that kid over to play the world's most beautiful baby," she told the new mother. That was stretching it, but April was alarmed by Sylvie's lack of maternal enthrallment.

"Did she at least open her eyes for you?"

"Yes. She was also cramming her fist down her throat. Don't they feed her?"

"My milk isn't in. She'll just have to wait."

Such a callous dismissal. Alicia Beck Straight, as the baby had been named, was in for some hungry days. April looked around trying to saturate herself in mother-hood, mothersmell and motherair. Gift flowers were strewn everywhere. Tucked between the vases were Tiffany boxes with silver accessories. There was even a little machine fitted with five cassettes to play mood music for baby. On each cassette was a baby with the correlating expression: sleepy, bored, cranky, happy, sad. Sad? Why would she be sad? "Is the music to change the mood or coax it out? Why would you want to tamper with happiness?"

"I know which one will get the most play," said Sylvie heavily. "The one that makes it sleepy."

"*It?* You wanted a boy?"

"Of course not. I have a boy."

"You didn't want another baby?"

"Oh . . . I did, I guess." Thirty seconds later, Sylvie burst into tears which quickly deteriorated into hard sobbing.

"Did I do something? Is it something I said?"

"No . . . " Sylvie waved her hand and cried harder. "It's just . . . oh . . . *everything.*"

"There's nothing wrong with the baby, is there?"

"No. God, no. That would be too much."

"Postpartum blues?"

"Oh, April, that doesn't come till much, much later." Almost as if to stop the amateurish diagnosis, she began to recite a litany of ills. Three people in her neighborhood had died. They were dropping like flies. Suicide. Leukemia. Heart. Any one of them could have been her. And her life . . . it really had no point . . . except to do as Spencer said she must do. And keep their social aspirations high. "He's openly ambitious. So am I." She lowered her voice and her head as if revealing something dark—a sexual fancy for the dead. "He wants to meet better people. Always better than the last. Our boat's named Ambition."

There was more. She had to start over every day with the same awful routine: carpooling, dinner parties—who owed you, who you owed. Nobody ever said what they really meant except—get this—for terrible jokes and cracks about Jews. "And now, with her," she pointed toward the nursery, "it'll start again. Except it'll be piano instead of violin. Horseback riding instead of hockey. Tennis instead of baseball. And none of it, absolutely none of it will leave *me* with *anything*."

April was stunned. Sylvie, the Queen of the Gots, unhappy? How could that be true? She might as well say she'd like to trade places with April, which is exactly what she did say.

"Now, you," she said in an accusing voice, "you've got a terrific career. You look so much better, I can't believe it's really you. And . . ." she took a big sigh for the finale, "you can screw whomever you want instead of doing it every Tuesday with someone who just sticks it in, and sometimes on Saturday, if we don't get home too late or drink too much."

If she had to credit anyone with changing her attitude about her job, it would have to have been Sylvie because it was that night, reeling from those revelations, that *she* decided to become openly ambitious. For all her woes, Sylvie had a small estate, a silver Mercedes—with a CB radio, she was Silver Momma—a membership in a yacht club, a near yacht, a one hundred thousand dollar stock portfolio, seeded with bonus money for each child, and two healthy children, one of whom would at least make it to be Secretary of State.

And what did she have? A studio apartment where the entry of the sun was so miserly, even shade-loving plants struggled to survive. An exhausting daily round trip to downtown Newark. If she chose to walk to or from the train, she feared mugging and turned down panhandlers and young bums who urged her to "help support an alternative lifestyle." What's more, she still had paralyzing memories of a failed marriage and sick daydreams about a man who probably had never entertained two consecutive thoughts about her.

Her new ambition must have sent out vibes because Missy began to give her more responsibility. Burdie's had never had a real fashion image. It was not, like the old Best and Company, a place known for classics. And it was not, like Bloomingdale's, expensive and trendy. Traditionally, ads were directed to faceless, nameless women with no discernible lifestyle. Headlines were blah: *Junior fashions take a step toward fall.* Or, *We like this sailor chemise for spring.* Or, *The three-quarter coat is set for the cold.*

With this new directive, April began to address her ads to a recognizable audience: young women coping with new ambitions, new personalities and new problems of identity. The business suit with the soft, gathered shoulders became *The Un-Stern Suit.* Feminine angora tunics were paired with briefcase-style handbags and sold under the reassuring message: *Dress softly . . . but carry a big briefcase.* The season's intimidating harem pants, knickers and jodhpurs were not solely for the anorexic: *Knickers and harem pants are good for your hips,* she told the less than perfect women of New Jersey.

There was a new playfulness that also instructed and reassured: *New easy-care wools you can wash with impunity (or a capful of Woolite). Peachy keen velveteen separates that won't lose their fuzz.*

Missy also asked her to sit in with the brainstorming group that met weekly in Ned Perkins's office, the vice president for advertising and public relations. The group included Don, Erica and Ray Nolan from the art department as well as herself and Missy. The president almost always dropped in. Luis. She liked to say it. I felt my hipbone today, Luis, she would say aloud in her bed in the morning. You want to feel? Go right ahead. Feel all you want. Does this mean a promotion, ha ha.

He was there to pump their creative juices (Missy's description) and encourage lateral thinking (his description). They thought laterally about a lot of things including the year's big promotion. They had done Italia Fabulosa, Paris à la Mode, Greek Fantasy, England Forever. The routine was tried and true. The buyers scoured remote European villages for cottage industries making *tchotchkes* (Erica's word) unique to the country. "What it is, is garbage," offered Selma. "Cute garbage." Still, it was a very good way to satisfy ordinary people's desire for the exotic and make the profit picture considerably brighter. *Burdie's is dedicated to your fantasies of fabled empires.*

Another problem on their agenda, traditionally the bane of the retailer, was the dead time of 9:30 to 11:00 A.M. when the fully staffed, fully heated or air-conditioned store was chronically underpopulated. The president wanted their thoughts on how to stimulate traffic in the early morning.

April made it a point to walk through the store in the early hours and look at the people who came in. Many were mothers with small children. They looked harassed and the children were often cranky and not pacified by the bottle of juice or milk the mothers offered. If there was more than one child, the one who could walk begged to get into the stroller and the one in the stroller begged to be held.

"I don't know what's worse," she heard a young mother say to a saleswoman, "staying home with them or coming out."

April decided that these young mothers were the most identifiable target group for early morning shopping and decided to speak about them extemporaneously the next time the brainstorming group met.

Don was already there when April entered Ned Perkins's office and when Luis came in, he nudged her. "Hubba hubba."

"Him?"

"Don't tell me you haven't noticed."

"Of course, I've noticed."

"He called me into his office this morning. I almost fainted."

"For what?" Her heart sank. Suppose he preferred men?

"He said, and I quote: 'Uh, Don, the Execu-cycle display . . . it looks like the rider's had a coronary. He's lying across the handlebars.'" Don grinned devilishly. "I pushed the damned mannequin myself. I know he walks that way but I thought he'd just phone. I didn't expect a facey-facey."

She tried to calm herself before speaking to the group, knowing that Luis would be staring at her, listening, judging. "There is a segment of forgotten women," she began, "there must be hundreds of thousands of them right here in Newark. Women who wake up each morning to the same old breakfast dishes, the same baby crying, the same crayoned walls, the same unremovable stains on the same . . ."

"We get the picture," Erica interrupted, "what are you driving at?"

"These are the women who watch Phil Donahue and David Hartman on "Good Morning America" because they feel that Phil Donahue and David Hartman are taking care of them. These women take care of everyone but Phil Donahue takes care of them. That's an irresistible idea to that kind of woman—to be taken care of. To be comforted."

"And the point is?" asked Missy pointedly.

She was about to give a deprecating shrug and finish lamely. I didn't mean it, folks. Here, take back the floor.

Instead, she kept going. It was a good idea. Even if they
didn't follow through, they'd know she was *thinking*. "The
point is these are the women we would like to have in the
store every morning. They're the ones who are available
at those hours. True?"

"True." Luis threw out the word loud and clear. He
also smiled encouragingly.

"Well, then, we have to take care of her, too. We have
to be just as comforting as Phil Donahue and David Hartman. We have to convince her it's better to get out of her
nightgown and into her car on a freezing morning or a
hot morning and come to Burdie's and be comforted by
humans instead of by a cold, glaring image. We can start
by taking care of her preschooler—that's right, a small
nursery. Let's say the first fifty children on any given day
. . . not just watched, but enlightened with educational
toys, games, companionship. Two hours each day. We
could use the community room as a part-time day school.
There could be a nominal charge, or nothing."

"How would we know that she stayed in the store? She
could just plunk the kid down and take off," said Ray
Nolan.

"Maybe she could claim the child with a sales slip," said
Missy.

"What if she didn't buy anything?" said April. "Would
we hold the child hostage?"

"No," said Luis. "It would have to be without any
strings attached."

"It might be such a success, we'll have to franchise,"
said Ned Perkins. "Burdie's Nifty Nursery. Burdie's Busy
Bee Nursery."

"We could put a baby shop nearby," said April. "Small
Blessings. We'll sell them the toys the kids like best and
children's clothes. It would be a natural."

Seeing that everyone was taken with the idea, Missy became excited, too. "What about scheduling special events

for the mothers? So it wouldn't just be for shopping? Maybe it could be a club. The Nine-forty-five Club."

"That's what I was coming to," said April. "It would have to involve either cooking classes or exercise tips or decorating ideas. We might schedule something different every day of the week on a continuing basis with the special merchandise of the event as well as whatever else they might buy on impulse."

As the meeting wound down, Ned told Missy that he thought the three of them should meet again and map out a rough plan that they could present more formally. April walked out with Don, who said: "Jane Armstrong saves the day. Boy, did you ever make points. He was staring at you the whole time. He hung on your every word."

"You're just saying that. I know for a fact that he looked at Ned and Missy much more than at me."

"Yes, but he looked at you with *emotion*."

"No, he didn't."

"Yes, he did."

She would have really liked to pump Don to tell her what nuance he had caught in the way Luis O'Neill had looked at her. But she knew that once encouraged, Don would go berserk with speculation. Instead she waved him away and returned to her cubby. She wondered if Luis equated the old her with the new her. At times he looked puzzled, as if he weren't quite sure where she had come from.

25

On August 15th, the Feast of the Assumption according to Eyewitness News, celebrating the Virgin Mary's being assumed into heaven without dying, April lost her fifty-first pound. Nine more and she'd be home free. It had been one hundred and one days since she had begun.

Pounds, inches, water and fat. Stored toxins, stored pains, stored humiliation and despair had wafted out of her every orifice. She had lain in bed at night imagining all those layers of fat—dazzling white slabs—peeling away from her dermis, or whatever they adhered to—softening, yielding to her efforts, liquefying and pouring out of her in so many ways. She had unloaded more than fifty pounds—a decent-sized six-year-old child, Don had observed solemnly.

At a plateau of twenty pounds, everyone had been admiring and supportive, obsessively interested in what she ate, how many miles she "wogged," how she felt—was she hungry? constipated? dizzy? happy? At thirty pounds, they showed surprise. "Oh. Still with it, huh? How long you planning to keep it up?" At fifty pounds, they turned hostile and suspicious. "Don't tell me you're going to lose *more*?" said Erica disapprovingly. "You'll look like a skeleton."

"You'll make yourself sick," prognosticated Gayle, a layout artist with adult acne.

"Nobody ever got sick from being beautiful," said Selma.

"I read about a man in South Africa," insisted Gayle, "he lost a hundred pounds and died. His body couldn't cope."

"Why couldn't his body cope with a hundred fewer pounds?" asked Selma.

"Look, I don't know. It was in the *Times*."

The most revealing jab of all came when she was within seven pounds of her goal. Gayle said: "What are you trying to be, a glamour puss?"

"How does it feel?" asked Don one morning when they were doing their exercises on the roof of Burdie's.

"Fine."

"Come on. You know what I mean. How do you *feel*?"

"As if I've taken a journey through a long, long tunnel."

"That's it? Like you took a journey? What else?"

"Taller. I feel taller. And fragile. And light. Light as a feather. Corny but true."

"You know your nose got bigger." He peered critically into her face. "You've got a big nose now. Sorry about that. No refunds." He cackled, then he looked up at her impishly from the floor. "I thought you'd feel horny more than anything. All those nerve endings are right up front now."

"All right. I feel horny."

"Good." He sat up. "Why should you be so happy?"

"What's the matter, have a fight with Pierre?"

"I never have a fight with Pierre. Pierre has fights all by himself. Which reminds me, he made an appointment with this man to give you a body wave."

"I don't want a body wave, thanks."

"You've got to have a body wave." He sat with his legs crossed like a swami or a thwarted child. "You need volume. Your hair just lies there. Too limp."

"That's my cross. I'll just have to bear it."

"Have a body wave. *Please.* You can look leonine. You owe it to us. We've worked so hard."

"Okay. I'll give you three months as a lion and then that's it."

"Some streaks, too. Ten streaks."

"No streaks."

"Seven."

"No."

Don and Pierre decided that the *only* hairdresser they would trust to give her a body wave without any kink was Carlo, formerly with Kenneth, formerly with Mr. D. It was a three-day process and like no permanent she'd ever heard of. The first day she went home with gook on her hair and a scarf. The second day, she went home with different gook. The third day, Carlo washed it and put more gook on. True to his word, he had doubled the volume without a single curl. He showed her how to bend over and blow-dry it over her head and then brush it back lightly the other way. It was the Jackie Onassis hairdo. The old Baby Jane Holzer hairdo. Dina Merrill, Jane Fonda. Imitative but impressive. He must have snuck a little peroxide into the last bit of gook, because her hair was definitely lighter. He also plucked a two-lane highway between her brows, which made her eyes look wide-spaced. Carlo was definitely a devotee of the "Jackie" look.

Each time she looked in a mirror, she jumped. She felt as if she was hogging the air rights for two feet around herself. On the other hand, she looked fantastic—and the new manipulated eyebrows really punched up her eyes.

A few days later she was walking to the Newark train station. It was twilight on a rare, dry August day. Luis's limousine pulled up beside her and he put his head toward the open window. "Why are you walking on these streets?"

"This is the way to the train."

"Don't get smart. Get in." And when she was in: "You could get mugged . . . pocketbook dangling, gold chain showing . . ." He looked her over for enticements to violence.

She looked around the limousine, which was overly upholstered in gray velour with deep, coffin-style shirred tufts. "This is a bit much."

"Yes, it is," he agreed. "But I must have a limousine. I'm the president."

"I know," she smiled.

"You live in New York?" He asked it as if he deserved to know. She could see his mind going ricketi-ki-tick, adding up her situation. It was what he did, she supposed. He was in merchandising. Was he looking for a way to sell her?

"Yes."

"Why do you work in New Jersey?"

She hesitated only a moment. "I couldn't get a job in New York because of my weight."

"Your weight?" He didn't understand.

"I was too fat."

"You look fine," he said as if he were defending her. He didn't even remember her as a fatter person.

"Not now," she said. She was brought back to him by the realization that she was near and he had nothing on his mind but her. It was a small miracle.

"Now that you're not fat will you get a job in New York?"

"No."

"Good."

He didn't ask her to sit with him on the train. In fact, he made a point of saying good-bye as they entered the station, took his dull cowhide briefcase and walked purposefully to the end of the platform as if he had a special reason for doing so. She bought the *Newark Evening News* at a kiosk just for something to do. It was not a paper she felt connected to. It had nothing to do with her. There was one of her ads for electroplated gold charms. A full page of tiny replicas: tennis rackets, irons, a Cuisinart, hearts pierced by arrows. She stopped at a tiny calendar of February with a diamond chip for the 14th. *Good.* He had said good when she said she wouldn't look for work in New York. Why good? Because she was good for the store? Because he liked her work? Because he liked her? Because he liked her ass? Because. Because. Because. If he had said bad, or nothing at all, it wouldn't have been polite.

The very next day, Selma came in and announced that she had taken a job with Grey Advertising in New York City. She was going to work on a large cosmetics account, do both radio and television commercials and receive a big hike over her Burdie's salary. Part of it, she said, was due to her abilities and the other part was that she was black and attractive. But, she also insisted, the New York agencies were *very* friendly to copywriters trained by the Burdie's chain.

They were not immediately happy for Selma. They felt that she had snuck behind their backs. "This place was always just a steppingstone," she told them. "I was always looking. What was I supposed to do, announce it?"

"When were you looking? How could you look?" asked April.

"On my lunch hour."

"You went all the way into the city on your lunch hour?"

"Sometimes. Sometimes I took a sick day. It's my career, you've got to hustle. You know what an extra fifteen thousand means to my standard of living?"

They were mad at themselves for not having thought of it first. If Selma could get an agency job so could they. If Selma could make fifteen thousand dollars more a year, they could make that and more. April felt especially chagrined. She had never even considered another job. Burdie's was her whole world. She hadn't even considered that she could survive anywhere else. Well, that was one more thing to keep before her. She had a fat portfolio to show and a slim body, just the opposite of how she had begun. That week she worked on her resumé and had a hundred copies reproduced.

26

"ARE YOU AN AMERICAN?" Luis looked down at the upturned face of Nell Burdette, aged five. He liked children. He especially liked plump, bald babies who stared silently, but he could find nothing appealing in Fred Burdette's children. He suspected Nell was a disturbed, highly sexual child. She squirmed on his lap and put her arms around his neck seductively.

Jonathan, the boy, asked loud, embarrassing questions. Is our father your boss? Do you have to do what he says? How old are you? The Burdettes looked very much alike: sandy-haired, pale, slightly freckled.

"We don't bring any help to Point O' Woods," Faith Burdette bragged. "I do everything myself." She did. There were corn flakes and Rice Krispies for breakfast, bologna and cheese sandwiches for lunch and, at night, hot dogs for the kids and a bony steak for the grown-ups. The drinks were plentiful and exotic: piña coladas made with Coco Goya mix and rum.

Fred and Faith's pride in their self-sufficiency was liquor-fed. They were devoted to drinking and slept quite a bit. They were sleeping now, at ten o'clock on a sunny

Saturday morning, while he sat in their damp, slip-covered living room with the two children.

He had spent one other weekend with them but Lisanne had been with him and it hadn't been so dismal. This time, alone, he had expected to talk seriously with Fred about the Burdette chain, its financial health, new projects—important issues they had in common. But Fred was bored with retailing and even more bored by money talk. He liked to reminisce about Princeton and was cranky because there was no fourth for bridge.

"Are you allowed to be here by yourselves?" he asked the children.

"You mean without mummy and daddy or anyone?" asked Jonathan.

"No. I mean with mummy and daddy sleeping," answered Luis.

"But you're here," he said, puzzled.

"Yes, but I've got to go out." He was desperate to walk down the narrow paths and through the gate that separated Point O' Woods—somber and conservative—from Ocean Bay Park—gaudy and liberal—to Alan Leeds's rented house. That was a better place for him to be. With people who had to work for a living. It was only a twenty-minute walk away, if he could just get out gracefully.

"Where do you have to go?"

"Out. Just out." He sounded too annoyed and gave Jonathan a friendly pat on the shoulder.

"Oh," said the boy, knowingly. "Feeling like you have claustrophobia?"

"Exactly," said Luis and made his escape.

He walked quickly toward the gate—would Fred come to pull him back?—and tried to sort out his reasons for being there. Fred was his college roommate; while Fred lived in California, they had spent five years without laying eyes on each other. Fred was the chairman's son; Fred couldn't do anything for him that he couldn't do for himself. Fred loved him; Fred had a sentimental view of their closeness. He would never tell Fred anything really sad or problematic. He was closer to Leeds or Merlow or Ned Perkins, men he had known barely nine months. They were self-made, except for Perkins who was rich as hell but smart and ambitious anyway.

Leeds was sitting on the deck drinking coffee when he arrived and was surprised to see him. "I thought you were at the Burdettes'."

"I am," he said sullenly.

"Why are you slumming?"

"No wisecracks." He leaned against the deck rail and took a deep breath of ocean air.

"Sorry. Want a drink?"

"At ten-thirty in the morning? That's just what I'm running away from—a lot of soused Episcopalians."

"Oh . . . want to go to the beach and meet some women?"

"What do you mean *some* women? Ten women? Twenty women? Why do we need so many?"

"Okay, forget the women."

"I just want to sit down and read the paper in the sun. Do you have a paper?"

Leeds went inside and brought the *Times* out on the deck. Luis chose a comfortable chair and stretched out. He liked the fact that Leeds was hopping around trying to please him.

Merlow Hess, yawning and stretching, joined them. "Do you have to go back? We can play tennis. Tobias isn't out this weekend and you can have his bed."

"I don't want to go back," he said stubbornly.

"Well, you certainly don't have to stay there if you don't want to," said Merlow, like a righteous parent. "Tell them a filling fell out."

"How many times have you used that one?"

"Here," Merlow picked up several pebbles out of a planter, "this is even better. When you're having lunch, jump up from the table, dig around in your mouth and pull out this little white pebble. Tell them it's a tooth." He put his hand to his cheek and looked horrified. "Say, 'My god, I've broken off a tooth.'"

"What makes you think they won't offer to help me?"

"The success of this plan depends on speed. Don't wait for suggestions or offers of help. Just leave. Vamoose. Don't wait for the ferry. Mumble something about grabbing a water taxi to Bay Shore. In fact, have your bags packed before the tooth breaks."

"And when I'm out on the sand with my suitcase?"

"Come here," said Merlow. "Come right here where your friends will be waiting for you."

"And if the Burdettes come strolling along the beach to find me?"

"They won't. They wouldn't be caught dead on this side of the beach."

"I'll give it a try." He was going to do it for the fun of it as much as anything else. He accepted a glass of orange juice, "for courage and high blood sugar," said Merlow, and headed back to Point O' Woods. He did exactly as instructed, packed his small bag, put the pebbles in his pocket and waited for lunch. A little after one, Faith Burdette placed five naked carrots on a plate, a prelude to the sandwiches. He bit into one, munched zealously, bit again and then jumped up, spitting out the contents of his mouth. There it was. Amid the brilliant orange of chewed carrot, a tiny, authentic-looking tooth. They all searched his palm and saw it.

"Who's out here that can help?" Fred asked his wife.

"Oh, no," Luis protested. "I'll get a water taxi and head back." He thanked Faith, kissed her cheek, and was gone.

Leeds and Hess congratulated him and thumped his back but midway in the afternoon, Merlow came up behind him on the beach and in his best Burdette lockjaw muttered: "You think we fell for the broken tooth routine?" Luis jumped and both men doubled over with laughter.

"There's a house three blocks down with two of our girls," said Leeds when they were returning to the house. "Dinner awaits. I don't think they'd mind a third."

"Why don't we eat out? I don't want to go to anybody's house for dinner."

"It won't be bad. It's Susan Scott's house. If you're uncomfortable, we can eat and run."

"This time *you* break the tooth."

When they reached the house, he was surprised to see April. "I wouldn't have thought you'd be here," he said.

"I wouldn't have thought *you'd* be here," she replied with the same inflection. "But why wouldn't I be here? Not the type?"

"The other afternoon, you were so specifically tuned in to the problems of the downtrodden housewife, I'm surprised to find you're single and . . . in such a carefree setting."

"You don't have to be a housewife to feel downtrodden," she said defensively.

"Oh . . .? Anything specific?"

"No." She sounded miffed.

"Well, we can breathe a sigh of relief." She looked surprised and he was sorry it had started so badly. He thought the dress she was wearing was hideous. It was long, dark and flowery—the season's god-awful Western look. "Is that dress from our store?"

"Yes. It's a knock-off of Ralph Lauren's prairie dress."

She smoothed the skirt in admiration. "The women wore them on the wagons west, I suppose . . ."

"I see." That she had been won over by her own clever copy made her seem touchingly vulnerable.

"Why are *you* out here?" she asked. "Aren't you too smart and serious?"

"Of course. But I'm not a regular. I'm a guest, an uninvited guest." He grinned. "I won't eat much."

"Eat as much as you like. It's chicken. I wanted to make a nice lemon sauce but Susan insisted on barbecuing. I hate barbecued chicken, so don't worry. There'll be plenty left over."

"You should have taken the chicken away from Susan," he advised and then had the ridiculous notion of marching to the kitchen and getting her the chicken.

"Susan wanted to barbecue more than I wanted to make my lemon sauce. She said the men would help with the cooking. Are you going to help with the cooking?"

"No."

"Good."

Leeds came toward them with a glass of wine, handed it to Luis and propelled him out to the deck. It was very pleasant, wide-planked and practically on the sand. The sea gulls came close by to grab bits of bread Merlow was tossing out. He greeted Susan, who was turning half gray briquettes with a pair of tongs. She was dressed in a skimpy ruffled halter and white shorts. When she bent over he could see her breasts, although today they didn't interest him. He sat with his arms across the railing, staring at the bay. The sunset was spectacular, but he felt restless. He thought of Lisanne, who was returning from Texas the following evening. He had promised to meet her plane, which meant he'd have to take an early ferry out.

April came out and began to shred lettuce into a large wooden bowl. Merlow was scattering Triscuits on the railing to entice some nearby birds. "Anybody dying to tend this fire?" asked Susan. Luis caught April's eye across the deck and winked. She smiled and popped a cucumber round into her mouth.

"Am I complicating things?" he whispered to Merlow. "Were you guys going to pair off?"

"Not me, buddy. I hardly know the ladies. I'm just along for the ride. It's Leeds who has the hots for Susan."

"I see." He tried to think where he'd rather be and what he'd rather be doing. He was happy to be away from Point O' Woods, and dinner alone with Leeds and Merlow would have degenerated into sloppy shop talk. Back in New York, he'd be alone, not exactly what he wanted either. Maybe this was the best place after all. He took a gulp of his wine and relaxed. April took a gulp of her wine, finishing what was in her glass and choking a little on the last swallow. She saw him watching and pushed the glass away.

Susan placed the chicken on the grill, retreating after each piece as if the heat was singeing her eyelashes. "Here, I'll finish that," said Leeds.

The chicken wasn't on the fire two minutes when a man dressed in pale gray fatigues and an infantryman's cap walked onto the deck, picked up the barbecue stand by two of its three legs, carried it the few steps to the water and dumped everything—chicken, charcoal and grill—into a lapping wave. "There's an ordinance against barbecue fires," he shouted. "Next time I'll fine you fifty dollars."

The five of them remained rooted to their spots.

"Are we going to let that guy get away with that?" Leeds recovered first.

"I guess not," said Merlow, dusting his hands from the Triscuit crumbs. "I'll go." Luis continued to sit there, undecided as to his role. He'd offer to take them out to eat when everyone calmed down. Susan burst into tears and ran inside. He looked over the edge of the deck and saw that the chicken had remained stuck to the grill and looked miraculously unscathed except for the water lapping up underneath.

Merlow returned. "He really is the fire warden," he said. "And there really is a serious ordinance against charcoal fires." He wiped his upper lip which was full of perspiration. "Here, I'll have some of that." He held out his glass to Leeds who had the jug of wine.

April went down to the water's edge and placed all the chicken into a big colander. When she came back to the house Luis followed her into the kitchen. "I'll remember never to cross you," he said.

"What do you think? Can we wash it off?" The chicken looked pretty normal. "According to "60 Minutes," there are much worse things that happen to our food every day. Mice droppings in the baby food. Human fingers chopped into our hot dogs. A little sand and seaweed are wholesome by comparison." She held up a leg and thigh that had been rinsed under the faucet. "See. Good as new." She dried the pieces with a paper towel, rubbed them with oil and squeezed lemon juice over them. Then she put them under the broiler and began a pot of rice.

He could see her mission to save dinner had transformed her. She worked with a prim efficiency, as if he weren't there. He had always liked the cheerful sounds of cooking and sat at the table.

"I'm going to have dreams about that guy, I know it." She stirred the rice grimly. "It was the violent way he did it."

"If you tell yourself you'll dream about something just before you go to sleep, you won't dream about it."

"That sounds like something your mother told you."

"Not my mother," he said. "A respected psychologist."

"Who? Joyce Brothers?" He didn't mind the hostility, he had done the same to her when he came in. It was strange because they had exchanged maybe fourteen sentences, tops, so why were they mad at each other? "If you want to be snotty about it, go right ahead and have your bad dreams."

"Who said it?" she demanded.

"Nobody. I just made it up."

"That's very nice." Did she mean it was nice of him to try and soothe her or was she being sarcastic? "How can someone just invade your property like that? Shouldn't he have had a search warrant or something?"

"He didn't have to search. He saw what he was looking for right away."

She glared at him as if he were condoning the whole thing. "Mrs. Beck was right. Fascism *was* right around the corner."

"Mrs. Beck? Who's Mrs. Beck?"

"My best friend's mother. She had the government's number all along. She was an activist before it was fashionable. When we were in fifth grade and couldn't keep the Spanish explorers straight, she told us, 'Remember, girls: Pizarro pissed on Peru.' Literally, he must have urinated—he was there for several years. And figuratively, he pissed on the Incas."

He smiled and refilled his wine glass. "Did Mrs. Beck also feel that America had pissed on her?" He could talk like that, too. If she was a bleeding liberal, he couldn't take it.

"Yes, exactly. She felt her ideals and rights were trampled on daily by General Motors, General Mills, General Haig and Frito-Lay."

"And your parents? The same?"

"Oh, no. Just the opposite. They had a full-color portrait of Eisenhower over their bed."

The chicken was half done and she turned the pieces with authority, gripping them firmly in her tongs. Her hair had come undone from its bun and framed her face, which was flushed. He had been watching her smooth, lovely neck as she cooked. She was a pretty girl.

"Did you always side with Mrs. Beck?"

"Not consciously."

"But you always root for the underdog?"

"Not always. Sometimes I like the topdog."

She saw right away that he might construe that to mean himself and became very busy with the dishes. "I better set the table. We'll be ready to eat in ten minutes."

Dinner was quiet. Leeds and Merlow were hopelessly drunk, although far from boisterous. They kept trying to cut their chicken with rubbery hands. Susan was overly cheerful but didn't acknowledge the virtues of the dinner, which Luis considered ungrateful. It wasn't the best dinner he'd ever had, but it was fine.

They skipped coffee and dessert and he steered the two men home. When he finally lay down on Jack Tobias's bed, his fatigue was almost sensual. He looked forward to a deep and refreshing sleep. The restlessness had left him. He felt calm and somewhat optimistic.

27

Exercise # 21 called for dumbbells, three pounds in each hand, to firm her upper arms and bust. It was called the "Slow Motion Clap," done flat on her back with her legs up on a chair. She did six slow motion claps and then sat up.

"What's the matter?" Don stayed up, too, after one of his sit-ups.

"I'm lonely."

"Huh," he grunted and continued down again slowly, "welcome to planet earth."

"No. I mean *really* lonely. I'm lonely in the mornings, I'm lonely on the weekends. Saturday nights were made to torture lonely, single people. All those couples look so smug . . . 'Ooooh, you're alone, well get away from us! You must be incomplete and n-e-e-d-y.'"

"You gonna judge yourself by a bunch of idiots who go out on Saturday night? You know how stupid it is to go out on Saturday night?"

"Don, forget about Saturday night. I'm alone too much. It scares me. Sometimes, I think there'll never be anyone in my life again. It really scares me."

"So what else is new? Everybody's scared. You know what Kafka said about life: Life is being seasick on land."

"I never heard that Kafka said that."

"Well, he did, believe me. He was a very unhappy person."

She ignored him. "I'm not doing enough to meet men."

He made an indecent sound with his nose. "Every other building on First Avenue is a singles bar. You want to go on the rack? Go right ahead. Just don't stuff your face after the first rejection."

"There's a woman who lives above me. She goes all the time and meets men. She says they can be very insulting. They say, 'Sorry, but you're just not what I'm looking for.' She calls them garmentos. The guys from the garment district are garmentos, the guys from cable TV are cablelleros and the ones in the stock market are Dun Quixotes"—she waited for him to ask her why . . . he didn't—"for Dun and Bradstreet."

"Veeery clever. Veeeery stupid. Don't you know how good-looking you are? And you're not pushy either, or loud. You're a very refined human being."

"Thanks. I felt my hipbone last week."

"That's another plus for you. Tragedy has given you a soul. Would you believe Susan Scott has a soul?"

"Well . . ."

"Exactly. She's never had to delve. Who needs to delve when the whole world wants to suck your toes?" He did his final sit-up and crossed his legs. "That's where you have the advantage. You're beautiful *and* you have a soul. Another few pounds and you won't have to worry about men. They'll be all over you. Including the guy upstairs. Well, actually, he's downstairs from here. We're upstairs."

"The guy upstairs? You mean god?" She knew who he meant.

"Don't play Mary Jane with me, sister. The guy upstairs. He's not a garmento or a caballero but he's got some Latino." He cackled maliciously.

28

Luis knew that if he stopped kidding himself, he would admit that he was looking for her during the day. It began as an aimless sudden awareness of wondering where she was. At night, he invaded Lisanne's body with everything but his invading rod, and during the day, he was looking for April. When he was driven to the train, he looked for her on the streets, but it was more than two weeks after Fire Island that he finally spotted her on the platform, waiting for the 6:03.

"You survived the dinner." She smiled shyly.

"It was fine. And yourself? Any bad dreams?"

She looked down demurely. "No. I did what you said."

"There, you see." She was dressed better today. Very chic, although he liked her hair better the other way. She still looked vulnerable but he knew she would take offense at such a view. She might think of herself as invincible.

In contrast to their previous meeting, she was talking nonstop. First she listed all the trains that passed through Newark—the Patriot, the Minuteman, the LaSalle. She talked about her first favorite, her second favorite, etc.

Then she itemized all the things she had found of value. An English-German dictionary, a Channel 13 umbrella, a stainless steel set of nesting measuring spoons. She had tried to turn them in, of course, but another man watching her had said, are you kidding, lady. Either you keep it or they do. Suddenly she looked over his head with great relief. "There's Muriel Sachs, are you waiting for her?" Muriel Sachs was the better lingerie buyer—pretty but coarse. He wasn't waiting for her.

"What makes you think I'm waiting for her?" She appeared so nervous he wanted to put his hand on her arm and tell her to calm down.

"Well, she waved. I thought maybe you were supposed to meet her." He turned around to see Muriel Sachs buying a newspaper.

"I have a policy," he said. "I don't take out employees." He had no such policy. He had said it instinctively to protect himself.

"Absolutely right." She bobbed her head up and down unnecessarily hard. "I do the same."

"You don't date employees?"

"No. I date employees. I just don't date *employers*."

"Oh?"

"No. Never."

"You mean if I asked you to have dinner, you wouldn't accept?"

"Nope."

"Hmmmm." This news was disappointing. "That's interesting."

"It's not interesting at all. It's sensible. It's smart." With each new modifier, she grew more self-righteous. He was beginning to recognize that tone in her voice. A clarion call that she had gained an edge and was running with it. "I don't believe in eating and being intimate in the same place." He stared at her, not expecting such a heavy message. "Eating is a metaphor for earning a living, of course," she said less smugly.

"And what is intimate a metaphor for?"

Her eyes were at half mast. "For intimate." She barely whispered it. She wasn't as brave as she liked to pretend.

"I see." He paused. "Technically, you're not my employee. You're employed by the Burdette Corporation."

"Mmmmmm . . . well, yes. *Ul*timately." She made it sound as if he were being childishly technical.

"So you really could go out with me. You wouldn't be breaking any of your rules."

"Are you asking me out?"

"Yes," he said emphatically. "I want you to have dinner with me." He surprised himself.

"All right."

"*All right?* All right, what?"

"All right, I'll have dinner with you."

He must have looked stricken because she protested that, of course, he didn't have to if he didn't want to. "You tricked me," Luis said. "Why?"

"Are you kidding? I'd have to be a mental defective to turn down dinner with you." She said it with such admiration, he felt undeserving.

"Okay, you've got it," he said, smiling. When they reached Pennsylvania Station in New York, he excused himself to call Lisanne and lie. She was staying in his apartment while hers was being painted. "I should be home early," he said, feeling like a heel. He'd treat it as a business dinner. He might even pick her brains. She was full of bright ideas. Tricky, too. But there would be nothing physical. No touching of any sort. What he had said in jest made sense; he didn't date employees.

She insisted on taking her own cab home after dinner, which should have been a relief to him but wasn't. It made him want to see her again. That very night wouldn't have been too soon.

He tried to pinpoint why he was intrigued. She was pretty but not that pretty. His mind kept returning to her at odd moments. You want to get her in the sack, he told himself. You feel like getting her in the sack because she's vulnerable and defensive. That wasn't all of it. He wanted to see her finally calm and still. And the way he wanted to calm her was with his body. All of his body over all of hers. This idea was so strong and provocative, he kept looking for her, even though he knew it was a bad idea. What would he do with her once her defenses were down?

29

DON TOOK AN EXPLOSIVE sip of his coffee and coughed for five minutes. "See how excited I am?" He had wormed everything out of her. The meeting on the train. The dinner. "It's better than *The Other Side of Midnight*. Remember when Bill, the rich, handsome boss, taps Catherine, the mousy, lovelorn secretary, on the shoulder and finally kisses her?"

"There wasn't any kissing," she said, alarmed.

"Why not?"

"I offered to take a cab home right after dinner."

"Very dumb."

"I had to give him a way out."

"You don't give him a way out. That's the first rule."

"But I tricked him. It was a cute trick, but a trick."

"Believe me, he must have loved it. It was clever and daring. It showed you had spunk. And it was flattering, too."

"Yeah . . . I've shot my whole clever, spunky wad."

"I want to know everything," said Don. "He didn't just suddenly *see* that you exist. It must have been working on him for a while."

She told him about the fiasco at Fire Island, including the part about picking up the chicken and washing it off. Don shook his head. "Disgusting. I can't believe you would do such a dumb, unclassy thing. What are you, the bag lady of the Atlantic Ocean?"

"He didn't think it was so disgusting. He sat with me in the kitchen while I cooked. Nobody glued him to the chair."

"Okay, so you were lucky. Through some lapse of sense, he considered it resourceful or thrifty. What are we going to do now?"

"*We?* We're not going to do anything."

"What are you talking about? Don't you feel excited?"

"Of course. He's a really exceptional human being. Not just good-looking . . . it's everything. He's kind and considerate."

"Well then?"

"It's frightening . . ." she paused and rubbed her knuckles against her teeth. "It would be so easy to love him. But then what?"

"It wasn't too long ago that you were ready to fling yourself to the bimbos on First Avenue, remember?"

"That was different."

"No. *This* is different. Don't be a fool."

"Let's see what *he* decides before we start arguing about it. Let's see what happens."

"*See what happens?* Are you crazy? You've got to *make* things happen. Do you know his schedule? You've got to park yourself in front of his face at every chance. Get on his train. Squeeze in next to him. Thumb a ride. Anything."

She did none of that. She slunk away in the opposite direction when she saw him approaching. She took an earlier train than the 6:03. She wasn't strong enough to handle anything as important as this. She needed her energies for fixing up the rest of her life. She needed a new apartment and . . . a new job. Definitely, a new job.

At night, near sleep, unguarded, her thoughts went wild. Suppose she hadn't taken the cab home. Suppose he had touched her. Kissed her. The thought of that kiss sent shock waves throughout her body. During the day she had a very good hold of herself. All those months of denying herself food had taught her something about self-control. Luis O'Neill was a wonderful man but he could also break her heart.

She didn't like what was happening that weekend. She was thinking about Luis in a way that spelled trouble. Instead of jogging along the East River or doing the hip-walk, she was staying in bed and brooding. Brooding was one step away from being unhappy over something she could do nothing about. It smacked of old bad times. She would go apartment hunting to distract herself.

When Pierre and Don had first seen her one narrow room, haphazardly furnished, dark and often dank smelling from some unresolved leak, they were appalled. They told her she had to move. "Ees not good enough for you, Avril," said Pierre.

In the interim, they rearranged her furniture to make the most of a bad situation. They put the sofa in the middle of the room, backing it with a barn-smelly early American dry sink which she had purchased on Third Avenue. The new arrangement *did* make the room more interesting but she couldn't fall asleep with the couch facing the windows. She was sure someone could see her sleeping and she moved it back against the wall. The dry sink was still in the middle of the room, which made no sense at all. She had to move.

She searched through the previous Sunday's *Times*

supplement under Manhattan apartments of three, four or more rooms. She circled one described as "large 3½ quiet, treed street, low 30's, 800." She also circled "Immaculate 1 br., tv sec. low 70's, 1050." And a floor-through on the West Side where the values were supposedly better.

Taking the paper with her, she looked at the 3½ first because it was within walking distance. It consisted of a large living room, a kitchen, and a recessed alcove supposedly for sleeping but with no means of ventilation. It wasn't different enough from her own apartment to justify twice the rent. The one bedroom in the Seventies was sunny and had all new appliances but the rooms were very small and she couldn't persuade herself to part with more than one thousand dollars a month with no return except for shelter and a television scanner that might keep out thieves and murderers.

She stopped at a coffee shop and continued to look through the paper but, instead of looking at rentals, she turned to the co-ops. The idea of owning real estate—which had not occurred to her until that moment—made her adrenaline shoot up. At the very least, it was a possibility. She still had her stock portfolio which she had kept throughout her marriage. And the settlement she had received from Harald was in a money market fund earning fourteen percent. Most of the co-ops advertised that they could be financed up to seventy-five percent. There were ads from two banks offering co-op mortgages. The idea appealed to her on several levels. She could live in more imaginative space. It was a better investment than the stock market, which was weakened by high interest rates. And, momentarily, it would be something engrossing enough to displace Luis.

Her price range, under one hundred thousand, put her on the West Side, but the West Side didn't have to be remote. There were loft buildings opening up in the

Twenties and Thirties, the flower district and the fur district. She scanned each column, trying for something this side of Eighth Avenue. She read the whole page twice and then noticed a two-line ad that said: "15th Street, off 5th. Raw loft space, good light. 1025 s.f. 78,000."

She took the Fifth Avenue bus downtown, feeling odd and daring and scared. As if she'd already bought it. She wondered if she was dressed too casually to be taken as a serious prospective buyer.

The building had one of those grimy facades that, upon closer inspection, reveals an astounding array of ornamentation. The entrance, a double door scuffed and pitted by a thousand hand trucks, was flanked by fluted columns with Corinthian caps. She looked up to see which windows looked empty. They all looked empty and dirty. But the real excitement was the windows themselves, which were double-storied, arched and heavily mullioned.

One of the doors was open and there was activity on the second floor, which was a manufacturing plant and showroom for knitted goods. They called out a man who said he could let her into the loft but couldn't give her details. The owners were away until Monday.

It was on the top floor, facing 15th Street. Six of the windows she had seen from the street wrapped around what was essentially a huge rectangle with bites taken out of it for the outer corridor. Each window had a deep sill about a foot off the floor. At the rear of the space was a skylight which was cranked slightly open and could be reached by an iron ladder. Outside of these two spectacular amenities—the windows and the skylight—the rest of the place was uninhabitable. The floors were filthy and falling apart, patched in places with linoleum. There were pipes but no bathroom or kitchen. There was an odd small sink with the drain two thirds rusted out and the remains of a toilet which had been disconnected long ago. Over the sink was the sole light bulb although wires dangled from open sockets. There were no partitions. No closets. The walls were painted a nondescript industrial green but they too were obscured by dirt and grime. Raw space, the ad had said—which was not strictly true. Raw space implied you could start from scratch, but here there wasn't any way to begin anything until you had dug the place out from the layers of dirt.

She dusted one of the window seats and sat and stared. She noted that the part of the room under the skylight was higher than the rest of the room, a natural division for a bedroom or a kitchen. *Her* bedroom or *her* kitchen. She took a key and picked away at the walls to see what was underneath and was surprised to find that they weren't plaster at all but wood. It was at this point that the whole place began to change before her eyes. If you could look past the dirt and the wires and exposed pipes, it was a miracle. A miracle of vast, potentially interesting space in the heart of New York City. Don and Pierre were away for the weekend, so she called Sylvie who was mildly interested but couldn't understand why April would choose to live in such an isolated situation when people were being killed left and right. "You should have a doorman," she said. "To screen visitors and take your packages and things."

By Monday morning she had twice decided to buy it and remained firm for a period of four hours and twice decided not to buy it. Around eleven o'clock when she reached the owner, a Mr. Shapiro, she was in her cooling off period and asked him if the price was firm or was he open to offers.

"What have you got in mind?"

"Well, it needs a lot of work. A kitchen and bath alone will run to thousands of dollars. And the floors . . ."

"It's raw space in a prime location. You don't want it . . you don't want it," he said philosophically.

"Are you open to offers?" she repeated, not having the vaguest idea what she would offer if he said yes.

"I'm open to anything. You want to make an offer, make an offer."

"Sixty-five," she said, waiting for him to scream.

"Make it seventy and you've got yourself a deal."

"Seventy." Her hand was trembling so, she could hardly hold the phone. She hadn't meant to say it. The momentum had built up and she was just a victim.

"You've got yourself a loft," he said. "Congratulations."

When she finally saw Luis again, it was the day she had received the keys to the loft. The closing wouldn't take place for a week but her hefty deposit entitled her to a key and virtual possession.

She was already on the train when he rushed in and squeezed beside her in an already crowded three seater. They were as close as they had ever been. His thigh pressed against hers, his arms perilously close to her breasts. It gave her no comfort that he, too, looked twitchy and unsettled. Suddenly and without warning, she was overcome with desire. A passenger one minute, a basket case the next. What was he going to do with his thigh from Newark to New York? His arm kept falling against her. And his hand. There was no place to put his hand except . . . She shifted. He shifted. He glared at her. "You've been taking an earlier train. Why?"

"I've been apartment hunting." It was the first thing that came to mind.

"Why are you apartment hunting?"

"Because my apartment is very small and very dark."

"I see." He looked around the train as if trying to orient himself. "Are you going apartment hunting tonight?"

"Not exactly."

He opened a newspaper as if her vague answers had suddenly annoyed him. Maybe she was being too coy.

Maybe he didn't like her answers. "I bought a co-op and I got the key today. I'm going to see it right now."

He turned back to her quickly, clearly impressed. He now felt differently about everything. "That's . . . that's a big step," he said, as if he were really thinking about something else. A much bigger step.

"Well . . . the worst is over. I know I did the right thing. It's huge . . . a loft. And there's plenty of light, lots of windows."

When they were off the train and he was ready to go his way, he put his hand on her arm. "I'll give you a lift. Which way are you going?"

"Just to 15th Street. Between Fifth and Sixth. Maybe you'd like to come."

"Why not? That's where your loft is?"

"Yes."

They began to walk south and she knew immediately that something was going to happen. They would be alone. Really alone. On the sixth floor, or the twelfth if you considered the double height ceilings. On the twelfth floor of a deserted building. She was wearing a soft dirndl skirt, a blazer and a silk shirt with chains in the neckline. She had on dark pantyhose and sensible navy pumps. Her pocketbook was a deep burgundy with a shoulderstrap. Her hair was pulled back with a Bill Blass scarf, she had gold shell earrings on her ears and an antique commemorative pinkie ring from England that said ASD had lived from 1871 to 1903. A mere thirty-two years. If *New York* magazine wanted to do a story on the quintessential career woman with nothing on her mind but her individual retirement account and a safe method of birth control, she could be an ideal choice. So why then did she feel so threatened and so sad? As if he had already kissed her and loved her and it had turned out badly? As if he had already left her? The sadness replaced desire, a good start. She definitely had to watch out for him. He had taken her hand as they crossed the street but now she let go.

The moment they entered the apartment, she started her pitch in case he had ideas about the desirability of the loft. "The floors are salvageable . . . maybe we'll have to replace a few boards, but they're solid. And the walls . . ."—she knocked on them—"wood, believe it or not. The old style paneling with narrower boards. And the windows . . . I really love the windows . . . with seats. See . . . the sills are wide enough to sit on. They'll need cushions, of course." She began to walk toward the rear wall, her voice echoing. "But the bonus of it all . . . really unexpected . . . is the skylight. It opens . . . and it gives you daylight way back here."

He stood there watching her, not paying attention to any of the details. There was a smile on his lips. When she had run out of sights and attractions and she was just flailing her arms, willing him to respond, he went to her under the skylight and took her in his arms. "Well, what do you think?" she asked in a small subdued voice. "Aren't you going to say anything?"

"It's the best loft I've ever seen in my life."

"How many lofts have you seen?"

"None, but I'm sure there's not another one as fine as this."

She began to hit his chest and struggle in his arms but he managed to put his mouth over hers and keep it there until she was finally still. He felt her back, her buttocks and her back in quick succession. He grazed her breasts. She held him, too, with her head on his shoulder. They stood together for quite a while.

"Now what are we going to do?" she asked with great concern.

He smiled and moved away. "It isn't as if we've killed someone and have to get rid of the body. What if we just went to get something to eat?"

"Everything is going to become very complicated."

"Not necessarily."

He touched her twice during dinner. She was aware of his every movement. Her senses were supercharged. As if she was about to witness an accident.

"I'm not going home with you," she announced abruptly during dessert.

"Why not?"

"If I do, I'll sleep with you and I don't want to do that."

"Why not?"

"Lots of reasons . . . plenty . . . a million rea . . ."

"Okay, okay . . . just one will do."

"I won't be happy about it in the morning."

"How do you know? I may not be bad."

"That's just the problem," she said. "You'd probably be wonderful and then think how awful it would be for me if it didn't work out."

"Well, now," he took a deep breath, "I think you're being unnecessarily pessimistic, but we'll do whatever you like. We can still see each other. How far can I go? Kissing? Hugging?" He was teasing her.

"No further tonight," she said primly.

He took her home and she insisted he keep the cab so he kissed her quickly while she kept her eyes glued to the driver's neck.

"See you tomorrow," she heard him call out cheerfully as the cab drove away.

The next time he asked her out, which was two days later, she told him she couldn't sleep with him while they both worked at Burdie's. "It would get too sticky," she said, seeing immediately that it was a poor choice of words. She also told him she would understand if he didn't want to continue the relationship under those circumstances. He told her to shut up in a rather loud voice, during the second act of the play *Amadeus*. The people in the row behind them told him to shush.

30

ONE MORNING IN SEPTEMBER, she decided not to go to work and called in sick. She wasn't sick. My internal clock is telling me something, she said to herself out of the blue. After the call, her internal clock nudged her into a "dress for success" gray suit and out to the Jerry Fields Employment Agency, specializing in jobs for the advertising profession.

She sat there numb and uninterested in what would happen. Maybe that was the perfect attitude because the male interviewer liked her portfolio and kept giving her sly happy looks while he turned the pages. He made her feel she had held out on him how good she was. "Retail experience is the best preparation for agency work," he said with controlled optimism. "Of course, this won't be your big move. It will be your middle move."

"Fine," she replied with equally controlled enthusiasm. "Do you have any questions?"

"No." Her only question, he couldn't answer. Suppose Luis stopped seeing her when she wasn't so handy. Well, if that were true, wasn't she better off without him? Only a jerk would accept such a wobbly connection. Yeah. A happy jerk.

Before the day was gone, the Jerry Fields man had found her three jobs or at least the possibility of three jobs. "Three very different company profiles," he said. "J. Walter Thompson is a behemoth but you can certainly move around. Donaldson, McKee is conservative, mostly financial advertising which is limiting but their salary is the best. Sinclair and Chewalt is a comer. Very loose. Very experimental. They would certainly let you do your stuff."

She didn't want any of the jobs—she wanted to stay with Luis—which probably meant she would get all three.

With the excuse of a sudden dental emergency, she took the morning off and kept all the appointments. By three o'clock, back at her desk at Burdie's, she found out that J. Walter Thompson and Sinclair and Chewalt would both be happy to have her. Thompson was willing to pay $32,000 but she would work on industrial and trade accounts whose ads only appeared in specialized magazines.

Sinclair and Chewalt would only go to $30,000 but they wanted her to work on spaghetti products and a toy doll that said thirteen things when you pulled a chatty ring on the back of her neck. The Jerry Fields man told her to sleep on it but by five o'clock her stomach was in such knots, she called him back. If he were already gone, she would take it as an omen and forget the whole thing. He answered on the first ring.

"This is April Taylor," she said quickly. "I've decided on Sinclair and Chewalt."

"Good choice," he answered cheerfully. "I'll call them right away and let them know."

On the way home that night she was thinking, well, it's not so bad. I'm not going to a different country. Maybe it'll be better. I can certainly sleep with him now. But she couldn't quite convince herself that things would be all right. She didn't know if she had done something very good. Or very bad.

When they got out of his limousine the following day, April took his hand in hers and whispered, "I can sleep with you now."

"Oh . . . Why? I mean why now?"

"I got another job yesterday."

"Another job? You're leaving Burdie's?" He stopped walking and turned her around. "You can't mean it. Why didn't you say something?"

"What was I supposed to say: Is it okay if I look for a better job with lots more money and more creativity? You're making it sound as if I did something underhanded. This is an agency. The big time. National stuff."

"What national stuff?"

"Spaghetti."

"Oh . . . well, spaghetti. Why didn't you say so?"

"And a doll."

"A doll, too?" His eyes widened with respect.

"And you can stop making fun of me. It's a wonderful opportunity. And anyway, you should be happy because now I can sleep with you."

"Great. How about next week?"

"Next week?" She looked ready to cry.

"Gotcha." He laughed. "That was for leaving Burdie's. If you insist, we'll make it tonight."

"I insist."

"Before or after dinner?"

"Before."

"Your house or mine?"

"Yours."

"Have I left anything out?"

"I don't think so." She was happy to see that he was nervous, too. They were both nervous and silent until they reached his apartment.

The first thing he did when they were alone was to put four fingers across the nape of her neck. His thumb indented her mouth and he maneuvered it across her cheek several times, as if the texture of her skin was irresistible. This unspectacular beginning opened every valve in her body. By the time he kissed her she had turned to liquid. Where were her bones? He was looking at her body, a body that was new to her and still made her shy. She blessed Don and god and her own bone structure for giving him pleasure. Finally, she searched his face for clues as to what was in store for her and was reassured. It was going to be all right. More than all right. She was finally living her life.

He made love to her at ten o'clock, eleven and now again at six in the morning. He was both strong and tender. Personal and impersonal. His tenderness and concern made her want to cry. Now he was staring at her back and half of her buttocks in the available light. The person she most admired in the world was free to look her over in the most vulnerable position. She continued to lie still, her head resting on her arms, her breasts half squashed beneath her. Once on the radio, a psychologist had described how ashamed women could be of certain parts of their bodies. Passion wasn't as important as to keep from being seen. They would contort and struggle to hide themselves and bless the dark. Bless the dark. This moment confirmed all that she had won.

There was stirring and a tug of the covers. "Why aren't

you married?" He asked everything as if he had a right to know. Executive privilege.

"Is that supposed to be a compliment?"

"No. Yes."

"Deep down, I knew you'd be coming down the road one day and how could I pass that up?" Her mouth was straddled over her forearm and the words were muffled.

"Don't be glib."

"Okay."

"Look at me."

"Okay." She sat up slowly poking one leg out of the covers and then raising it slightly before sending it down again as an anchor to help her up. She put her arms around her leg as if she loved it and played with her ankle bone, momentarily transfixed by its boniness. Then she rested her cheek on her knee and stared at him. "I was married."

"You were?" He sat up.

"First you're surprised that I wasn't married. Now you're surprised that I was."

He ignored her. "What happened?"

Her hair now hid her face. "Easy come, easy go," she said ruefully.

"Not funny."

"You said it," she agreed soberly. "He left me."

He wasn't prepared for that and didn't respond. She felt her moment of contentment ebb away. The phone rang. The phone had rung twice the previous night but he hadn't answered. Now he seemed relieved to be interrupted. Who could be calling at seven in the morning? She got no clues from his responses—a series of grunts and assents, a blatant yawn and a goodbye. She lay back down, pulled the sheet around her and covered her eyes with her arm. He was quiet. She could feel him mulling over the fact that her husband had left her. If Don had heard *that. You told him what? Why didn't you just add that you had a record of mental illness?*

"It must have been very painful for you," he said finally.

She kept her arm over her eyes and bobbed her head up and down. "Want to talk about something more cheerful?" Again she bobbed her head. "How about Mrs. Beck? I haven't forgotten her thoughts on Pizarro."

She took a deep breath and sat up. "Well . . . Mrs. Beck wouldn't go for this scene. She was all for sex but not for free." She tried to sound lighthearted.

"She wanted you to get paid for it?" He feigned shock.

"No. She wanted us to get married for it. She made up a song to help keep us pure: Be Kind to Your Openings."

"Oh, my god. I don't want to ask which openings she had in mind."

"Want me to sing it?"

"No, thanks."

"I guess it's time to get up anyway." She picked up her clothes and handbag and headed for the bathroom. The sink was sculpted into the shape of a shell set on a slim pedestal. There was a single faucet which didn't respond to pushing or pulling or twisting. Suddenly, it tipped backward and a gush of water hit her in the stomach. She left the sink and sat down to pee. The toilet was low and sculpted, too, but—thank god—flushed in an ordinary way. There was no evidence of a medicine cabinet. Didn't he ever get a headache? Her first glimpse of the apartment the previous night had been a surprise.

"Okay, I give up," she had said. "Where's the furniture?"

"This is it."

"Which is it?"

"The platforms *are* the furniture."

"Where do you sleep? Where do you eat? Where do you put your clothes?"

He began to show her all the ingenious carpentry—tables that flipped out from the wall, clever decorations that pulled out hidden doors which, in turn, revealed rows and rows of recessed shelves and drawers. "The bed," he said sheepishly, "is completely undetectable by day."

"Why is it such an advantage to hide everything?" she asked mystified.

"You've just put your finger right on the dilemma," he said. "It's of no advantage. It's repressive and a nuisance." Having said this, he led her to a platform nearest the window wall which, as it turned out, was the undetectable bed. Staring at herself now in his overly mirrored bathroom, she felt as if all of it had taken place several days ago. She had another go-round with the faucet, washed her face and rubbed her index finger vigorously over her teeth. Then she got dressed, put on mascara and, unable to find her blusher, pinched her cheeks until they hurt. With her handbag slung carelessly over her shoulder, she went to say goodbye.

"Thanks for a wonderful evening."

"Where are you going?"

"Home."

"I'll get you a cab."

"Thanks. I can get one." She waited for him to say something about seeing her again but he didn't. He had put on a terrycloth robe and followed her to the door. With her high heels, she was only a couple of inches away from his eyes, which looked puzzled and concerned.

"You okay?" he asked.

"Sure. Perfect."

"I don't think so."

"Why don't you think so?"

"I shouldn't have asked you about your marriage."

"It's okay . . ."

"I couldn't understand why you would still be unattached."

"Yeah . . . well, don't say anything nice to me or I'll start to cry."

"Why would he leave you . . . you're a terrific girl."

"There. Now you've done it." She pulled a Kleenex out of her handbag and wiped her nose. She waited for him to say something else that was nice but he chose that moment to clam up. They stood awkwardly, staring at each other.

"Well, so long." He kissed her solemnly on the cheek.

"So long."

She didn't hear from him for several days. "Wonderful," she chastised herself in the mirror. "You were wonderful. Now all he can think of is that you sleep around and your husband found you unlovable." Then she became angry with herself for thinking that way. She hadn't done anything wrong. She looked and felt better than she had ever looked and felt in her life. Just because he wasn't bowled over didn't mean she was damaged goods. Anyway he had too much on his mind to be bowled over by anyone. What she wasn't going to do was sit around waiting for a call. That would be stupid. After work she went shopping for the loft and bought two occasional tables in blonde oak and some fancy sheets. The following night she returned the sheets (they might not fit her new bed) and cancelled the tables, realizing they were out of scale with her outsize apartment.

For four days she avoided Don, unwilling to confide in such a harsh critic, but on the fifth day, after half a glass of wine before dinner, she spilled everything.

"Have things . . . uh . . . progressed?" he asked carefully.

"What do you mean?"

"Have you gone . . . how shall I put it . . . all the way?"

"You're going to ask me questions like that?" She tried to look harsh and put off.

"Why not? We're all adults." He waited. "Well . . ."

"Yes."

"Oh, my god, really?"

"Why are you so surprised?"

"Not surprised. Just excited for you."

"Well, don't get too excited, right after that he dropped me."

"Dropped you? What do you mean?"

"He hasn't called in five days."

"*Five days!* That's bad. You must have done something really awful."

"Thanks for leaping to my defense."

"Oh, don't be silly. I'm only kidding. He'll call."

"Why are you so sure?"

"I'm not. I'm just trying to make you feel better. What did he say when it was over?"

"He said I was a terrific girl."

"Uh oh. That doesn't sound good. When a man says you're a terrific girl, it's like finding a dead canary on your doorstep or your favorite horse's head in your bed. It's the kiss of death."

She finished her wine in one gulp. "Let's change the subject." She didn't know if he was kidding or serious and she didn't want to know. Before she left for home, however, Pierre kissed her cheek and said, "He weel call tomorrow. I feel eet here." He dug his finger into his diaphragm.

The following day when she returned to the office from lunch, there was a message on her desk: Mr. O'Neill called. Next to Wants To Be Called Back was a black check.

"I'm just back from Harvard," he offered casually. "I attended a seminar for executives. On ethics."

"Good," she said. "I thought you didn't want to see me anymore."

"Why would you think that?"

"You said I was a terrific girl and everyone knows that's the kiss of death to a relationship."

"I take it back," he said. "You're not terrific. You're crazy."

"Now you're talking," she laughed in relief.

That night he kissed her with a hunger that made her sober and contemplative. The last five days had shown her how painful it could be. He slept with his head burrowed into her breasts and clung to her all night. He trusted her enough to show his need, yet she couldn't help feeling apprehensive. She had to guard herself against him.

31

Indian summer was generous and lengthy. The dry, golden weather lasted past Halloween and All Souls' Day into late November. Everyone talked about it as if it was someone's happy mistake. April and Luis saw a lot of each other but still within certain boundaries—they didn't go from stage to stage. She was sure she was more aware of the details than he. There were certain hours when he never called. Days when—for business reasons (her assumption)—he was unavailable. There were subjects they never discussed. Was he as fastidious about doping out her habits? Probably not. Still, she was pleased at the way she had handled the whole thing. He was part of her life but not the whole of it. There were no tears at night. No false hopes.

If she hadn't had a love affair and a co-op to occupy her mind, her job at Sinclair and Chewalt would have been a decent substitute. It was a medium-sized agency with three copy and art groups each with a supervisor reporting to Herb Sinclair for copy and Morris Chewalt for art. April's group head was Larry Sugarman, ambitious and coarse, but not mean or stingy. He didn't waste time putting things in a nice way, particularly criticism. If something stank, he said it stank. On the other hand, if something was good, he kissed you and patted your behind, man or woman. "Clio, Clio," he would shout. "For sure, a Clio." The Clio was the Tony Award of the advertising industry.

He had only said "That stinks" to April twice, but he had kissed her and patted her behind more times than she cared to remember. "You ever hear of sexual harassment, buddy?" she'd ask in a menacing voice.

"You want to talk sexual harassment," he would throw her on his couch, "I'll show you sexual harassment." She liked him and he liked her. He didn't mind if she learned to be better than he. He gave her a mountain of old story boards to study in preparation of her first spaghetti commercial. "Just remember one thing. It's like doing *War and Peace* in 58 seconds."

When she wasn't thinking about her job and Luis, she was thinking about 15th Street. She was paying $368 a month maintenance but she couldn't move in without a sink and a toilet. She had called two floor men from ads in the *Village Voice* to give her estimates on the floors. On weekends, she scraped paint off the walls. When she finally reached the wood, she buffed and caressed each bit of paneling like it was a child.

Don and Pierre were crazy about the apartment. On his first visit, Don had headed straight for the ladder that led to the skylight. Then he went through the skylight and onto the roof, something that had not occurred to her. "You can plant tomatoes up here," he shouted down to her. "It's wonderful. It's unbelievable. How could you have found this all by yourself?"

She was thrilled that he liked it and followed his advice even when she didn't quite agree. She would have done a lot to make him happy. Both Don and Pierre insisted on helping her scrape the walls. They worked together as long as they could keep the windows open because of the remover fumes. Even so, it was such tedious work, they only had the back wall done when the weather turned suddenly cold and they had to stop.

Her days were full and some of the nights were memorable. There was nothing in her experience that compared to making love with Luis. Nothing. It was both sweet and dangerous. Dangerous because it wrenched her out of the world as she knew it. She was floating somewhere above all the mundane. And yet, before and after, there was incredible sweetness. He had a habit of rubbing her jaw. She knew he wasn't thinking of what he was doing. He was probably thinking about his grosses and his nets or if they should do Ireland In Our Midst or Shanghai Holiday for the fall promotion. Still, rubbing her chin helped to soothe him. Like a pacifier. "I don't mind being your pacifier," she said softly, "as long as I'm not your doormat."

"What are you talking about?"

"Nothing."

If she stayed overnight, which she seldom did, she left immediately the next morning. She didn't make his breakfast or offer to make the bed. It was his bed, let him make it.

She would have loved to make his bed, plump the pillows and hang up his clothes, but that wasn't why he liked her—for her housekeeping abilities. He liked her independence and her cheerfulness. And the fact that she was too busy to hang around all day. She never ate breakfast there either. "Don't have time," she would mutter. Even on a Saturday.

On the third occasion she did this, he stopped her. "I don't get it." He was sitting up in bed with no pajama top and it was difficult for her to look at him without getting back into bed. "Come here," he patted the side of the bed. "I want to have a talk with you."

"Look, Luis," she was brushing her hair as Carlo had taught her—all the way over her head, bending over, and then all the way back. "If you want to discuss something with me, just say, 'I want to discuss something with you.' Let me decide whether I sit on the edge of the bed or not. But don't pat it as though you're going to talk to a pet. Or a child."

"Of course," he tried not to smile, "I just want to know why you run out of here like a bat out of hell every time you sleep over."

"It's morning," she said reasonably. "The night is over and it's a new day."

"And? . . . what? You just signed on for the twelve to eight shift? What's wrong with staying a little while? Stay all day. Spend the day with me."

"Oh, I couldn't do that."

"Why?"

She sighed and sat next to him on the bed. "Luis," she began slowly, "I'm sure it's not news to you that you're a desirable man. Forget that you look like a movie star. Forget that you could be a gigolo and get by on your looks alone. Forget that you are a generous lover. Forget that you're wealthy and have a sense of humor and are kind and smart. For—"

"All right. April, will you cut it out! Get to the point, for godsakes."

"I could fall in love with you for your eyes alone, but then where would I be?"

"What's wrong with falling in love with me?"

She ignored the question. "I could fall in love with you like that." She snapped her fingers. "If I gave my imagination the slightest leeway, it would, every day, see us married with ten little guys that looked just like you. I'm smart and I'm pretty and I'm a terrific copywriter, but I don't have the emotional clout that you do. Not in this situation. I'm going to be the one left crying my eyes out and you'll go on to someone else or something else." She rose. "That's why I don't stay all day. I can't depend on you for my happiness." She struggled into her coat and looked around for her handbag. "You should be thrilled with the arrangement. Someone to screw who's not hanging on to you. It's ideal."

"Don't say screw."

"Why not?"

"It's not . . . Just don't say it."

"Sorry. I was being practical. I got carried away."

One morning as she was leaving, he sat up, shook away the sleep and called to her. "I can't see you for a week. I have to go out of town today."

Two fat tears rolled down her cheeks, surprising her as well as him.

"You don't have to take it so hard. It's only a week." He was teasing her in a gentle way, wiping the tears away with a corner of the sheet. "Why are you crying?"

"You've never told me before when you couldn't see me. You just didn't see me."

"You're crying because I told you that I wasn't going to be able to see you?"

"Yes."

"But you're happy I told you?"

"Yes."

"You're crying because you're happy?"

"Yes."

There was a big difference when a man told you when he couldn't see you as well as when he could. He was letting her in on the particulars of his life, which put everything on a different footing.

If she had known that day why he was going to be away for a week, she would have cried for a very different reason. When he came back he told her he had been offered a job to head a small conglomerate in California. They had offered to pay him $360,000 a year, one thousand for every day. They were prepared to give him a three-year contract if he would accept, and he was thinking very seriously of accepting. In fact, he was ninety-five percent certain that he would.

To his credit, he told her all of this in the dark and when she didn't answer or ask any questions, he made love to her twice and then held her to him for the rest of the night.

She understood why he couldn't ask her to go with him. It was one thing to have a loose relationship in New York. If it didn't work out, each went his own way. But when you had to transport someone across the country— ask them to give up their job, their co-op, their entire life—well ... that was a very serious thing. Very different.

32

NEW YEAR'S DAY WAS on Thursday and Luis was to leave on Saturday. The last night they were together, she was determined not to make any reference to his going. "This is just another evening out," she told him in his foyer. "No sad looks. No sad words."

He helped her on with her coat. "You don't have to take it *that* casually," he said. "Go ahead and cry your eyes out."

"If I did, you'd hate it. Men," she addressed the two Art Nouveau prints on the wall, "they don't want you to be serious but they're hurt if you're casual."

"What do you want to eat?"

"Something light, I guess, in case I really break down. How about that little Chinese restaurant where they make the pancakes?"

"I thought you weren't going to cry?"

"See? Just what I told you."

"Suppose I cry?" He said it softly and seriously, which pleased her.

"Over me? I'd like that very much."

"You know the choices in this situation really stink." He was going to explain it to her all over again.

"If I followed you out there, it just wouldn't work. You'd hate it and I'd hate your hating it. It just wouldn't work." Actually, it was he who had said all that. She was parroting it, thinking perhaps he hadn't meant it. That he would say he wouldn't hate it. But he didn't say anything.

Dinner was very quiet and brought no new resolutions except that she would go with him to the airport after all. She cried and waved furiously until the airplane was probably over Ohio. They went so fast. She stayed at the airport for hours—as if that would bring him back—sitting in a row chair next to a black woman with four small children. She wanted to tell the woman her troubles. One of the children kept dropping her bottle so that April would pick it up. It was a game.

The worst part of his going was not the deathly stillness that enveloped her, but the thought that she was not going to fall apart. She had prepared herself well, an adult woman who wouldn't be undone by love.

"Well, I think that's veeery weird," said Don. "You *should* fall apart. Just don't get fat again. Drink. Turn to drink."

She had been careful to set a full life in motion just for this eventuality. She had begun to exert some influence at Sinclair and Chewalt. Her spaghetti commercial was in production. She had requested and received a sofa in her office which amused her because she hadn't really wanted the sofa, but merely to test the extent of her clout. A nice, tailored, black and brown tweed sofa had arrived within ten days. It had round bolsters at both ends to cradle your head if you wished to lie down. She was lying down a lot because she didn't sleep well. This only made her seem more valuable to Herb Sinclair, who considered idiosyncratic behavior a true measure of creativity. He often walked in on her lying down and diplomatically closed the door after timidly whispering, "Oh . . . you're thinking."

The loft was looking more beautiful every day. The only walls she had put up were to enclose the bathroom. Her friends loved the idea of no walls but the workmen considered it peculiar. They said hers was the worst job they had ever had. She stopped listening to what they said. The plumber was nice. He installed a toilet, sink and stall shower for precisely the price estimated. Encouraged, she hired a cabinetmaker to make pine cabinets for what would ultimately be her kitchen. It looked as if she meant business. This was going to be a home.

Even with the real progress in the loft, January crept along. She couldn't move in until the Department of Buildings issued a certificate of occupancy which seemed to take forever. It was a busy time for news. A new president, the release of the hostages. One day while she was in the supermarket, the Muzak was interrupted by a news bulletin: three hostages had gone shopping in Wiesbaden and caused a minor riot. Mayor Koch had announced that the hostages would receive the biggest ticker tape parade ever.

"So how about the veterans?" said an old man on line. "When they came home from Vietnam, nobody looked up."

"Virginia is the state with the most hostages," said a young girl.

"That's because all the spies live there," said the same old man.

Instead of the perennial *Have A Nice Day*, her register printout said *Welcome Home 52 Americans*.

On the thirty-first of January, the telephone rang at 11:45 at night, scaring her out of her wits. She could have sworn later that she knew by the ring that it was long distance. Very long distance.

"It's me," said Luis sheepishly.

"I know," she said.

"How are things there?"

"You should be happy you got out. We're having the worst crime wave ever. Murders are up eighteen percent. How's the work going? How are the sushi stands?"

"You know about the sushi stands? How?"

"Are you kidding? I read the business section cover to cover."

"Everything's fine. Really fine. How about yourself?"

"Oh, great. The apartment's livable. I have a bathroom with a door and the floors are in. It's very big. Much bigger than I imagined. It's pretty. Have you stopped thinking about me yet, because I haven't stopped thinking of you."

"No. I think about you every day."

"That's good."

"It's not good."

"It might not be good for you, but it's very good for me because . . . because . . . well, it's much harder than I thought it would be. Much harder . . ."

"I know." Silence. "I thought you'd like my address and telephone number. In case you need something or . . . you know . . ."

"Of course. Just hold on, I've got to get a pencil." While he held on, she went into the bathroom and looked at herself in the mirror. "I can't believe this is happening," she said aloud. "I can't believe my life is being dribbled away over the telephone wires. Please, somebody. Help me." She went back to the phone and took his address and telephone number, after which he wrapped it up and said good-bye.

After the call, she began making bargains with god. She would be good. She would be very good and maybe he'd call back. She took Harlan and his wife, Agnes, out to dinner to a French restaurant, which was a mistake. They felt uncomfortable and unable to order with confidence. Her father looked remarkably young and she had put her arms around him when they met. He laughed an embarrassed laugh and looked sheepishly at Agnes. The evening was a flop and she could feel Harlan separating himself from her all through dinner. He was put off or frightened or overextended. During dessert, she remembered how he had told her that trees would grow inside her if she swallowed pits, unless it was apples—in which case the cyanide would kill her first. She had been terrified of swallowing a random seed.

She tried telling them about her job, but, just as Marty Bell had warned her long ago, Harlan's wife kept asking: "You mean somebody writes those words? *That's* what you do?" This revelation made Agnes's confidence shoot sky-high. "Your father and I are going on a cruise for Thanksgiving," she put her hand on his arm. "The poor man hasn't had a real vacation in years." She said it as if April had personally kept her father from enjoying life until that moment. "That's wonderful," said April. She had not been to Queens for nine months and it looked as if she wouldn't be going soon again. Mrs. Beck had moved to Israel and was living on a kibbutz. Greeks lived next door.

Twice she visited Sylvie, who had either recovered her appreciation of Ardsley-on-the-Hudson or resigned herself to the old life. She had even gained some weight and looked terrific. So did seven-month-old Alicia.

"I've never known you to be anything but thin as a stick, you look wonderful," April told her.

"Really? It's the breast-feeding. It made me thirsty for beer and milk shakes." She washed some lettuce in silence. "I'm going back to work in the fall," she said, as if sending out a trial balloon.

"That's wonderful. Is that your idea?"

"Yes. The baby will be over a year and Bradford is six. I'm going to be a paralegal . . . you know, like a para-medic . . . like 'Emergency,' the TV show."

"I know."

"I might even go back to law school. In a couple of years, maybe I'll run away and we can be roommates in the city." She said it jocularly but there was a new cyn-icism in Sylvie's voice that April found more difficult to bear than her former smugness. Why did she feel that Sylvie wasn't strong enough to survive anything really bad? Perhaps she was the one who would not survive. Her heart felt leaden every day. California appeared in her dreams and in her imagination as the end of the world. She could barely believe that it really existed.

It was Don who finally convinced her she had to go to California and plant herself in front of Luis for one last try. "It's more courageous to go than not to go." He said if she didn't go, he would never speak to her again. "He can't ask you to come there unless he asks you to marry him. That's the kind of guy he is. But you can go. There's no law that says you can't just show up."

It sounded so simple. "And if I go? Then what?"

"He'll be so happy to see you he'll beg you to stay."

"That's what you say but you're on my side."

"So is he. He's on your side, too. I feel it right in the gut." He turned to Pierre. "You do too, don't you, Pierre?"

"Ees true. You must go to heem."

"Just show up? Don't ask or anything?"

"Just show up. The shock value will be good."

He dialed and made the plane reservations. When the

tickets came she almost went right to the terminal and
turned them in. She told Herb Sinclair that her mother
had died and she had to go to California and make fu-
neral arrangements. She begged god to forgive her for
telling such a gruesome lie. In just four hours, if the
plane didn't crash, she would see him again.

33

IN THE FIRST WEEK, Luis knew California was the wrong setting for a man like himself. He didn't prize body hair or casual dress. He liked wearing ties and somber suits and serious shoes. He missed his old neighborhood with the yelping dogs and skinny trees. He also missed the discipline of hard work which, in Southern California, was looked upon with grave suspicion.

Quite soon, Luis stopped working, too. It didn't seem to matter what he did for his thousand dollars a day. He could play golf or tennis or spend the day in the stress-relief center situated within the corporate park—or the corporate campus, as they liked to call the acres of evenly green lawns that surrounded the Whitestone Corporation building.

Perversely, his indifference to his position and its responsibilities reaped him sizable rewards. Two casual decisions—acquiring a chain of sushi stands and a small chemical plant that would make the chemicals for their existing paint division—proved to be pure gold. In spite of himself, his stock rose.

His moodiness and lack of volubility made everyone as-

sume he was hard to please and they tried harder to
please him. When he visited the chairman's house—a
spectacular minipalace—the chairman's wife asked over
and over: "Do you have everything you want? Can we get
something for you?"

There were plenty of distractions for a wealthy, attractive man, although here he wasn't as attractive as he had
been in New York. Amid the spectacular-looking, affable,
athletic male population, he was merely okay.

He visited his associates in their homes and swam in
their pools built around natural rock formations. There
was often a woman invited to be his partner. He dutifully
took them home, kissed them lightly on the lips and
thanked them. Most of the women he met were very thin
and wore their hair pulled out in short, separated wisps
that floated back in an unnatural way.

Unlike the men, the women were underactive. They
organized their actions to lead gracefully to the ultimate
activity, which was sex. Their voices were geared to sex—
throaty and difficult to hear. More than talking, they
liked to smile—they had a repertoire of smiles which they
used to answer questions. Facial expressions were big,
too. Pursing the mouth to one side meant indecision—
usually over what to order to eat. Pulling in the lips while
looking to heaven meant disapproval—someone was
being tacky. Raising eyebrows while pushing lips outward
and chin upward signified confusion or ignorance.

There was little sarcasm and no one wanted to disagree
about politics, art or religion. Even so, with life so pro-
scribed and their future assuredly sunny, the women
cried a lot in California. More than once he had seen evidence of tears on the face of a girl he had passed at a
party or in the office.

He was sure his attitude would improve. What's not to
like? he asked himself over and over. A woman—a certain kind of woman—would make it personal. Then it

would begin to make sense. But where was he to find such a woman?

He missed his mother. He felt as if he were in a vacuum. No, no, forget the vacuum, it was more like a dream. He was disoriented. He missed his grandmother. He missed her as if she were already dead and he would never see her again. Maybe he missed all the safe women in his life to keep from missing the one unsafe one.

You know what Kafka said, she had told him at the worst moment at the airport: He said life is like being seasick on land. He didn't believe Kafka had ever said that but it was a fine line nevertheless. He now felt seasick on land.

There were so many moments that could have stuck in his mind but the one that did was very ordinary. The look on her face when she was rushing to leave his apartment in the early morning. "The night is over and I've got other things to do." And when there was no response from him: "What's wrong with that? What's wrong with having a nice, friendly night and then going your own way in the morning?"

She had been right to protect herself. As it turned out, he had left her. He had left a strong, vulnerable woman with a lovely neck, compassionate eyes and a generous body. But how could he have done otherwise? Brought her out here like a pet while he made up his mind? Come out, I miss you. Come out and let me see you again so I can make up my mind.

They had rented him a prim Victorian house high on a cliff. It was probably the only Victorian house in all of Los Angeles, filled with Mission furniture which was expensive and scarce. A nice black woman came every day to make his breakfast and his bed. In the afternoon, if he was coming home, she fixed his dinner and left it on the stove.

On one particular night, he drove up to his house and left the car in the driveway. The view was spectacular and he felt like standing there and taking it all in. He stayed out for quite a while before walking up to the door.

He didn't see her right away but thought he saw something familiar on the porch. It was the skirt. He was amazed that the skirt looked familiar and made him think of her. He had seen that skirt every day for two weeks on a mannequin at the entrance to Better Sportswear. How could he forget it? But then she rose from the hard Mission bench and came toward him. She was looking at him anxiously, waiting for his reaction. His lungs felt unnaturally full.

"I'm here on business," she said quickly.

"Oh? What business?"

"No business," she confessed. "Just for a visit . . . but I can't stay long," she added quickly.

"Are you going to start that again? You just got here."

"Yes. But a visit is a visit. It's not the rest of my life. I want to call the airport in the morning and confirm my flight back."

"Of course. You can call tonight, if you like."

"Tonight?" She looked surprised.

"Better than that, I have a plane at my disposal."

"You would." She had regained her composure. "They do things in a big way here in California." He was tracing her face with his finger. "You can't imagine how much I've missed you."

"Could you say that again, please?" Her voice began to quiver.

"You can't imagine how much I've missed your dear, sweet face." He felt like an old man. He felt as if he had already lived his lifetime, but without her. He held her tightly, as if she might disappear. His best efforts weren't enough to keep two tears from sliding down his cheek, but it was dark and she couldn't know.

"It's certainly a relief to hear that," she said in a strong, cheerful voice. Then she sighed deeply and asked to go into the house.

In the morning they were both very quiet, as if there was too much at stake to talk casually. The housekeeper's arrival saved them from having to start. He urged her to use the pool and suggested sending a chauffeured car to show her around but she insisted she would manage on her own.

The moment he left for the office he began to feel uneasy, as if that would be the last he would see of her. She was such an impulsive person. She was capable of anything. Maybe she wouldn't even be there when he returned. By eleven o'clock he was sure she was already boarding a plane back to New York and he left the office for home. He drove faster than was safe and tore through the house looking for her. The house was empty. There were no telltale towels at the pool, not even a chaise out of place. The housekeeper was nowhere in sight, either. He went to sit at the edge of the pool, his briefcase still in his hand. She could have waited, he told himself over and over. She could have waited one rotten day. There was nothing he could think of doing that would help ease the emptiness he felt.

He had been sitting there about twenty minutes when he heard the housekeeper's ancient Chevy chugging up the hill. When it reached the driveway, they both stepped out.

"You're still here!" he yelled in relief.

"Of course." She was confused. "We've been out buying things for dinner. Why aren't you at the office?" she asked sternly.

"Oh, god," he grabbed her arm and pulled her roughly toward him. "I was sure you'd gone."

"Why would I be gone?"

"It's not unlikely given your past behavior. You have a history of rushing out . . . remember?" He looked at her face and saw a glint of something new. Was it power?

"You were upset when you thought I'd gone."

"I thought it was crazy . . . and unnecessary."

"You don't want me to go?"

"No."

"You don't want me to go so soon, is that it?"

"No, that isn't it."

As quickly as it came, the gleam of power was gone and her face was painfully vulnerable. "You don't want me to go . . . ever?" He had to lean very close to hear it but his own answer was strong and clear.

"I don't want you to go ever."